Edmund Clerihew Bentley was born in 1875 and educated at St Paul's School, London, where he met eminent critic and author G K Chesterton, who became his closest friend. Bentley began a lifelong career in journalism in 1902, working for ten years on the editorial staff of the *Daily News* and for a further twenty years on the *Daily Telegraph*. In 1905 he published *Biography for Beginners* (under the pseudonym E Clerihew), which was a volume of nonsense verse consisting of four-liners called 'clerihews' (in his honour) and became as popular as the limerick form. Bentley's masterpiece, *Trent's Last Case* (1913), was written in exasperation at the infallibility of Sherlock Holmes and marked the beginning of a new era in detective fiction.

D0169483

BY THE SAME AUTHOR
ALL PUBLISHED BY HOUSE OF STRATUS

COMPLETE CLERIHEWS
TRENT INTERVENES AND OTHER STORIES
TRENT'S LAST CASE
TRENT'S OWN CASE

BIOGRAPHY
THOSE DAYS

ELEPHANT'S WORK

AN ENIGMA

E C BENTLEY

HOUSE OF
STRATUS

This edition published in 2001 by House of Stratus, an imprint of
Stratus Books Ltd., 21 Beeching Park, Kelly Bray,
Cornwall, PL17 8QS, UK.

www.houseofstratus.com

Typeset, printed and bound by House of Stratus.

A catalogue record for this book is available from the British Library
and the Library of Congress.

ISBN 0-7551-0323-8
EAN 978-07551-0323-2

I DEDICATE THIS STORY TO THE MEMORY OF
JOHN BUCHAN

because, among other reasons, it was he who advised me to write it. That was long ago, but I have a very clear memory of the occasion. It was at a chance meeting outside Blackwell's bookshop. We had not seen each other since the publication of his romance, *The Thirty-Nine Steps*, about a year before. When I told how much I had enjoyed it, he said, "Why don't you write a shocker yourself? It is twenty times easier than writing a detective story, like *Trent's Last Case*." His argument was that, in writing a shocker one need not bother about probabilities, hardly even about possibilities – all that mattered was the shock.

Before beginning to write this story I bought a copy of the latest of the numberless editions of John's shocker, which has been shocking readers without intermission for so many years. I read it again, and tried to take to heart its lesson, but I cannot claim that this story attains at any point to so high a standard of improbability as is reached in *The Thirty-Nine Steps* in some places. But I have done my best.

August, 1949.

CHAPTER I

It was, Severn thought, the most formidable face he had ever seen.

Not that he minded. On the contrary, one glance as he entered the first-class compartment, where the man sat alone on the corridor side, had decided Severn to take the place diagonally opposite, so that a roving eye could, from time to time, casually light on those regular features. Passing by the man to get to his place, he had caught a slight, inoffensive whiff of some toilet preparation. As he settled himself by the window and placed a raincoat and a few papers on the seat beside him, he took in more of the man's appearance. His clothes were good, perhaps a little too good – smart, in fact, and much more recently pressed than Severn's. The leather suitcase on which his right elbow rested was, to a discerning eye, an expensive article. He might be an American – something about the hat, perhaps, with its brim a little wider than the brim of Severn's own soft hat. He looked thirty or so, in hard condition, and the face which had made that immediate impression on Severn was long and tanned.

It was refreshing to Severn, as he called to mind the faces with which he had to do every day of his life, to think that this was not a commonplace face, or a good-humoured face, or a sad face, or a silly face, or a theatrical face, or a suspicious face. Most faces told you something, even if it was only something you were expected to believe. This man's face was totally without expression; yet its complete blankness, the coldness of the steady, close-lidded blue eyes, the immobility of the lips, produced more of an effect than the most speaking countenance. It was the effect of a completely ruthless spirit more so than any Severn had ever met with.

And yet he had come from time to time in contact with desperate characters. Even now, he reflected, stroking his chin with a thumb and forefinger, he saw something of decidedly bad men; but they were not men who had ever done anything criminal, seldom anything even actionable; they were weak men or hypocritical men. The man in the opposite corner was very far from giving an impression of weakness, or of putting on an act. He just looked formidable.

The man, Severn perceived, was unobtrusively observing him, as he was observing the man; and he wondered idly, in this interval of precious leisure, what conclusions the man might be forming about an Englishman in rather crumpled grey flannels and a blue jacket, with an open collar and no tie. Now that he came to think of it, he probably did not look like anything in particular. He supposed that he looked like an educated man. He assumed that he looked at least ten years younger than he was, because strangers always thought so. He knew that he had a frosty blue eye, because a well-known gossip-writer in the Press had mentioned the fact; but he didn't believe that this made him look formidable. He hoped that he looked as considerate and good-tempered as he felt, but he could not be at all sure about that. The thought crossed Severn's mind that if he had had a wife, he would probably have gained from her much clearer ideas about his personal appearance. He would also, perhaps, have had a different one.

Presently their eyes met, and the man's hard face achieved a brief, mechanical smile. "I was wondering," he said, "just how long this train stops here." Severn's guess that the man came from across the Atlantic had been right, but only an expert could have put a name to the very faint trace of accent in his speech; to Severn, it might belong to anywhere north or south of the Great Lakes.

"There's usually rather a long wait at Bridlemere," he said. "As much as five minutes sometimes. That isn't just because it's a sleepy little country station, it's because this train has to wait for another that makes a connection with it."

"Uh-huh!" the man said. "I'll say it's a sleepy little dump, anyway. Lying in the bottom of a gully, and woods running right down both sides. Well, I've nothing against scenery, as long as I don't have to live in it."

Severn laughed. "The people who do live in it find it pleasant enough. I'm a town-dweller myself, and a busy man, but I have a cottage here in the outskirts of Bridlemere, and when I have a lot of writing and thinking to do I come down here for a few days. Then I finish off with a visit to my golf club, where I'm going now." He glanced out of the window beside him. "What interests me at the moment is this train of boxcars on the up line. I don't remember anything like it being here before, at this time, and it sounds as if there were horses in this car just next to us."

The man nodded decisively. "You said it – horses. I can tell you something about that train, though I never saw it before, and I've only just landed in your country. That's a circus train. I had an eyeful of it as it was running in here – got the smell of it, too. I have travelled in quite a few of them. This is a pretty big outfit, too – hell of a lot of animals."

Just then the guard of the train came along the corridor and, seeing Severn, touched the peak of his cap. "Afternoon, my lord," he said. "Going to Molesworth, I suppose. Well, you've got a fine day for it."

"Yes," Severn said. "An occasional round of golf is all that stands between me and a mental hospital. Tell me, was that my old friend Inspector Owen I saw in the distance, getting into a carriage near the front with two other men?"

"Owen it was, my lord," the guard said. "One of them with him's a chap from London, the other you may have come across perhaps – a big man in the county force, Superintendent Paulton."

Severn shook his head. "No, but I've heard of him, of course. They're after somebody, I suppose. Yes, Paulton – it was Paulton who got himself shot last year, wasn't it, arresting the Whitway murderer?"

"Ay, 'twas," the guard said. "Ought to've got him a medal, that did. Hit three times, and then knocked his man out – good work, that."

"Bad shooting, too," Severn observed; and he noted the momentary twitch of a muscle in the frozen profile of the American traveller. "Well, if it comes to pluck, Owen's a useful man to have at one's elbow. He's a VC – I suppose you know that. He was one of my NCOs in my soldiering days. Is it a specially dangerous ruffian they're after this time, I wonder?"

"Dunno, my lord. Owen told me that Scotland Yard have just been notified from New York that somebody who's wanted over there has just crossed in the *Queen Anne*, and that he must have a forged passport. They guessed he would be taking the first train to London, which is this train. As soon as we get started, they'll be going through the passengers looking for that passport. They don't expect to be long about the job, Owen said."

"I hope there won't be any shooting this time," Severn commented. "And talking about being long about it, when

4

is this train going to get started? This gentleman was asking me. He is a stranger among us, and he takes an interest in our transport problems."

The man in the opposite corner smiled bleakly. "Don't get me wrong," he said. "I am not discontented. I am not in any hurry, and this seems to me just a perfect train for persons who are not in any hurry."

Recognising an intelligent foreigner, the guard returned his smile. "We do our best, sir. But you'll find," he added tolerantly, "you'll get to your destination at the scheduled time, barring accidents." He turned for a backward look out of the window behind him. "We should be off in about a couple of minutes, gentlemen. Good-day to you."

He moved along the corridor.

Somewhere a small dog began to yap.

"He's quite right," Severn said. "This train starts late sometimes, but it always arrives on time. Everything is for the best on the best of all possible railways. Good lord, what's that?" he broke off, as a splintering crash and a series of heavy thumps resounded from somewhere down the line.

The American met his look with blank unconcern. "It sounds to me," he said, "as if something not exactly for the best was happening at the hind end of that circus train."

Again came the noise of smashing wood and thudding blows; then a sound of quite another quality – an unearthly, blood-freezing roar and scream combined, filling the air again and again with fury and menace.

CHAPTER II

Chuny was feeling bored and irritable.

For one thing, she hated travelling. She had no feeling that it improved her mind, and it did not even offer, to Chuny, a change of scene. On the contrary, travelling usually offered to her no scene at all but a view of the wall of the boxcar in which her railway journeys were as a rule taken; and to a healthy young elephant keenly interested in life this in itself was annoying enough. Besides this, Chuny loathed the monotonous and senseless clacking that accompanied the boxcar's passage by rail, and when it was at rest, the sound of voices and movements outside, of which she could make nothing, was more disagreeable still.

Moreover, Chuny had that day a special grievance: in fact, two special grievances. Her particular man, who had looked after her and been her constant companion from childhood, had not appeared at all that day. Chuny felt as much lost without him as Beau Brummel without his valet; and she did not possess Beau Brummel's serenity of temper.

She could not know that Nanuk Chand had broken one of his fragile legs in a collision with a porter's truck the night before, and now lay in a hospital, muttering obscenities beyond the range of the most uninhibited English bargee against the fate which had parted him from the animal that

6

he cared for as much as it cared for him. His place in Chuny's life had this day been taken, most unsuccessfully, by James Reynolds, the under-keeper of the menagerie, a man whom Chuny knew well enough, but whose appearance she had the misfortune to dislike, and whose personal smell – imperceptible to his fellow men – she detested.

This was one grievance; and Reynolds, with the best intentions in the world, had made bad worse that day by attempting to propitiate Chuny with a bunch of bananas as a dessert after her usual sixty pounds of oats and three trusses of hay. He knew very well that Chuny loved bananas: what he had failed to observe was that when bananas were given to her by Nanuk Chand they were always in an advanced stage of ripeness, not in that hard and insipid condition in which they are preferred by British palates, and which to Reynolds seemed perfection. The natural consequence was that Chuny, after one glance at the objectionable canary-coloured fruit, had snatched the bunch out of his hand, flung it on the floor of the box-car and trampled on it, squealing.

These were Chuny's special grievances; and she treasured them, as her kind are known to do. As the circus train stood at the up platform in Bridlemere station, she was shifting about on her feet, her ears twitched fretfully, the end of her trunk wandered from side to side on the floor blowing up sawdust, and there was that in the sidelong look of her quill-fringed eyes which would have told anyone familiar with Chuny's habits that a storm was brewing.

Unhappily, there was in the absence of Nanuk Chand no one who could read the signals of her disposition. Chuny was a problem elephant. She and her attendant were both of them recent acquisitions of Appleseed Brothers' Colossal Circus; and those brothers' joint experience of the brute creation, large as it was, had not included temperamental young female elephants, not yet schooled by the passage of years to that immovable sobriety which contributes so much to the charm of the greater pachyderms.

Chuny's previous owner, of course, had lied about her age; and he had been backed up by Nanuk Chand, who thought only of her future, and knew that Appleseeds' represented a step up for her in the trouping world. She had been offered for sale as having reached the trustworthy age of forty; and as she stood ten feet at the shoulder, the Appleseeds had not suspected that half that figure would have been nearer the truth, and that there were moments when the management of Chuny presented difficulties even to Nanuk Chand – when she was, as he had been heard to express it, a *pukka Shaitan ke bachha*. Without him she was at such moments, as James Reynolds had epigram-matically put it that morning after the banana incident, three tons of perishing dynamite.

So here Chuny was in her boxcar at Bridlemere station, simmering with wrath, listening to the to-and-fro of feet and to unknown voices from the platform side, annoyed, above all, by the strange sounds from the other side, where a good deal of incomprehensible clanking and hissing and shovelling and slamming was going on.

Her car was, in fact, immediately next to the engine of the train on the down line, and on the footplate Judson Rogers, the driver, and David Hopkirk, the fireman, were getting ready for the start that was almost due. They had just failed to reach agreement on the question whether the disappointing display given by Wales in the last Saturday's International had been owing merely to bad luck or to the selection of Frank Rudge to play at inside-right; and Rogers, changing the subject, had remarked that the wild beast in the neighbouring boxcar seemed to have something on its mind. To this the fireman had rejoined that he, Hopkirk, would feel like doing a bit of trampling and snorting himself if he were shut up for hours on end in a bloody box on a fine day; and he had added that anybody who treated dumb animals that way ought to be 'ung.

It was at that moment that Miss Susan Dorking, with her Pekinese Rollo on a lead, happened to stroll on to the platform near the end of the circus train. The distinctive odour of elephant, shut in though Chuny was, could not escape the notice of Rollo; and he did not like it. Always a demonstrative dog, he barked like mad, straining at his lead in the usual Pekinese display of frantic anxiety to tear limb from limb something which there was not the least chance of his being allowed to get near.

For Chuny this was the last straw. Like all elephants, she loathed small dogs, and was distracted by their noise. In a blind impulse to get into the open and away from this final outrage, she kicked backwards at one side of the car and drove with her tusks at the other, the side next to Roger's engine. They were the small tusks of her sex, but they were strong and unbreakable. Half a dozen blows were enough to smash through the wood, and Chuny began with tusks and trunk to tear away the side of the car.

The sight of a furious elephant's head suddenly thrust out and overlooking them was too much for the composure of the men on the footplate. Both of them yelled at Chuny in a way that, even in the sweetest of tempers, she could only have considered provocative, and Hopkirk was so rash as to strike wildly with a spanner at the threatening trunk. The next instant he was seized by the slack of his waistcoat, plucked from the cab and flung on the permanent way. The driver did not wait for his turn to come. At the moment of his colleague's disappearance he dived from the cab on the opposite side, while Chuny filled the air with clamour – not the normal trumpeting of her kind, for trumpeting may be a sound of pleasure or courtesy or not disagreeable feeling of one sort or another. The scream and bellow combined of a seriously angry elephant is, so the hunters tell us, one of the most terrifying sounds in the world.

Back in Severn's compartment he and his fellow-traveller stared at each other, the one face alive with excitement, the other without visible emotion of any sort.

"It's an elephant!" Severn cried.

"Sure is," the other agreed, opening one corner of his mouth slightly. His lean hands lay relaxed before him like the hands of a graven Buddha.

"It must have gone mad!" Severn exclaimed, springing to his feet and seizing the window-strap. He let the window, which was already half-open, fall with a bang, threw his hat on the seat, and adopted the posture which is discouraged on German railways by the printed notice, *"Nicht hinauslehnen,"* or on those of France, more affably, *"Messieurs les voyageurs sont priés de ne pas se pencher en dehors."*

What he saw, as he gazed forward past a score of other protruding heads, was enough to occupy all his attention – a man lying, to all appearances insensible, on the ground between the two trains, and a great head, with ears extended and trunk darting here and there, stretched across from the wrecked boxcar to the cab of the locomotive. He could even make out – for he had vision as keen as a young man's – the dangerous show of white in the animal's eye, that eye so tiny in relation to its huge bulk.

The thought flashed across his mind, how much more fearful a beast an elephant would be if its eyes were larger; as large in proportion as a man's, who can strike terror into faint hearts with a glare of rage. An elephant with eyes the size of dinner plates, charging at one out of the jungle! If it came to that, how about the hunting of the whale – a furious cachalot, Moby Dick with eyes like cartwheels, rushing at the boat!

But this elephant was bad enough, in all conscience. What was the animal doing?

Chuny, screaming still, was by this time in that state of mind commended by Moltke as the only proper one for soldiers – she felt that her business was to destroy, and destruction was her sole thought. She was making what hay she could with the multitude of bright steel devices which Judson Rogers had so hurriedly left to their fate; but with these it was proving difficult, even with the mass of muscle that was Chuny's trunk, to do a really satisfactory job of wrecking.

She tore off a few dials, some cocks and levers and small, exposed pipes; she produced a deafening blast on the whistle; but there were many more gadgets on which she could make no impression. Finally she caught hold by the rim of a substantial wheel which she could not drag from its pillar, and wrenched it half way round. Then at once Chuny got action.

The train began to move.

If Severn, staring at the incredible sight, could have known what was happening behind him in the compartment, he might have been hardly less astonished.

The moment his head was outside the window and his gaze turned towards the proceedings at the forward end of the train, the demeanour of the man in the opposite corner underwent a startling change. Although not a muscle moved in his face, and his cold eyes remained fixed on Severn's back, the rest of him shot from inertia to activity as if a spring had been released. He sprang erect, and his hands with animal swiftness tore open his waistcoat and were busy at the buckles of a leather attachment beneath his left armpit. He jerked free a strapped holster, from the mouth of which jutted a revolver-butt ornamented with

11

mother-of-pearl, snatched from his inside breast pocket a small, green-covered booklet impressed with the arms of the United States and bearing the title, PASSPORT.

He thrust the holster and the booklet one into each of the capacious pockets of Severn's raincoat as it lay untidily by his place. He flung his own hat into the rack above the coat, caught up Severn's hat and put it on – a very fair fit it was – then, grabbing up his suitcase, the man with two strides of his long legs reached the corridor and disappeared.

Some ten seconds after his evasion, Chuny's work was done. The train jerked into movement, and Severn, turning round in high excitement to address his fellow-traveller, found no fellow-traveller there. What had been done to the engine he could not know, but could reasonably guess at the nature of it from the rapidity with which the train put on speed, until it was going more rapidly than that train had ever travelled before. Faster yet it went, while shouts and screams resounded from the corridor as fields and hedges, trees and cottages flew past.

Severn had sometimes been in deadly danger in the past, but never with such a sense of total helplessness as he felt now. Instinctively he sought to guard himself from a coming shock that might smash him against some part of the hurtling coach; with all his strength he gripped a luggage-rack in either hand and held himself erect. Nothing, he felt, could avert a disaster of some sort. He recalled indistinctly one of Zola's novels, read many years ago, which ended with a driverless troop train roaring on through the night to destruction with its freight of light-hearted conscripts all unconscious of their peril, *"qui chantaient"*. On that merry note, he remembered, the story had broken off short. There was no singing, no ignorance of the impending danger, for the people in this train.

Severn did what human beings in such a situation always do. He prayed. In the past he had not thought it reasonable to expect miraculous interventions of Providence; but now his prayer included petition for a miracle, because there was no reasonableness left in him, and he still had hope.

So the fact that the other man had vanished from the compartment made no impression on his mind. He did notice the train's rushing past the place where he should have left it – Molesworth station. An instant later the end came, when the engine jumped the line at the curve under Rowan Hill.

All that Severn experienced was the instantaneous, sickening change from dizzying flight to a tattoo of inconceivably violent bumps, the somersaulting and the instant crashing of the little environment that enclosed him.

Consciousness left him like the blowing out of a candle.

CHAPTER III

There were four men in the big black car that sped along the road heading westward from the scene of the Molesworth disaster.

A squat chauffeur sat silent at the wheel. Behind him a tall man of powerful build and another as noticeably small conversed as they supported between them a drooping figure, apparently unconscious, bandaged about the head so that only the closed eyes and mouth were visible.

"I'm glad that's over," the small man said. "Lugging bodies about, alive or dead, is too much like hard work – when you're my size, anyway. You look as fresh as paint yourself, though you were hard at it all the time I was patching up our friend here."

"You showed no sign of fatigue, *chico*, while lugging the bodies," the tall man rejoined. "One of the other rescuers, a passenger on the train – he was an American I think – made a remark to me about it."

The other looked gratified. "What did he say? That's the sort of compliment I appreciate."

"He said 'That half-portion there seems as strong as a horse.' I suppose you might call it a compliment, at least it was true. Well, it was a duty to do what we could until there were other helpers on the scene."

"It was devilish lucky for the Chill," the small man said as he smoothed a bandage on the head of the motionless figure, "that you had the first-aid outfit in the car."

His companion looked across at him with a flashing smile. "Not lucky at all. No car of mine is ever without it – it is the rule. As you know, I am a man whose whole life is governed by prudence."

"I've heard you say so," the other answered drily. "You didn't look like it when you were dragging casualties out of the burning end of the train. Well, perhaps you'll admit it was lucky we found your man so quickly in such an appalling confusion as that. As it happens, I've never assisted at a railway smash before, and I shan't mind if I never see another. I must say, General, it's a mystery to me how you got on to him with so little trouble."

The big man waved one hand in an airy gesture. "It is no mystery, and no chance. All was provided for. It was arranged that he should travel in the forward compartment of the first-class carriage – there is one first-class carriage only on that train. In broad daylight it could be seen easily in the midst of the wreck – at night, it could have been more difficult. As it was, I knew where to look for him without any delay. A small matter of staff-work – which at one time was my business."

The small man nodded. "So you made that arrangement when you wrote to Farewell Billy – I see. Quite simple when you know. But you never told me – you love to stage a surprise, General, and you had me thinking it was all very wonderful. And it was all arranged, I suppose, that this chap should get off with concussion and a few superficial head-injuries, when the guard of the train and a dozen more people were killed and incinerated, and a lot more badly damaged."

"You are among those who are permitted to laugh at me, Barlow *de mi alma*," the General said mildly. "That he is not damaged badly is most fortunate – could I deny it, I who have always so much good fortune? It is most fortunate, also, that a doctor of the first order happened to be staying with me just at a time when his skill was unexpectedly called for. Ah yes! There has been plenty of luck, *gracias a Dios*! It was lucky that he was alone in the compartment – no one to take notice of what happened to him. It was lucky that there were two of us for the not very easy job of getting a senseless man out of a railway-carriage lying on its side. It was lucky that we were able to get him away before there were any police on the spot to make themselves nuisances, as I suspect they would have done."

The doctor laughed shortly. "You're damn right they would. For one thing, they would have taken an interest in that gun of his – and especially the harness. Even the bad men in this country haven't got around to wearing holsters under their arms, I believe. And from what you tell me, that passport wasn't made to be examined with too much attention. Besides, they would have pointed out that it wasn't for us to be carting off one of the casualties without a word to anyone."

"To act quickly," the General said with satisfaction, "cuts out so many difficulties as a rule. We are waiting for my friend at the station – we suddenly see the train rush through like a brickbat in a fight, and go to smash a quarter of a mile away – *al instante*, we turn the car, we burn the earth, we are on the scene immediately, our car is the first to be brought near the track. It is nice work."

"What isn't so nice," the doctor said, "is that we can't get him to Mrs McBean's place and bed him down till it's dark. He'll be all right as he is, but we shall have to waste another three hours or so cruising about the landscape, or lying up in by-roads. I suppose Newlove" – he nodded towards the silent chauffeur – "knows what to do."

"He has his instructions," the General said. "Nothing has been forgotten." He glanced at the motionless figure between them. "I wonder, *chico*, what sort of a bird we shall find the Chill to be when he comes out of his concussion. I had him wished on me by Billy, and for one reason and another, I was willing to take him, but I cannot help wondering how we shall get on. A man that all the worst characters in New York were afraid of may not turn out to be the most agreeable of companions. A man does not get a name like the Chill given him for nothing, as you say."

"Yes, I've thought of that," the doctor answered. "But from what I could hear he never gave any trouble when he was with Rawlins's circus outfit – "

"Aha!" the General broke in with intense appreciation. "Six-Gun Pete, the Wyoming Wonder."

"Yes, well, the Wyoming Wonder was perfectly harmless so far as Rawlins's lot were concerned. They were all afraid of him, I was told, but that was simply because of his manner. As far as I could make out, he never did a thing to anybody and never talked tough, but he looked – "

"Like a Wyoming Wonder, I suppose," the General laughed. "There are men who have a way of looking dangerous all the time, they cannot help it, because they really are. I can remember quite a few. And usually the consequence is that people are very careful not to offend them. For my part, I always feel inclined to pull their noses, but it is a bad plan, I think, to pull a man's nose just because you do not like his face."

"It is not advisable, I agree," the doctor said. "But my idea is that a man who has that sort of effect on ordinary harmless people is likely to seem even more terrifying if he gets promoted to a high position in the gangster world, where violence and recklessness would be quite in order, so to speak. So, as they all have nicknames, he gets a sinister one."

The General tapped his friend on the knee. "Just the same, *chico*, we cannot put him away as a completely innocent character. If he was, he would never have joined up with Billy, also Billy would never have wanted him. Besides, we have to remember that the Chill has done something which made it a good idea for him to get out of the United States. But it does not matter, he must be ready and willing to play ball with us, or Billy would never have sent him, and that really is everything – you can always trust them if you belong. Well, now, we have to get through a long time of cruising about the landscape, as you have expressed it." The General felt in a pocket of the car, and took out a large flask. "A little telque, taken from time to time, will make it more endurable." He drank, and shook his head regretfully at his companion. "It is a pity, *chico*, that you do not care about this cool, refreshing drink. Truly, it is an acquired taste, as you say, but the acquirement is worth the trouble, believe me. You have tried it once only. You do not give it a chance."

"I'd sooner drink furniture polish, if it was left to me," the doctor said with feeling. "Besides, I've just had a good go of the first-aid brandy. As for acquired tastes, there are people who have trained themselves so that they can get lit on methylated spirit. I've tried that once, too, and in my judgment it's nectar compared with telque. Never mind, there'll be all the more for you, General."

"You cannot think that that is any consolation to me," the General said reproachfully. "I do not care to drink alone, but if it must be so..." Again, with resignation, he resorted to the flask.

CHAPTER IV

When the injured man came to his senses he was lying in a bed in a strange room. It was like an awakening from deep sleep; he took in his surroundings slowly.

The bed, though small, was very comfortable, with a dark green eiderdown quilt. It stood out from the wall in a room of moderate size, carpeted with dark green, its walls colour-washed in a lighter shade. Against the wall opposite were a wardrobe and a small, plain bookcase. To his left were a fireplace and a door, to his right a window; the boughs of an apple-tree in blossom, very close at hand, could be seen through the half-open sash, and sunlight poured into the room. Wherever it was that he happened to be, he liked the look of things.

Beneath the window stood a large table with a white enamel top, a small, rectangular leather case with a handle, a glass jug of water, a tumbler, a graduated glass and some small bottles and boxes. Flanking the table were two green-painted rush-bottom chairs, by the fireplace was an arm-chair. No picture, flower or ornament of any kind was to be seen.

The whole set-up, he thought, looked very civilised, rather austere and slightly medical. It was an invalid's room, and he, obviously, was the invalid. This conclusion was fortified when, seeking to account for a faint feeling of soreness and stiffness about his head and face, he lifted a hand and found that they were swathed in bandages, leaving not much more than his eyes, mouth and nostrils exposed.

Certainly, he was the invalid. He had been injured, though he now felt well enough. But was anything else about him certain? Or was anything known at all? Nothing to speak of – that was the disconcerting answer, so far as this invalid in this bed was concerned. He did not know who he was or what he was. He could not remember his own name, or anything else whatever about himself, but for some recollections of boyhood and youth when he had, as it seemed to him now, been happy and healthy and sane.

The realisation of all this did not altogether demoralise him. It shook him, but not profoundly. The man who had forgotten who he was possessed a strong and well-controlled mind. Although most of his personal past seemed to have been entirely blotted out, there was a good deal of mental experience remaining. He knew what was the matter with him – loss of memory. He knew that it was fairly common. He had, too, the reassuring knowledge that recovery from it was also common. And after all, he appeared to be bodily sound but for the injuries – not now at all painful, if they had ever been so – to his bandaged head.

It was clear enough that someone had been looking after him, and doing it well. He felt clean, the sheets were clean, he was in clean pyjamas – which he noted with interest, were of purple and white striped silk, and several sizes too large for him. A movement of the head told him that a small brass bell stood on a table by the bedside. Accepting its mute invitation, he rang gently. Perhaps it would be answered by a nurse – he knew about hospital nurses – but he hoped rather for a man, to whom he could talk as a man.

In a few moments the hope was fulfilled. A man entered the room, a small, dark man; he might be set down as a youngish man, in spite of the much wrinkled forehead that made his bony face look like a good-tempered monkey's. His black hair was cropped close, and he wore a suit of black-and-white checks of a pattern that would have looked vulgar on someone fat and coarse, and was clamorous enough as it was. The man who had lost his memory observed that the checks of the trousers were slightly smaller than those of the jacket and waistcoat, though the pattern was otherwise exactly similar – a detail of sporting dandyism that pleased him, for no particular reason.

This odd figure stepped quickly to the bedside, took hold lightly and expertly of the bandaged man's right wrist, and gazed into his eyes. After a short silence, the dark man nodded his head sharply, thrust his hands into his pockets and observed. "So you've come out of it at last."

The man in the bed smiled. "Somehow I didn't think," he said, "you were going to begin with, 'And how are we today?' And I don't think you are going to finish by saying you are very pleased with me. Yet you must be a doctor."

"So I am," the small man said. "And a damned good one, too. I'm wasted on a simple case of concussion like yours, ending up with the patient in complete possession of all his faculties, and getting fresh with his medical adviser. You've been out for just upon a fortnight, it's true, and I've had to attend on you like a baby, but there doesn't seem to be anything wrong now. Your face won't look very pretty when the bandages come off, which most of them are about due to do – probably it'll never look very pretty. But perhaps it never did. I wouldn't know, because it was nothing but a mess when I started on it. Your passport photo gives you a presentable set of features, but no more expression than a cake of soap, so you may have looked like the most damnable brute unhung."

The bandaged man sat up in bed. "Passport!" he exclaimed, "I've a passport, have I? And you've seen it. Then you can tell me who I am, and what I am. I don't know. I can't remember anything."

The doctor gazed at him with a new expression in his eyes. "So you are a case after all," he said slowly, rubbing his hands together. "You're beginning to look one, too, now that we've begun to touch on the trouble. The worried look. Well, try to snap out of that if you can – it isn't anything deadly that's wrong with you.

"So you don't know your own name?" the doctor resumed after a moment's thought.

The other shook his head.

"Or anything about yourself?"

Again the head-shake.

"Well, you'd better have a name, I think, just for convenience, so we'll call you by the name on your passport, which is Taylor. And I'll say this for you, Taylor: you take your memory trouble better than most of them – starting to josh me, I mean, with a thing like that on your mind. You take it better than most of the genuine ones, that is, and far better than any of the frauds. Half of those I've come across were putting on an act, and the frauds always overdo it – always! A very useful act it can be, too, as you may imagine – if it goes over, that is. But if the doctor knows his stuff, not many of them get by nowadays."

During this jerky discourse the doctor had gone to the table and, unstopping one of the small bottles, had shaken a tiny tablet into his palm. "Open your mouth," he said; and when the man called Taylor did so the tablet was deftly flicked to the back of his tongue. "Swallow that now. It's good for what I expect you're beginning to feel, and if it went on you wouldn't enjoy it, believe me. The black night of the soul, they used to call it long ago."

"Who are 'they'?" Taylor asked.

"Mystics," the doctor answered briefly.

Taylor looked puzzled.

"Well, don't worry yourself on the subject, for God's sake," the doctor advised him. He seated himself on the edge of the bed, the sunlight strong on his cadaverous features. "The blokes who gave it that name got it trying to squint through the keyhole in the door of heaven. *You* never got it that way, though, if my information about you is right. It comes from too much nervous strain, which can be the result of a lot of things. It will pass away. Now, will you be treated by me as a patient? My name's Barlow, MD, FRCP, if anybody asks you. You haven't any other doctor, I can tell you that. You're in good hands, including mine; you're among friends. I'm staying with the General as a holiday from my own work, and I shall be with him long enough to see you over your little trouble."

Taylor smiled; he was beginning to feel drowsy. "All right," he said. "I don't seem to have any alternative; but I am quite willing. And I hope the treatment will begin with something to eat."

The doctor rose to his feet. "As a mind-reader," he said briskly, "I stand in a class by myself. The moment I heard your bell ring I passed the word to have a bowl of soup got ready for you. I'll go and fetch it now. That's all you can have at the present juncture of affairs. When you've swallowed it, you will feel an inclination to go to sleep. You will yield to that inclination. That is the start of the programme."

He left the room, and the door shut quietly behind him. In a few minutes he appeared with a well-appointed bed-tray, and Taylor, after disposing of a pint of heart-warming chicken broth, with few words on either side, fell into a deep slumber.

His waking gaze fell on the doctor, who, sprawled in an armchair, was busy with a writing-pad and pencil. Some books, one of them open, were on a small table before him. As Taylor stirred, he looked up sharply and rose to his feet. "A little under three hours," he said, glancing at his wrist-watch. "How goes it?"

"Very well, thanks," his patient said, stretching his limbs. "Ought I to feel bad? I don't. In fact if it wasn't for a slight soreness about the head and face I should feel quite right physically. Why have I got a slightly sore head and face? I suppose you can tell me that."

"Railway smash," was the curt reply. "Train derailed near Molesworth station – if that means anything to you. A friend of mine was expecting you at Molesworth – I was with him. When he saw the train jump the track and pile up, he decided to go to it and snatch you out of it. It was he who found you in the wreckage, but getting you out wasn't by any means a one-man job. Having a petite and beautifully proportioned figure, I was cast for the part of crawling through the window of the carriage as it lay on its side, and disentangling you from the debris and heaving up your lifeless form so that he could draw it out. So there you have the sketch, and now you know why you have a sore head and face."

Taylor nodded and passed a hand over the bandaged surfaces. "I don't need to be told," he said, "who it was who plastered me up – and saved me from bleeding to death, perhaps. Thank you, doctor – I shan't forget that."

Dr Barlow shrugged impatiently. "Don't get the idea," he said, "that I'm the person to be thanked, if you feel thankful. The whole scheme was the General's – that's my friend who was with me – you'll meet him later. I only did what I was told. Not that you weren't quite a job of surgical work. You see, the roof of your compartment was stove in, and your head would have been, too, if you hadn't been devilish lucky. As it was, you had a comparatively slight attack of steel and splinters, and your clothes were ruined. That doesn't matter – I've got together another rig-out for you while you were unconscious – reach-me-downs, which ought to do you pretty well – fortunately you're one of the stock sizes. As for the pyjamas, we put you into the only spare suit that was handy, and you may have noticed that they're a little roomy. You won't wonder when you see the man they belong to. Meanwhile, how do you feel about a bath? We've got one, though it fits the bathroom rather more snugly than the pyjamas fit you, and I shall have to superintend the operation. No false modesty, I hope. The reason is that you're sure to be wonky on your legs after being in bed so long, and I shall have to hold you up."

Taylor's reply was to throw off the bedclothes and begin the turning up of a large extent of superfluous pyjama leg. He stood up, staggering slightly, and the doctor produced from the wardrobe a dressing-gown of dark red fleecy stuff. "Straight off the peg," he remarked as he held it to be put on. "There you are – might have been made for you – neat but not gaudy. I'd have liked something a little livelier for you, because cheerful surroundings are good for every sort of illness, even if it's only a crack on the skull, and a really larky dressing-gown is a cheerful surrounding, of course. But they had nothing at all stunning in your size. My own dressing-gown would have been just the thing – when I appear in it, children run screaming to their mothers, and dogs bark themselves into convulsions. But you couldn't have got it on, even with a shoe-horn, so this will have to do."

Still talking, the doctor swiftly dragged off the bedclothes, flung them over chairs, and supporting Taylor on his arm, led him out of the room and into a very small bathroom adjoining it. The house itself, as a glance about the landing told him, could be no more than a cottage. But the things essential, including very hot water, were in the bathroom, and soon a much-refreshed patient, towelled and re-pyjamaed, was having his injuries examined.

"Most of the cuts are all right now," the doctor said, "but your scalp isn't quite fit to be seen yet, and I'll have to keep you mummied up round the jaws to keep the bandages on top where they belong. But before we do that, how about a shave? You can see for yourself" – he waved a hand towards a small mirror on the wall – "what a gorilla you look."

Taylor, gazing at his reflection, passed a hand over the stiff stubble on his cheeks and chin. "I never saw anything more hideous," he admitted. "Can I shave it off now? It looks as if it might be rather tough, but I shan't feel easy until it's gone."

"Much better let me do it," the doctor said. "I've got the things ready. Surgical shaving is rather a speciality of mine, as it happens, and probably you don't realise how much like a hedging-and-ditching job it's going to be, with those scars. Shove on the dressing-gown and sit on this stool."

Taylor did as he was told, and submitted to a very long and vigorous lathering. "Lucky you haven't a train to catch," the doctor remarked. "This is a job that takes time, and needs a lot of thinking out, as the artisan said when he was asked to drive a nail into the top of a post." After the lathering came the dexterous stropping of a cut-throat razor. "No safety razor for you until the undergrowth is cleared away. The brushwood sheaf on the elm tree bole, mentioned by the poet, was nothing to this. Do you remember Mark Twain's first experience of being shaved by a Parisian barber? The first rake loosened his hide and lifted him out of the chair. Now, if you feel anything like that, let me know."

The patient, however, felt nothing like that. On the contrary, he felt that deep relief and satisfaction that an artistic shave brings to a skin which has for some time been suffering from an unaccustomed growth. At length, after a final bathing with hot water and something cool out of a bottle, Dr Barlow stood back and regarded his work with a judicial eye.

"Not so bad," he observed. "I haven't drawn blood anyhow. As I said, you'll be no beauty to look at for some time, but I can assure you, as one who knows, that a man can get along without beauty. In fact, a few scars are a positive advantage – they lend distinction to the human countenance. And be thankful that you've got a countenance – that knocking-about might very well have left you looking like the faceless fiend in a horror story. You certainly looked like him before, with the full set of bandages on. Now I'll attend to the new lot."

When they returned to the bedroom a black-haired, red-cheeked matron was putting the last touches to the making of the bed. "This," Dr Barlow said, "is Mrs McBean, our housekeeper, who is the best cook I know. Mrs McBean, meet my friend Taylor, formerly the faceless fiend. He is longing for a cup of tea, and so am I."

"It's a shame to talk that way," Mrs McBean said, smiling largely. "And if it comes to faces, I know one that wasn't behind the door when ugly ones were given out. But I am very glad to see you are yourself again, Mr Taylor, and up and about, and I will say you owe a lot to Dr Barlow for that, if he does call you a fiend. Now, while you're dressing I'll get you your tea, and I hope you will be ready for a real tea, with some things of my own making. I won't be long if the shop doesn't keep me." And Mrs McBean left them.

The outfit which Dr Barlow now produced from the wardrobe included some blue shirts and collars of a pattern more in keeping with his own tastes than the dressing-gown; but he had shown some restraint in the choosing of the tweed suit, an affair of brown and yellow checks which might pass unnoticed at a cattle show, and arouse no more than a fleeting interest at a golf club. The tie of reddish yellow was nearly matched by the socks.

"Your own underwear will do until you get some more for yourself," the doctor said. "It wasn't damaged in the accident except for a lot of blood on the vest, which has been washed for you. Your shoes, too, weren't hurt, so you will be more comfortable in them for the present. Being black, they don't go perfectly with the clothes, which I selected with an eye to cheerfulness; but after all, you aren't going to Buckingham Palace. I don't know what happened to the baggage you were travelling with – it wasn't with you in the train. There was a hat and a raincoat, and the hat's all right, but the coat wasn't worth saving; I brought away what you had in the pockets of it. Those are your own cuff-links and studs in the shirt you're putting on, and here are the things from the pockets of the clothes you were wearing – money, notecase, pencil, penknife, keys. You ought to go on keeping all those things in your pockets – you never know, the least trifle may remind you of something."

Taylor, feeling himself to be entirely in the hands of his only friend in an unfamiliar world, dressed himself in silence. He was contemplating himself, with a slight feeling of distaste, in the mirror on the inside of the wardrobe door when Mrs McBean entered with a large tray. The tea provided by her was indeed real in the popular sense of being substantial; Taylor had no fault to find with the array of buttered and butterless food, and the sight of a teapot stirred within him a vivid gustatory memory.

"How do you like him, Mrs McBean," Dr Barlow inquired as he filled their cups, "now that he is dressed like a gentleman again?"

Taylor, who had not felt any certainty on this particular point, was not entirely reassured to hear her say that he did not look like the same person; but it was evidently a difference that pleased her, and he wanted to be on good terms with another companion in this strange new life.

"What did you mean, Mrs McBean," he asked, "by saying that the shop might keep you? You know I don't yet realise where I am."

Mrs McBean beamed at the prospect of enlightening him. "It's the tobacco and sweetshop, sir. I keep the only one in Abbot's Dean. If you care about anything in that way, you might step down and look at the stock after closing time – that's if the doctor says you can. There now!" she broke off as a faint tinkle came from below stairs. "There's a customer wants me." And Mrs McBean vanished like a comfortable spirit.

Dr Barlow, busy with a buttered bun, nodded as he handed his patient a plate of adorably thin ham sandwiches. "These," he said, "are recommended by the faculty – made with slightly stale bread, on my instructions. If I were you I should hog the lot – you want to catch up on your eating, and you can't do better at this stage than home-cured ham and butter that was inside the cow only this morning. Yes, this is the village sweetshop – in a small cottage just a little apart from the others, with an orchard – also small, but quite good cover – at the back of it. Just the place for us, Taylor. Nobody on God's earth would ever imagine anything interesting could be happening behind the scenes of Mrs McBean's sweetshop."

Taylor, munching thoughtfully, considered this statement. "Why is it just the place for us?" he asked.

Dr Barlow grinned. "You'll hear all about it from other lips. I mustn't spill too many beans – it's not my campaign. But I've just told you one thing – what marvellous moral camouflage a place like this is. You can suspect the worst, if you're feeling that way, about any fairly prosperous-looking house – love of money being the root of all evil, as you may have heard – but you simply can't suspect anything about a poky little brick box that nobody would live in who wasn't poor but honest, especially when it has a small, dark shop on the ground floor, with a cracked bell rigged over the door. I remember when I was a student in London I used to pass every day a row of dull little undetached houses that looked as if there wasn't a ha'porth of crime in the entire outfit. One day there was a policeman at one of the doors when I went by, and a crowd goggling at the upper windows. A man had murdered his wife in there, and not knowing what to do with the body, had lived with it for ten days, all alone, until the police got on to it somehow."

Taylor, who had obediently finished the sandwiches and was busy with a second cup of tea, grimaced at this. "Well," he said, "you're not concealing a dead body, anyhow, though you say I look like a corpse. But I can tell you something that you are concealing – I've just thought of it."

"What's that, Taylor?" Dr Barlow asked.

"My passport," Taylor reminded him. "You said I had one, and I want to see it."

"I haven't got it," the doctor said tartly. "But I can tell you – "

A deep voice, speaking from behind them, interrupted softly: "I beg a thousand pardons – for having taken possession of your passport, *amigo*, in the first place. For overhearing some of your conversation in the second place."

CHAPTER V

Neither Taylor nor the doctor had heard a sound, either from the opening door or from any footstep; yet there was nothing quiet or furtive about the appearance of the man who had spoken, and who now approached them as they sat at the table.

He was tall and of powerful build, dressed in a close-fitting dark blue tunic and trousers. His head, thatched with short black curls, was held high; black brows were arched over large, thoughtful eyes and a long nose, slightly hooked; a black moustache bristled upwards from a mouth that was smiling now, but still looked far from harmless. In spite of this, his expression was open, sincere and friendly. He looked like a stage Gascon out of *Cyrano de Bergerac*; yet he was obviously very real indeed.

Taylor felt an immediate attraction to this personage. If looks meant anything, this was a man of immense vitality, a positive, vigorous and resourceful character; to have him on one's side would be of advantage in any difficulty. So Taylor, whose difficulty was serious enough, felt immediately; if he was, as the doctor said, among friends, he was glad that this should be one of them.

"I wish to God, General, you wouldn't pussyfoot about like that all the time," Dr Barlow exclaimed peevishly. "It's all right with me – I'm used to it, and I haven't any nerves,

31

anyway; but this patient of mine – anything sudden is enough to make him jump through the roof."

The man addressed as General heard him with an appearance of great interest. "So! You have not any nerves. Well, as a man of science, you should know. Just as your Postmaster-General, he should know if he comes to me and says, '*Amigo*, I regret to say that you are mistaken in me, I must confess to you that I have no telegraph wires, no telephones.' But I am compelled to disagree with you, Barlow *mio*. The truth is, you have a hell of a nerve, telling me what I must not do. Overhearing your conversation, as I have said, I get the impression that your patient is not now so ill that I must break myself to him gently."

The man in blue turned to Taylor. "Just the same, I apologise to you for what our doctor calls my pussycat behaviour. He is not the first to give it that name. It has become second nature to me – a custom of long standing. I am a man whose whole life is governed by prudence. So often my safety has depended on my not being seen or heard, I have formed the creeping habit. In my own country, in the Republic of Peligragua, they have a name for me – *El Gatillo*, the Little Cat. They call me other things also, it is true, but if you mention *El Gatillo* it is known by everyone that you refer to General Justo Hernando de la Costa." And the General bowed in self-introduction. "I may say that the name has passed into our political history. When I was a candidate for the Presidency, attempting to overthrow the corrupt scorpion Verdugo, the walls of every town and village in the country had written on them, '*Queremos El Gatillo*' – We want the Little Cat. *Desdichadamente*, they did not get that quadruped." Here the General exploded in a loud laugh, which was checked abruptly when Dr Barlow hissed, "Silence!"

"Talk about quadrupeds!" the doctor went on bitterly. "Mrs McBean is going to get the reputation of keeping a laughing hyena concealed on the premises if you're not more careful. Suppose Johnny Jones has just come in for three penn'orth of toffee crunch, what's he going to make of a peal of Peligraguan merriment coming from upstairs?"

The General smote himself heavily on the chest. "You are right, *chico*, and I am a triple idiot." He turned to Taylor. "I must tell you, my dear Taylor – so I hear our doctor call you, and it is a good idea – I must tell you that we are in a situation of some delicacy here. As I have just heard the doctor telling you, this is the sweetshop in the Hampshire village of Abbot's Dean, a little isolated from the other cottages. The tenant of it is Mrs McBean – invaluable woman! – the widow of a late friend and assistant of mine. It is believed by every one in the place that she lives alone here, and I wish to encourage that idea. But in fact, she has from time to time a guest or guests. At present there are three – yourself, in this room; Dr Barlow and myself, who sleep in the next room. And all three of us are *escondidos*."

"He means we are lying doggo," the doctor translated. "We wouldn't have to tell you this, you understand, if you hadn't had that knock on the head. You'd been told all about it already, before that happened – before you came to England, in fact."

"Lying doggo," the General said thoughtfully. "A nice expression – I must remember it. Sometimes it happens, my dear Taylor, that I am for the moment at a loss for the right English word, though I speak English well enough, I believe."

"You do, indeed," Taylor said. He had been wondering how anyone so emphatically un-English as this man was, in manner of speech as well as in appearance, could speak the language with no trace of any foreign accent. "You speak it better than most Englishmen do – in a way."

The General smiled. "In a way, yes! You mean that I am more careful in speaking. That is because I think in another language. I think in Spanish. In my childhood I learnt English, or rather English came to me – for the best of reasons. Often in my life I have spoken only English. I have lived some years in New York and in other parts of the States, and some years in England. But the language of my heart and mind is the language of Castilla la Vieja, as it was brought to the lovely land of Peligragua by Pedro de Alvaredo so long ago. So it happens that sometimes I am at a loss for an English term, as I have said. Or sometimes I use a Spanish expression, just for..." He hesitated.

"Just for the hell of it," Dr Barlow suggested.

The General shook his head. "Or for the heaven of it, perhaps," he said gently. "What would you? One is not ashamed to be of Spanish descent. On the contrary."

"As the Frenchman said," added Dr Barlow.

The General's only response to this was to lean his head back and close his eyes.

Taylor, who had a sense that all this explaining should have included something from his own side, spoke up a little uneasily. "I have heard of Spanish pride," he said. "It is one of a thousand vague recollections. But you ought to be told, General, that I remember very little of my own life. Dr Barlow will tell you."

"But has he not told me!" the General exclaimed, spreading his arms abroad. "I know everything, *amigo*, and I have no words to express how deeply I feel with you in your misfortune. When you came to yourself the first time, this morning, I was sleeping in the next room – for me the night had been a busy one. I had been paying a visit to Glasminster. Some hours later, when you were again asleep, I rose refreshed, my first question was about yourself, I heard of your affliction with sorrow, and, I will confess it, with some disappointment. Then I slept a little more, until

I heard the sounds of activity in the bathroom. I rose, I made my toilette, then I came to this room to make your acquaintance, my dear Taylor, omitting so unpardonably to make a noise like an Englishman. I am, says our doctor, a pussycat. Also I lie doggo. It is a regrettable throw-back, as you say, to more early stages in the evolution of our species. Dr Barlow would never retreat so far. He is satisfied to look like a monkey – is it not so, Barlow *mio*?"

The doctor grinned. "I got used to being told so when I was at school," he said. "But never mind about the brute creation just now. We were explaining to you, Taylor, about our living here in concealment. The fact is that the General has several hide-outs dotted about the country where he can go to ground when it seems advisable. They are all kept by friends or retainers of his, and he has made even the smallest of them – like this place – pretty comfortable, if not what I should call ornamental." He waved an explanatory hand about the room. "The General is keeping you here until you are well enough to move. There you have an outline of the situation."

The General, with a smile like a benevolent wolf's, nodded his confirmation of this, while Taylor continued to stare at him in fascination.

"All right," he said. "If that's your idea of an explanation. It seems a little superficial to me."

General de la Costa looked at the doctor. "*Toma!*" he remarked. "What did Farewell Billy write about him? He talks like an Englishman, Billy said."

" 'Like a limey,' was what Billy actually wrote," the doctor corrected him. "Just the same, I wasn't quite prepared. I don't know if Billy thinks all Englishmen talk like Taylor. Perhaps he does – he probably never met one before."

"But I'm not bothering about the details just now," Taylor pursued. "Here I am, and you are quite right,

General, about my not being an invalid any more. I'm most grateful to both of you for having looked after me so well. But the only thing I care about at present is that I have lost my memory, and that you can help me to get it back. You said you had possession of my passport, I think."

The two others exchanged a look; then the General facing Taylor, pursed his lips and wagged a forefinger slowly from side to side.

"I regret most deeply to have to tell you," he said, "that your passport is no good. It would not help you to establish your identity. It was intended for a purpose quite different."

"How do you mean?" Taylor asked in bewilderment.

"I mean that it was intended to conceal your identity. It is," the General explained, "a forgery – passport, visa, the whole works. It is not a bad job, at that. It would get by any ordinary frontier official, it has not the faults which they look for. In fact, it has got by already, at Southampton. We owe to that happy circumstance the honour of your presence here. But an expert police examiner would see through it, and if such a person found it in your possession you would be arrested *al instante*. Therefore, as you were not in a state to be consulted about the matter, I took the liberty of destroying your passport as soon as we reached here. It was an incriminating document, as you say, and the sooner it ceased to exist the safer you would be."

Taylor gazed at him for a few moments in silence. "Then," he said at last, "the name on it was not my name, but a false name?"

"It said," the General replied, "that the holder of it was named Dwight Philip Taylor. That is a perfectly good name, and our doctor, as he tells me, has agreed with you that it shall be your name for the present; but it is not your true name. The document went on to say that you were a mining engineer, and that you resided at Boulder, in the State of Colorado. These were, as I am positively assured, untrue statements. The description of your person was, of course, not untrue, and the photograph was, we may believe, a fair likeness – as to that, *que se yo*? You are much altered in appearance now, and I never enjoyed the pleasure of meeting you in the past."

"Yes, but evidently you know who I am, and something about me, at least," Taylor said. "Or at least this Billy Somebody, who told you I talked like an Englishman – he must have known all about me, I should think."

The General shook his head. "Farewell Billy, who lives in New York, moves in circles in which it is quite usual for a person's true name, and the facts about his past life, to be unknown to his associates. It is also considered to be in very bad taste, it may even be not very safe, to question him about these subjects. I myself know Billy well, and I know what his straight family name is, but he may not know yours, or anything about your origin. When writing to me about you he said only that the name and other details of your passport were fabricated. He left it to you, we may suppose, to tell me your right name if you should choose, or a wrong name if you should prefer it. He mentioned that you had a nickname, as you say, a name by which you are known to one and all – like Billy himself. That name – "

Here Dr Barlow intervened, raising an admonitory finger. "In cases like Taylor's," he said, "it is thought to be more healthy to let the trouble cure itself, to let the memory come back gradually, or at any rate in its own way, by contact with circumstances. I should say," he went on, with a significant glance at the General, "that that would certainly be the right method in this case. Our friend has recovered his senses, his mental balance is much better than might have been expected, he is not in bad health, he does not seem to be unduly depressed now he feels he is among friends – that is the important thing for him. I see no reason why he shouldn't begin to live a normal life and – what was it the rhymester said? – 'do the work that's nearest, though it's dull at whiles.' That's my view."

"It is a wise view," the General said with enthusiasm. "To live a normal life – not to be a vegetable. You are in agreement, Taylor, I hope."

Taylor rubbed his chin. "I suppose so," he said. "What shall I remember, I wonder, when I do begin? It's pretty evident that my record is not all that could be wished – not the part of it that your friend Billy knows, anyhow – or I shouldn't have come here with a forged passport."

"Not all that could be wished – but wished by whom?" the General said softly. "Is not that the point, *amigo*? Must we wish all that is wished by that admirable Scotland Yard? And need I tell you that there are many men in high positions – statesmen – diplomats – who have travelled in their time with forged passports? Not for nothing do we live in an age of revolutions."

Taylor looked blank. "I know nothing about that," he said. "But if you want me to be a conspirator, I can tell you at once that it won't do. I don't believe I ever was a conspirator. In the days of my youth, which I remember in a vague sort of way, I used to hate anything of that sort, and you can't persuade me that I didn't."

The General, who had been moving gently about the room since his first appearance, now pulled forward a chair and seated himself astride of it, facing Taylor. "Do not misunderstand me," he said earnestly. "The words I used were no more than an illustration of my meaning. You have come to me – I may tell him about this, doctor, if I take it slow, may I not? – you have come to me to help me, not as a conspirator, but in defeating a conspiracy. What

38

else will you call a plot by a band of criminals to deprive me – Justo de la Costa – of my liberty?"

This, then, was a part at least of the truth about the position which Dr Barlow had sketched with so light a hand. "You mean that they are trying to kidnap you," he asked.

"I mean that exactly," the General said. "Not merely an insult and a challenge to myself, but a crime."

"Against the peace of our sovereign lord the King, his crown and dignity," Dr Barlow added.

"But why?" Taylor asked.

The General looked at the doctor, who nodded briefly. "You'd better do a little more explaining," he said. "Only don't rush it too much."

CHAPTER VI

General de la Costa frowned at the ceiling as if marshalling his ideas.

"*Escuchad!*" he said at length. "To answer your question, my dear Taylor, I must tell you something of my own affairs, hoping that you will not be bored too much. I am a man of many interests. One of them is a form of production, which is in a high degree profitable, and which is my own exclusively. Without this, I was not a poor man – my property in my own country is extensive. But with this, I am not ashamed to say, I am enormously rich. Why not? It is the reward of my researches, of my technical ingenuity and of the work of these hands."

He extended them proudly palms upward, but Taylor could see nothing notable about them beyond their being large and well-shaped.

"It is some invention that you have patented?" he suggested.

"By no means," the General replied. "It is not the sort of invention that is suitable for that. I alone know the process. I alone sell the product and pocket the money. It is better so – the one-man business, as you say. But you must know there are others who in their swinish greed do not agree that it is better so. They know what I am doing, they know that my business – what shall I say? – that it invades the territory of their business. They know that if I choose to produce in great quantity, or if for some reason I make my secret known, then it is all over with their damned business, which is for them a source of great wealth. You see?"

"They are your enemies, then?" Taylor asked.

"*Yo lo creo*! They are indeed," the General said with feeling. "All of those who control that very prosperous business are my enemies. Most of them are good citizens, however, excellent creatures, they would do no more than wish me at the devil with all their hearts. But one of them is a bad man, a man without scruple, who cares nothing for law or convention – he will not commit any crime himself, ah no! but he will pay others to do it for him."

"He would hire them to murder you!" Taylor exclaimed. "Is that what you mean?"

The General waved the suggestion aside. "Bah! To murder me – what is that? In my forty years of life, I have been very nearly murdered forty times at least, and the chances are I may be cooled off yet, as you say. But this man whom I speak of does not want my corpse, *amigo* – at least, that is not his immediate object. What he wants is my secret – that is to say, he wants me, in person. So, his agents who are trying to get me have been strictly ordered to get me alive and in good condition. They might knock me cold, perhaps, or put me to sleep one way or another – they have had several tries already – but certainly they are expected to deliver me, as you say, in good order. And that is quite a difficult assignment, as I and my friends have shown them."

"Apart from that," Dr Barlow added, "in this little country of ours professional criminals draw the line at murder. They will take almost any risk if you pay them well enough, but a swinging job is in the class of things that are not done – not for money, that is. If the General's trade rival seriously wants him murdered after he is through with him, he will have to attend to the matter himself."

The General nodded. "Our doctor puts it with admirable clearness, my dear Taylor. This rival, as I have said, wants my secret. He figures, quite correctly, that I will have kept it entirely to myself, so he wishes to get from my lips the way of getting rich that I have, in addition to the much slower and far more expensive way that he has already. If I may speak figuratively, it would broaden the base of his position, it would take care of any falling off in the natural resources on which he relies. In fact, my dear Taylor, your first suggestion was the right one – kidnapping. He would get me into his possession and make me talk. You see?"

Taylor heard this with a slightly sceptical air. "So it really is kidnapping that you fear," he said. "And being tortured to make you talk, as you put it. Are such things possible in these times?"

Dr Barlow stirred in his chair. "You don't know anything about these times, do you?" he said. "It's a point to be borne in mind. They may not be all your fancy paints them."

"Just so," the General said. " Pardon us for referring to your disability. The truth is that I am a man in a peculiar position, and that for a man in such a position, to be kidnapped is not at all impossible. And as for the kidnappers compelling me to talk, I must tell you that in these times, in which you have a confidence so touching, that sort of thing is by no means unheard of. As for me, if I were once taken I should not refuse to talk, it would not amuse me. *Vaya*! A money-making secret, it is not as if it were a matter of honour. Of course, the problem of getting away alive afterwards would be another matter, to be dealt with in its turn."

The General shrugged his shoulders lightly. "And as for having kidnapping to fear, as you say," he continued, "I may tell you that fear is not an emotion from which I suffer greatly. I do not mean that I am the kind of imbecile who does not know what fear is – ah no! But I do not let it throw me. On the contrary, I smack it around and make it wish it had never been born. What Newman wrote about himself is what I feel – 'My spirits most happily rise at the prospect of danger.' But perhaps you have not studied the works of Newman."

Taylor stared at him. "Do you mean Cardinal Newman?" he asked, frowning. "I believe I have heard of him."

"He did in the end become a Cardinal," the General answered with an air of faint distaste. "He wrote what I have said at a time when his opinions were in a more healthy state. But I am wandering from the point. I was saying that danger stimulates me. At the same time, my dear Taylor, I am a prudent man. I like to play a dangerous game, yes, but if I play it I play to win. Is not that what it means to be a soldier? To make life interesting, that is my aim, and if life is not organised so as to be interesting, I try to correct the mistake."

"It's an ambitious plan," Taylor said, laughing. "But doesn't it lead you into trouble with the police some-times?"

The General glanced sharply at him, then at Dr Barlow, who shook his head decisively.

"Not so often as you may think," the General said. "From time to time, I admit it, there are misunderstandings with the police, but that is a sort of risk which I wish to reduce to a minimum. To fulfil my duties to society – that is for me a counsel of perfection at least. Now take this matter of kidnapping me, my dear Taylor. What is wrong with my side-stepping that little arrangement? And what is wrong with my refusing to sell out my secret to the tarantula who is paying for that little arrangement? And is the world much the worse if the obscene carrion who are trying to carry out that arrangement get bumped about a little now and then? You cannot tell me that you think so."

The General spread his arms abroad in an eloquent gesture, and Taylor laughed again. "I don't think so, certainly," he said. "But who are they, anyhow? If they are professional criminals, aren't they known to the police? Aren't you entitled to protection against them? Surely it isn't a private war between you and them."

"Are they known to the police?" the General repeated, looking at the ceiling. "I regret most deeply to say that I am not in the confidence of the police. But I believe that in what is called the underworld that pack of brutes are referred to as Ketch's crowd. Ketch is an interesting specimen, a criminal in a large way of business. His interests include, as I have been told, counterfeiting and housebreaking and blackmailing, but I feel sure that the kidnapping of Justo de la Costa, which would be so handsomely rewarded, stands high on his programme. I have reason to know that he is very well served with information, for which he pays generously. Some of his people are always looking about for me. When they find me, they organise a snatch, as I believe they call it. You see?"

Taylor reflected for a few moments. "I seem to have heard of people like your Ketch," he said. "In my boyhood there were stories written about sinister organisers of crime, men of brains and education who sat in the background and pulled the strings. They never appeared to get much out of it for themselves, as far as I remember. They didn't seem at all life-like."

Dr Barlow laughed shortly. "I know," he said. "You're thinking of Professor Moriarty in the Sherlock Holmes tales. Life-like! Didn't he spend most of his time in the degrading slavery of coaching pups for maths exams, and run his gigantic network of highly profitable crime in his leisure hours? Is it likely? Loud cries of No! No!"

The General wagged a forefinger. "Nobody wanted him to be life-like, or even possible. But in the world of hard facts in which we move Ketch is a very genuine personage. He is a crook and a ruffian. He certainly is not of the educated class, though he has a good intelligence. He has built up a remarkable organisation, but he does not sit in the background. Several times I have met him, so I can tell you, my dear Taylor, how to know him, for it is possible you may meet him too. For one thing he is completely bald, owing to his having had as a young man an attack of typhoid fever, which unhappily was not fatal. Another thing which distinguishes him is a long nose, very much on one side – it is not to be mistaken. I knocked it sideways myself, about a year ago. It has remained so ever since, and I dare say it will always be so. Unless," the General added thoughtfully, "I knock it straight again for him one day, perhaps."

"It must have been a terrible punch," Taylor remarked; and Dr Barlow again laughed shortly.

"It wasn't a punch, strictly speaking," he said.

"Not precisely," the General agreed. "I did it with the heel of my right boot, swinging round on the left leg – they call it the *coup de pied tournant* at the school of the *savate* in Paris, where I studied the art. To do it with precision, at the height of a man's face, is not an easy thing to learn, but it is worth the trouble."

The doctor nodded. "I doubt if we could have made our getaway without it that time," he said. "There were five of them to two of us. I wasn't bothering much about the Queensberry rules myself, either."

"When one is dragged unwillingly into scraps where nothing is barred, what would you?" the General sighed. "And our doctor is pretty good as a square fighter, at that.

But this recollection, Taylor, brings us to the point which I wished to make clear. What I need – what I was needing on that occasion, in fact – is a specialist in that sort of thing, one whose mind is not occupied with other matters. In short, a bodyguard. Now, some time ago an American visiting this country called on an English friend of mine – an intimate friend, whom other friends of mine know to be in touch with me. This is a great convenience to me, living as I do in retirement."

Taylor nodded his understanding of this delicate form of words. "You mean that messages can be sent to you through him."

"Precisely – messages or letters," the General said. "Now this American visitor left with my friend a letter from Farewell Billy, of whom I have spoken already. In that letter he wrote to me of one of his associates who was coming to England, who had had experience as a bodyguard, and who would be willing to join me in that capacity if I needed him. Billy paid the highest tribute to this man's skill and courage. He mentioned particularly his loyalty, a virtue to which great importance is attached in Farewell Billy's world, and which is, in fact, looked upon as compensating for the absence of any other virtues. He made it plain that this man had urgent reasons for wishing to come to England, or to leave the States anyway. He added that this man would be travelling with a passport in which he was described as Dwight Philip Taylor."

"I was beginning to expect that," Taylor said grimly. "So I am the man who was Farewell Billy's bodyguard."

The General shrugged his shoulders. "Billy did not say so. But, like yourself, I am inclined to think so. Well, my dear Taylor, that was the position. Billy had written that I should be doing him a favour if I enlisted your services. I never miss a chance of doing a favour to a friend, and besides, I thought that I could use just that kind of assistance, as I have told you. Therefore I wrote to Billy accepting his proposal, and I mentioned a day when I should be expecting to meet this friend of his arriving at Molesworth station by a certain train from Southampton. This left ample time for him to make the journey and keep the date. So it was settled."

The General spread his hands abroad, then rose to his feet and looked at Taylor with attention.

"Yes, I see," Taylor answered slowly. "And when I came to keep that appointment – well, Dr Barlow has told me what happened. He insisted that it was you, General, whom I had to thank for my being saved from the wreck. Well, I thank you now. I am deeply indebted to you both, and I wish I knew some way of repaying your kindness."

The General threw up his head impatiently. "*Disparate!*" he exclaimed. "How could I do anything less, my dear Taylor? You had come to keep an engagement with me, and you understand – do you not? – that you were in serious danger of trouble with the authorities about the matter of your passport? Naturally I was obliged to take action. I did not like the thought of your recovering consciousness in a hospital, and finding a large man in uniform sitting beside the bed."

"Instead of a man of moderate dimensions in a tasteful civilian get-up," Dr Barlow added. "He's quite right, Taylor. If you'd been found with that passport on you, the consequences would have been unpleasant. We knew you would be found with it, and Farewell Billy had made it quite plain in his letter that the only kind of passport you could get would be a phoney one."

The General nodded. "A home-made one – that was Billy's expression. And, as I have said, quite well made. But not good enough to be left in the hands of the police for careful study. Now, unhappily, all that has passed out of your recollection, together with so much more. But you, my dear Taylor, are still the same man. My requirements are still the same. The question is, are you still willing and able to carry out the arrangement that was made?"

The General, his hands behind him and his feet apart, rocked himself slightly on his heels as he gazed earnestly at Taylor, who returned his look with bent brows. All that was quite clear to him was a conviction that he must not part company with these two men – his only companions in a world of which he was entirely ignorant, yet which was, it seemed, disposed to be hostile. What the business was in which the General and his satellite were engaged he could not guess. That it involved secrecy and danger was evident, and it appeared to mean, in the General's delicate phrase, not being in the confidence of the police.

But that was, certainly, Taylor's own position – the position of the man who had been travelling in that train. Nothing explicit had been said about the pursuits of Farewell Billy and his associates in New York, but from what the General had let fall it could be guessed that they were not model citizens, and if it were true that Taylor's passport was forged, the fact told its own story.

All that he knew about General de la Costa and Dr Barlow was that they were friendly. But to him that meant everything. It was the dread of isolation that had been overshadowing him more and more ever since he had realised the truth about his situation. Both these men, too, had impressed him in their different ways as men to be liked, and on whom he could rely. With nothing but instinct to guide him, he gave them credit for fundamental decency. They had helped him; should he not help them – in particular the General, to whom, for all the oddity and extravagance of his personal style, he found himself irresistibly drawn? But if he was to commit himself blindly to act as a hired fighting man, could he – setting aside all other considerations – play that part?

As these thoughts passed through Taylor's perplexed mind, the General struck his forehead lightly. "Pardon my forgetfulness," he said. "I should have mentioned the terms of your engagement which I suggested when I wrote to Billy. You were to live as my guest while under my command, with pay at the rate, in English money, of £200 a month. And the living – may I say it? – would not be so bad."

"You needn't have any doubts on that point," the doctor assured him. "I'm a fair judge of food and drink myself, but the General is an expert. He can live on anything or nothing himself, if he has to, and he has a liking for telque, which is the favourite poison of his native land, but he knows how to look after other people's creature comforts. Though I don't believe you care a tinker's damn about that," he added shrewdly.

Taylor shook his head. "No, I'm not thinking about the terms, but about the job," he said. "I don't know that I'm the right sort of man for it."

The others exchanged a smile. "All *we* know is," the doctor said, "that you have the reputation of being a wonder at it. Farewell Billy's testimonial means something, believe me."

"I used to be good at boxing long ago," Taylor said, frowning. "Very good, I believe. Wrestling, too – I used to enjoy anything of that sort, it's one of the things that I remember. But I feel certain kicking people in the face was never in my line – standing up or lying down."

The General waved the matter aside. "It is a rare accomplishment," he said. "In this country practically unknown. It was not expected of you, so do not let your ignorance of that technique weigh on your mind. There is another matter, however."

He made a sign to Dr Barlow, who was seated by the table under the window. The doctor, pulling open a drawer, produced a large revolver, and the General, taking it from him, weighed it in his hand.

"It is an excellent gun," he said. "Smith and Wesson .32. There is much to be said for the automatic and the other modern firearms in general, but for me, I am like yourself conservative in these things. I have found that some of the best men are so." Holding the weapon by the barrel, he extended the pearl-ornamented butt to Taylor, who looked at it dubiously.

"This is no good to me," he said.

"It is your own rod, *amigo*," the General assured him.

Taylor shook his head, and Dr Barlow, after fingering his chin for a few moments, came forward.

"This is interesting," he muttered. "Let me have it, General." Taking the revolver, he placed it gently in Taylor's right hand, which closed on it at once. "Now is it any good to you?" the doctor asked.

Taylor, staring at the weapon in his grasp, still shook his head; but his forefinger slipped easily into the trigger guard and he stroked the barrel gently.

"There you are!" Dr Barlow exclaimed. "The mind has forgotten, but the fingers remember. It often happens in cases like yours."

Taylor looked at the others with a rather sheepish smile. "I believe it must be so," he said. "I think I must have used it, or one like it, a good deal at one time."

The others exchanged a smile.

"You did," the doctor said drily.

"*Indudiablemente!*" the General exclaimed. "A good deal, my dear Taylor, as you say."

"It's a sort of patch," Dr Barlow went on. "In your memory, I mean. Things come back little by little."

"But we had better be clear about this," Taylor said, still playing with the weapon. "If killing people is part of my duties as a bodyguard, I'm not taking it on – that's definite."

The General held up his hands. "My dear Taylor, I must entreat you not to get me wrong. I have tried to explain to you that killing me is not on the programme for Ketch's crowd, and assuredly I would not set a bad example. I wished to secure the services of an expert gunman, for the very reason that he can use his revolver without killing people."

"That's the idea," the doctor said. "If at any time Ketch and Co. seem to have got the game in their hands, and the resources of civilisation look like being exhausted, the General wants to have an ace up his sleeve. This is the ace." He tapped the revolver as Taylor held it. "You see, anyone with your talents could lay out half-a-dozen men in no time at all without damaging them seriously. The General himself isn't exactly poor with a gun, but he doesn't feel he could trust himself to that extent. As for me, I'm no good at all – I should merely blast into the brown of them, and very likely set a bad example, as the General expresses it. It would be different with you. Of course, if we can get along without gunplay, so much the better – it's so noisy, for one thing, and we don't want to attract public attention any more than they do."

It seemed to Taylor that the time had come for putting plainly the question that had been shaping itself more and more clearly before him. He laid the revolver on the table, and addressed the General with more firmness than he had yet felt able to show.

"If you want me to join you," he said, "you must tell me more than I have heard so far. Don't you agree that I ought to be taken into your confidence? For instance, there's the question I asked some time ago – why aren't you being given police protection against these people? Surely I've a right to be told that."

The General stepped forward and laid a hand on his shoulder. "You have every right," he said, "to be told that and more than that. Reassure yourself, my dear Taylor, I wish you to know everything, I shall place my cards on the table. But there is a good deal to explain, and I am advised by our doctor not to rush it too much." He turned to Dr Barlow. "Shall I begin by answering just that question – about my relations with the police?"

"Might as well," the doctor grunted. "The truth about that wouldn't have been any shock to him as he was before the railway smash. Not knowing it now worries him, and we don't want him to be worried. If when he knows it he is still worried, you'll just have to call the whole thing off. He wouldn't be worried if he knew Cowdery, I should say."

The General shrugged. "Well, he is not acquainted with that obscene coyote, so we must do our best. Why, my dear Taylor, do I not claim the protection of the police? It is because I am myself a fugitive from justice, as you say."

CHAPTER VII

"That doesn't seem to surprise you," Dr Barlow observed with a grin.

Taylor, leaning back in his chair, kept an expectant eye on the General's face. "It doesn't surprise me at all," he said. "I don't believe either of you thought it would. Both of you have said things that were meant, I suppose, to lead up to it gently, and apart from that the whole situation prepared me for something of the sort. The question is, what the police have against you, and the General was just going to tell me that."

"As you say, my dear Taylor," the General agreed, with a courteous inclination of the head. "It is a pleasure to find myself so well understood."

"A little while ago," Taylor reminded him, "you told me that your plan of making life interesting did sometimes lead to misunderstandings with the police. I thought that probably meant you had done something illegal."

"I did allow myself that – how do you say? – that euphemism," the General admitted with a radiant smile. "Yes, my dear Taylor, I have done something illegal. In fact more than once I have been guilty of offending against the law. It has always been with the best of motives – need I assure you of that? – but such motives are no defence, I know it. Still, most of these offences have never been reported to the authorities, as far as I know. But in one case information has been laid against me before a magistrate, saying that I have given a thrashing to the contemptible animal who made the charge. If I had been present at the time, I should have admitted the fact, I should have done so with pride, but as being present would have interfered with my arrangements, I chose to be absent. A summons was issued against me. It was served, as I have been told, by leaving it at the hotel at which I had been staying. As I never saw the summons, and so did not obey it, a warrant for my arrest was issued. So far it has not been executed, because I have always been a few hops ahead of the police since that time. In other words, I am a fugitive from justice, as I have said."

Taylor drew a breath of relief as the General paused in his confession. "Well, that doesn't amount to very much," he said.

The General seemed not to be highly gratified by this comment. "It was an aggravated assault, *amigo*," he pointed out. "So it was described. And the assaulted person did not think it amounted to so little, believe me."

"Oh, I didn't mean to make light of it," Taylor said. "But is that all they have against you?"

"Nearly all," the General said. "I had not quite finished my story. After the warrant had been issued, when I had been missing for a few weeks, I drove down to his place in the country, where he usually spent the weekends, and gave him another licking, just to make the first one stick. Since then I have not appeared in public. And now, my dear Taylor, the evening draws on, it is almost half-past seven, at that time precisely Mrs McBean will have dinner ready for us in the other room, where the doctor and I have our beds. What would you? One must live as one can – still, I have better places, where I hope to enjoy your society in the future. And when we have dined, I shall tell you more about my affairs, and you shall say at last how you feel about accepting the post I have offered you."

Dr Barlow rose to his feet and stretched his arms luxuriously. "And you can say now," he suggested, "how you feel about saddle of mutton. Have you forgotten what it tastes like? If you have, I envy you from the bottom of my heart – you have a wonderful experience in store." He went to the window, which he closed quietly.

The General strode to the door and opened it, just as the red-cheeked matron came, empty-handed, out of the opposite room. "Thank you, Mrs McBean," he said. "You are punctuality itself. Let me show you the way, my dear Taylor."

The room where the dinner was laid was rather larger than the one they had quitted. It looked out, as Taylor could assume, over the road before the cottage; but the window was efficiently blacked-out with a blind and curtains, and a large oil-lamp over the table gave the only illumination.

Here, too, the effect of the room was one of civilised austerity; but there were, besides the two low beds and the three chairs at the table, three other chairs of a more comfortable sort placed about a small table before the fireplace. A blue-and-white checked cloth covered the larger table; the table furniture, though sufficient, was of a simplicity to match, but for the presence of wine glasses and two bottles, already opened. From one of them the General at once began to dispense the appropriate wine, while Dr Barlow took charge of the carving cutlery.

"We may not be Caledonians," he said with relish, "but our claret is sound and our mutton good. This joint was chosen by one of the General's friends, who understands these things, and it was delivered here two nights ago."

The General raised his glass. "*Brindis*, my dear Taylor," he said with an all-embracing smile.

Dr Barlow joined him in the pledge. "Your health, Taylor. There! I felt certain you weren't a teetotaller, somehow" – as Taylor, nodding to each of them, drank in his turn. "It's easy to see you were properly brought up."

"I think it has a good nose, as the French say," the General remarked modestly, savouring his own glass. "I must apologise for offering you only this wine. In this place we live very simply, as you have seen. There is nothing but this Beychevelle, but there is brandy, which our doctor considers good, and there is telque, for which he has not enough education, but which you shall try, if you will, later on. Meanwhile, let us dine, and God be thanked for food and fellowship."

Conversation at the table dealt at first with the subject of mutton, which seemed an inexhaustible one for General de la Costa and Dr Barlow. The General drew upon an astonishingly wide experience of mutton in all its forms and varieties of treatment; and he pronounced English saddle of mutton to be by far the best of all. Dr Barlow had a store of memories of mutton in English literature, from the song of the heroes of Dinas Vawr – "The mountain sheep are sweeter, but the valley sheep are fatter" – to the lines describing Mahbub Ali's feast in the Khyber Pass – "A cinnamon stew of the fat-tailed sheep."

"That I have never tasted," the General said, shuddering, "and I cannot pretend that it sounds to me very palatable. Cookery, my dear Taylor – that is the insurmountable bar between the West and the East. No one of European blood could ever enjoy that stew, just as no Oriental – so I have been told – can look upon even the most delicious of Burgundian snails as tempting food. Yet we can borrow from each other all kinds of excellent things. Polo, for instance, which I have played on both sides of the Atlantic, was known in Persia when Europe was a wilderness of howling cannibals. On the other hand, many Indians have taken seriously the game of cricket, discovering in it a charm which, I confess, remains a secret to me."

"Taylor is a cricketer," remarked Dr Barlow, who had noted a lighting up of the guest's eye at the mention of the game; and for the first time Taylor found himself talking freely and naturally on a subject that he understood, in response to the General's mischievous prodding. The doctor, posing as a neutral, grinned with appreciation as the argument developed; and he nodded judicially when Taylor firmly declined a third glass of wine. "Temperance is a habit with you, I can see," he said. "If you find you have a habit, stick to it. It all helps."

Saddle of mutton was succeeded by apple-tart, Dr Barlow calling attention to the exquisite balance of firmness and tenderness in the slices, and the ambrosial lightness of the crust. Mrs McBean, when she had put the coffee and a bottle of brandy before them, was complimented by him and the General on the dinner.

"So you always say," replied the matron, with the composure of conscious worth. "You will spoil me if I get nothing but praise."

"It is because you spoil nothing, Mrs McBean," the General said. "In this imperfect world something or some one must be spoilt, so it seems it must be yourself." He measured out three portions of brandy. "Gentlemen! to the health of our *cordon bleu*! Now let us take our places in the armchairs. One lives as one can, my dear Taylor, in a two-room establishment. Do you smoke? You do not. Then pardon us while we cultivate that insidious vice." Producing a small sack of black tobacco, he rolled a cigarette with magical dexterity, while the doctor lighted a cigar.

As Mrs McBean cleared the table, the General smoked with half-closed eyes, frowning slightly. "I tax my memory," he said when she had left them to themselves. "Will you tell me again, Barlow *mio*, the lines in which that disgusting mess of sheep's fat and cinnamon is held up to admiration? I do not recall them perfectly, and I should like to bear them in mind."

" 'So we plunged the hand to the mid-wrist deep in a cinnamon stew of the fat-tailed sheep,' " Dr Barlow recited, " 'and he who never hath tasted the food, by Allah, he knoweth not bad from good.' "

"A very proper God," the General opined, "to invoke in praising such a repulsive *olla*. But certainly that might have been truly said of the English saddle of mutton, and it is a reminder of our fallen nature that your Kipling, when he wrote that, cannot have forgotten the taste of the noblest of all mutton dishes. But that was his way – writing of India and Indian peoples, he would try to be more Oriental than the Orientals. For example, I cannot believe that in India the whole population – even the brutes in the jungle – talk the language of your English Bible. Does Kipling's Indian servant at table say, 'Curried eggs, sir'? Ah, no! He says, 'These be curried eggs, sahib.' And travellers at the end of a journey do not say, 'We are tired.' They say, 'We be tired men.' No! It is a compliment to the style of the great writers who produced your Authorised Version – but it will not wash. Indian novelists, writing in English of their own people – I have read two or three – do not make them talk like Elizabethan clergymen."

Dr Barlow, who had attended to the General's flight of criticism with an appreciative air, now offered his own contribution. "I don't know," he said, "that those clergymen you mention were really great writers, as you call them. I think they were just Elizabethans. It seems to me that everybody in those days wrote wonderful English without trying – they couldn't help it, somehow. You get it in their letters and private papers as well as in what was published. Even an ass like Lord Essex wrote wonderful

English. So did Francis Drake, who probably never wrote a line that wasn't absolutely necessary, and would have claimed to be a low-brow if he'd ever heard of the word."

"I didn't know that he'd ever written anything," Taylor said. "From all I remember of Drake, I should have said he was a very rough diamond."

To Taylor's surprise, a brief silence followed upon this commonplace remark. The General looked searchingly at Taylor, then met the eyes of Dr Barlow, whose lips pursed in a silent whistle, and who now raised questioning eyebrows, with a motion of his head towards Taylor. The General, in answer, nodded slowly. He held up a forefinger, and seemed about to end this dumb dialogue with speech.

At this moment a light knock on the door was heard, and Mrs McBean, her colour somewhat heightened, came quickly into the room.

"I had better tell you gentlemen at once," she said. "There is a man watching the house."

Instantly, but with no appearance of agitation, the General and Dr Barlow rose to their feet.

"I went out a wee while ago," Mrs McBean continued, "to take a letter to the post up the hill. Before I opened the door I saw a man through the shop window, standing on the other side of the road. There was moonlight enough for me to see him. When I opened the door he was dandering down the hill, and I went on to the post as if I hadna noticed him."

"Good!" the General said softly. "And when you came back?"

"He was in the wee wood nearly opposite the house," Mrs McBean said. "I should not have seen him if I hadna been looking out for him with the corner of my eye, but I could make out his face keeking round a tree near the edge of the wood. I didna stop or look that way; I came into the house as if I had seen nothing. I shut the door and bolted it as I always do, without any hurry, and came straight up the stair to you."

While she was speaking the General had gone swiftly to a cupboard by the fireplace and set it open, so that Taylor could see on a shelf within it a small oblong box with an attachment of earphones. "It was well done, Mrs McBean," he said.

"Like the dinner," Dr Barlow added. "You couldn't see enough of the man to tell us what he looked like, I suppose, Mrs McBean? – even when he was close to the house."

"When I saw him through the window," she answered, "I could see that he was tall. His hat was pulled down so that I couldna see his features. While he was walking down the hill I saw nothing but his back. When he was hiding in the wood I saw only the white of his face peeping round the tree and then going behind it again. But he was there – I have good eyesight. There is one thing more, gentlemen. This afternoon, just after I brought up the tea, a man came into the shop for cigarettes. He was not one who lives in these parts; I have never seen him before – a coarse creature, with his nose all sideways, and he was tall, like the man I saw just now. It might be the same."

"There is ground for your suspicion, Mrs McBean," the General said, baring his teeth in a ferocious grin. "We must move, my dear Taylor. If you wish to join us, as I hope, the doctor will help you to get ready," he added, as he fitted the loop of the earphones round his head and turned to the cupboard. As Taylor, with the doctor's hand on his arm, hurried into the other room, he heard the General's voice, low but clear: "Granada calling, Granada calling, Granada calling, listen to the gipsy's warning, listen to the gipsy's warning, Granada calling, Granada calling..."

CHAPTER VIII

In the other room little could be seen in the half-darkness until Dr Barlow, taking one of the brass candlesticks from the mantelshelf, placed it on the floor beneath the table and put a match to the candle. This done, he hauled a large canvas kit-bag from under the bed. "How do you feel about a little action – even if it's evasive action?" he asked. "You can stay here if you like, you know. It isn't you they're after, and you'll be all right."

"All I want," Taylor declared with conviction, "is to be with you and the General. You're the only men I know, and if he wants me to go with you I am more than willing."

Dr Barlow nodded, and took from the table drawer a small leather harness, the look of which puzzled Taylor until he saw that part of it was a holster. Into this the doctor fitted the revolver, which had been left on the table top.

"We'll put this in its proper place," he said. "We don't want to leave it behind, and as it's your gun and your harness, you ought to carry it, I think."

Taylor looked at the weapon with distaste. "I suppose so – yes," he said. "But I'm not shooting at anybody – that's understood."

"Of course it is," the doctor said. "You needn't go over it all again. Come on, take your coat off." Taylor did so, and the harness was swiftly buckled over his chest and left shoulder, so that the stock of the weapon lay snugly under his armpit. "Coat on again," the doctor said. "That's right – a nice fit for a new jacket."

He now began rapidly to throw into the canvas bag the articles of Taylor's outfit. "Fold up the dressing-gown to go on top, will you?" he said briefly. "I ought to have done this before – the General and I are always packed up ready to go at any moment. You heard him just now – he's getting a man by short-wave wireless 'phone, telling him where to meet us with a car near here. Probably it won't be less than twenty minutes or so from now, so there's plenty of time really."

Taylor was conscious of a by no means disagreeable thrill at these signs of urgency. "What does it mean exactly – that man watching on the road?" he asked.

"Hard to say," the doctor replied, fitting the small bottles and boxes into the leather case and cramming it into the bag. He laid the dressing-gown on the top of it and snapped the bag shut. "There we are – all ready to fade away. Yes, Ketch is on to us all right, but, as you say, what does it mean? I don't think myself he can be ready to make trouble yet, if he's only just got on to the scent, which is what it looks like. You see, there was nobody about last night when the General came in through the orchard – he always scouts round thoroughly. It was just his marvellous luck that Mrs McBean wanted to post that letter tonight, and spotted the watcher by the threshold. But, whatever Ketch's intentions may be, it's boot and saddle for us. The General has nothing more to do here, anyhow – we were only waiting for you to get right, and now he will be glad to have you string along with him, as you know."

"And I ask for nothing better," Taylor said with feeling. "So we shall all be happy."

Dr Barlow seated himself on the table and swung his legs. "Yes, but you've got to remember," he said, "that we're not always very safe company to be in. To be quite candid, the General doesn't like safety – most of his life he's been looking for trouble, and usually getting quite a lot of it. You've heard him talk about being a prudent man, but all that means is that he plans ahead, and that once he's manoeuvred himself into a thoroughly hot spot, he is as cool as Christmas, and never misses a chance of winning out. For instance, to hear him talk about his performance in the war with Riesgador you wouldn't guess that he made himself the idol of the army and the public because the personal risks he took were so appalling. In Peligragua they love that sort of thing."

Taylor shook his head. "I don't remember much of my own past," he said, "but I feel sure there was never a time when I didn't admire reckless bravery, and I believe most people are the same. Isn't that your experience?"

"Of course it is," the doctor answered. "But, believe me, in Peligragua – and in Riesgador for that matter, or anywhere else where there is Spanish blood in the ascendant – risking one's life is at least twice as much admired as it is where there is a larger dose of ordinary sanity in the national make-up. In England we have some idea of where to draw the line. The only line the General knows anything about is the line that is the shortest distance from one bloody row to another."

Dr Barlow paused and looked towards the door. "While we're by ourselves," he continued, "I'll tell you a little more about him. The reason why people love Justo de la Costa is not because he's a pugnacious devil; it's because he is also the most unselfish, generous, chivalrous character they have ever come across in their lives. That's how I feel about him myself, and I have as little use for sentiment as most people. There is literally nothing he would not do that he could do for a friend. I came across him first when I was doing some research work at the Rockefeller Institute in

New York. There was a man in hospital there who had been bitten by a snake in Peligragua, he was one of a party of Americans who had been making themselves useful to the General's political friends, smuggling some goods that were banned by the Verdugo Government. Well, the only place where this bloke stood a chance of being cured was at the Institute, where snake-venom cases were being treated by a new technique. The General brought him by air to New York, got him into the clinic, and stayed with him until he was out of danger."

Dr Barlow paused a moment, looking quizzically at Taylor. "It was you being here, my lad," he went on, "that made me think of that example of the General's way of behaving – because it's possible that you may have known that very man in those dear, dead days that you don't recall. You see he was one of a New York gang that made a speciality of smuggling operations, it was the General himself who had hired him and his party to do that job, and consequently it was a point of honour to get him cured of his snake-bite if money and trouble could do it. For just the same reason he was determined to get you out of that spot you were in, travelling with a faked passport as he knew you were."

"Yes, I thought of that," Taylor said. "The safest thing would have been just to forget about me and go home."

"Exactly," the doctor said. "A point of honour, with some risk thrown in, was just the General's dish. And your case was really tied up with the other in a way, because the General's looking after that snake-bite case made a terrific hit with the smuggling gang, and Farewell Billy, that you've heard us talking about, used to have a business interest in that gang's operations. So Billy, who is quite an important person in illegal circles over there, introduced himself to the General and thanked him, and they quite took to each other, each being a desperate character in his own way."

"Yes, I see," Taylor said thoughtfully. "It was Billy wanting to repay the General's kindness that led to me being sent over here to act as bodyguard. I wondered what the connection between them was."

Dr Barlow nodded. "That's it. Also, of course, Billy wanted to do *you* a bit of good. As you remarked yourself, it's clear the cops over there must have been sored up at you for some reason or other."

"Did I say that?" Taylor inquired with interest.

"Well, words to that effect," Dr Barlow said. "And now I've tried to give you some idea of the sort of character the General is. You'll hear more about him from his own lips – I know that, because he was just getting ready to spill the story when the alarm was given by Mrs McBean. Now, while I've been talking he has been reconnoitring – you can be sure of that. Doing a crawl round the back door, I dare say – the Gatillo touch."

The doctor paused, then resumed as one changing the subject, "You know, it was very interesting to me – you remembering all about cricket when the word came up. You seemed perfectly clear about it – more so than about anything else so far."

"So I am," Taylor said. "I suppose I must have been devoted to the game – in fact I know I was. And remembering it has made all the rest of that time – my school days – clearer than it was. Only I can't remember any names."

"Not any place-names?" the doctor said. "No? Well, don't try – it will all come of its own accord. But it's certain you were at an English school. We assumed that was so, anyhow, because Farewell Billy told the General you had emigrated to the States as a young man, and had never lost your accent, as he put it. Anyhow, I'm glad you didn't pick up Billy's, which is the most debased kind of New Yorkese. Before I met Billy I'd never heard the language at its loveliest, though I'd lived in New York for a couple of years. The first time – "

Dr Barlow broke off as the door opened silently and the General appeared in the dim light. A black cloth with eyeholes covered his face. As he came in he removed this, and began to strip off a pair of black woollen gloves.

"Accept my apologies for having kept you waiting so long," he said quietly. "I had to interrupt my talk with Newlove while he was getting through to Mewstone by the ordinary telephone, giving a message from me to Fielding. We are expected at his place tonight; he and his wife look forward to making the acquaintance of our friend Taylor. When that was settled, I gave detailed instructions to Newlove. He is on his way to us now, driving the Fendlair, and Gunn is coming from his place, driving the Antelope. So much assistance will make things more easy, because I rather think Ketch is ready for action if we should venture out of doors tonight. I have been up on the roof, looking around, and I could make out three men near the cottage. Probably there are others I could not see, and a car somewhere not far away."

"It does look as if they were here in some force," Dr Barlow said. "Just the same, my guess is that Ketch has only just got on to this place, and still isn't certain we are here. He was out on the road watching the upstairs windows for signs of life, I suppose – why should he do that if he knew there was any life?"

"We are going to show him some, anyway," the General said, laughing softly. "We should be doing so in quite a short time. You may think all this is small-time stuff, my dear Taylor, but, after all, I have to think of my liberty. Besides, making a monkey out of Ketch, as I hope to do, is quite a game. I have done it before, and enjoyed it greatly."

"When you told us to get ready," the doctor said, "you meant we should take our baggage, of course."

"We take nothing with us," the General said, "but we abandon nothing. Newlove has orders to call for our effects when the coast is clear. I have explained everything to Mrs McBean; she is staying in her room – she will not be in the way. We are going to move our quarters like *caballeros*, we carry no bags, we leave quite openly and by the front door, though we do not loiter about chatting of this and that."

Dr Barlow looked at Taylor. "That means he has a plan, of course. And I can make a guess at the sort of plan it is if there are two cars on the way."

"It is usual with me to have a plan," the General pointed out. "Newlove and Gunn are to meet at Hobb's Corner and come on together; they are to separate where the road forks at Hansell; they will converge again on Abbot's Dean, Gunn coming from the south and Newlove from the east. Gunn should arrive three minutes earlier than Newlove; he will make a demonstration of waiting for us at the back of the orchard. If Ketch has been reconnoitring this place, he will know that we always enter and leave by that way. When we hear Gunn, we shall have a little time while the enemy is concentrating at the wrong spot; we shall take up our positions at the front door, ready to step into Newlove's car when it comes down the hill. That is the general idea. When we leave, Barlow will go first, to open the front door and the door of the car outside. Taylor will get into the car first, then Barlow, then myself. For Newlove it will be a halt of a few seconds only. Is everything understood? Then let us wait here in silence, thinking about our sins."

The opportunity for this meditation was of the briefest. Almost at once two long-drawn hoots, followed by a short hoot, were heard in the distance. "It is the overture," the General remarked. Then came, from down the hill, the sound of a car being driven at speed.

As it approached, the car slowed down. Taylor, listening intently, could make out that it had turned up a by-road on their own side of the highway just before reaching the cottage, and was now moving at a foot-pace; soon, at a point in their rear, it stopped. Then silence.

"Now, my friends," the General said, "we go down the stairs, Barlow going first. I shall light the way for you from behind with this candle."

They left the room in that order, and Taylor noted that there was a thick carpet under his feet on the stairs.

Suddenly the General whispered, "Halt!" His hand fastened on Taylor's shoulder with a steely grip. "Do you hear – and you, Barlow? There are sounds of movement outside the back door – quite close, I think." He blew out the candle.

Taylor, listening intently in the darkness, heard nothing at first; then there came to his ear a slithering, shirring sound.

"Something is being lugged over the grass, I should say," Dr Barlow murmured. He took from his pocket something which made a metallic clink.

The next instant there was a loud crash from the back of the house, and the General, vaulting over the bannister rail, darted down the passage leading in that direction. Dr Barlow was at his heels, and Taylor, in high excitement, followed them into a back room where, by the dim moonlight from the window, a half-shattered door could be seen still holding by the bolts at top and bottom.

"Drive them out when they rush!" the General shouted. As he spoke there came another crashing blow on the door; it started from its bolts and hinges, falling in fragments, and the leaders of the assault charged into the room. One of them, springing at the General with head down and arms open, was instantly knocked into a corner by a blow which made an ugly sound, and there followed a half-blind mêlée around the open doorway.

Taylor, before he knew it, had whipped his pistol from the holster and was laying about him with the barrel; once it descended with a crack on the wrist of an arm that clutched at the General's collar. He could see little of what his companions were doing, and they made no sound, but from the small bunch of men who were attacking came savage oaths and stifled cries that had in them a note which delighted Taylor's heart. One of the invaders, felled, went down under his feet; the rest, giving way suddenly, were forced out at the door by hard hitting.

The General flew at the big kitchen table which occupied one end of the room, pulled it with one tug across the doorway, and up-ended it, legs inward; then dragged against it a heavy chest and another cumbrous piece of furniture that could be heard to rattle. As he worked he panted to Taylor, "Follow the doctor – the other door – quick!"

As Taylor hesitated, the General turned, seized him by the shoulders, whirled him round and ran him through the room and along the passage. As they came into the shop beyond it, the improvised barricade tottered under a tremendous thump; but before them the shop door stood open, and beyond it the moonbeams glinted on a long car with Dr Barlow holding the door of it open. Taylor, half running, half thrust by a great hand in the small of the back, stumbled inside, the doctor whisked in behind him, and the General's bulk was distributed over both of them as the car went off to a flying start and the door slammed. As the doctor thrust him into a back seat, Taylor had a vision of a heavy-shouldered man at the wheel of the car twitching off, with one hand, an earphone band from his head.

CHAPTER IX

The General lay back in the seat beside him, breathing deeply. "*Madre de Dios*! my dear Taylor," he said, "I must ask you to answer more promptly to the word when I find it necessary to give an order. I know! I know! You did not like leaving me, you did not like to run." He placed a hand on Taylor's knee. "I thank you for your intentions, but in these affairs someone has to take control, and when I am that person you must assume that I know what is best. If you had cleared the line of my retreat, we might have saved a couple of seconds – and a second is a long time when the other side are pretty sure to come again – as they did. Now that I have said that, let me say also that your share of the work was magnificent. In fact it was decisive. You waded into the scrap like a raving mad cannibal."

Dr Barlow, who had opened his waistcoat and was feeling under it cautiously, remarked with emphasis, "When Farewell Billy sent you Taylor for a bodyguard, he certainly picked a lulu." He switched on the light in the car. "Now then, what about injuries? General, you sound as if you were all the better for the battle – as usual. Have you anything to declare?"

"Someone banged me rather hard over the left ear," the General said. "It is my good fortune to have a skull made of teak; there is a little singing in progress, nothing more, except bruises on the body. I had the advantage of height, also of a brass candlestick. My dear Taylor, are you hurt at all? It seemed to me that you were doing nothing but dish it out, but I was too much occupied to observe very closely."

"I believe I have a few bruises, especially on the arms," Taylor said, "but I don't think I was attacked very much, as the General says."

Dr Barlow laughed. "You're damn right, you weren't. They don't like the look of you at all. They hadn't expected there would be three of us, for one thing – perhaps they thought there would be only the General. But when it came to a walking corpse joining in the scrimmage – you can't think what you looked like in the half-light with those bandages on – and your long arms and that very useful weapon, it was enough to put them off. As for me, I stopped a light one with my chin, and I thought I had a rib or two cracked, but it seems to have been a false alarm. In fact we got off devilish easily – considering that there were seven of them."

"Seven, yes," the General agreed. "Probably we have met them all before, I could recognise three of them to swear to, beside Ketch himself. Do you agree, *chico*?" Dr Barlow nodded, and the General went on, "The affair was handled properly, I should say – getting them all bunched up in the doorway and keeping them there. If they had been able to deploy, there would have been more difficulty; they would have been all round us. As it is, the only serious damage suffered by our side is the destruction of Mrs McBean's back door, and I shall ask Newlove to interview her about that tomorrow. An admirable woman, my dear Taylor; she and I have complete confidence in each other. I heard no sound from her from the beginning of the trouble to the end."

Dr Barlow, who had produced a box from under the seat, was busy with a bottle and a pad of cotton wool. "Nor did

I," he said. "She is more likely to have been chucking crockery down on them from the bedroom window."

"Let us hope that she did so," the General said as the side of his head was explored by the doctor's delicate fingers. "There, *chico*, you see I have saved my skin as usual; there is only a bump, and not much of a bump at that; even the singing is now *pianissimo*. Do me the favour of disregarding it and attend to your own chin."

"My chin will wag as freely as ever, never fear," the doctor said, cupping it in the hand that held the cotton wool. "I don't think Ketch will be able to say the same for a day or two, from what I could see."

The General shook his head gently. "I must say I am a little disappointed in Ketch; he was a fool to try tackling me as he did. He needed to be very sure of his support if that was to succeed, but as it was the man behind him was slow – perhaps the awful spectacle of our friend Taylor confused him. Anyway, you got home on his jaw nicely, Barlow *mio*; I have to thank you for this last of so many kindnesses."

"So that was Ketch," Taylor said, "who ran at you with his head down."

"That was Ketch, yes," the General said. "With his hands he is of the first order, but when it comes to the all-in stuff he stacks up short, as you say. Coming at me like that, he got my knee in his face, I dare say his teeth were a little disarranged, and at the same moment my candlestick put him out for the count, at least. It is worth remembering, my dear Taylor, that no home is really complete without a few brass candlesticks, heavy at the bottom. If they are hollow at the bottom, as happens so often, the cavity may be filled with plaster of Paris."

"I shall bear it in mind," Taylor said. "Well, General, it all seems to have passed off quite successfully."

"Yes, it is nice work," the General said happily. He raised his voice. "Newlove, you heard me say it is nice work? You and Gunn had your movements timed beautifully, and what is there in the world that matters more than perfect timing? It is the law of the universe, the stars obey it, even the comets arrive on time, Newlove and Gunn are in celestial company."

A hoarse laugh came from the man at the wheel; it was echoed by Dr Barlow, sitting with his back to the engine. "That's the company we shall all be in," he said, "if you take the driver's attention off his job. There is a happy land," he hummed, "far, far away, where saints in glory stand, all, all the day. It isn't my idea of a full-time occupation, as at present advised, but perhaps I shall feel differently when we get there."

Taylor, who had been in mounting high spirits ever since the opening of the night's activity, joined in the General's laughter. "We all seem very jolly," he said. "I feel as if we were a team going home after a rugger match – including the slightly knocked-about feeling. Besides, going at a pace like this makes me happy. What is it about rushing along at high speed that makes us happy?"

"It's another of the General's laws of the universe," Dr Barlow explained.

"Not my laws of the universe," amended the General, "but God's, and perhaps none the worse for that. It is a law also that when we are happy we wish to sing, even if we have voices like the sharpening of saws, Barlow *mio*, and even if we blaspheme the blessed saints in doing so. Now I will sing something more gay at least." And the General, in a deep voice, chanted a stave in Spanish that went to a rollicking air.

"Hear, hear! – whatever it means," Dr Barlow exclaimed.

"What does it mean, General?" Taylor enquired.

"It was our little campaign song in the contest when I opposed the re-election of Verdugo to the Presidency," the General said. "The words mean, 'What is that which I see coming down the steep hill? *Ta-ra-ra-ra-ra*. It is a dog with a portion of Verdugo in its mouth. *Ta-ra-ra-ra-ra*.' There is more of poetic imagery, I think I may say, in our political songs than in those you have in the English-speaking world. This one has always remained in my memory, it has a haunting tune."

"The only English one that remains in *my* memory," Dr Barlow said, "is one that was sung during a London County Council election in my student days. It was written for the party which had just covered itself with deathless glory by linking up the tramway systems north and south of the river. It began, 'Trams, trams, trams across the bridges. Cheer up, comrades, they have come.' If that isn't poetry, I don't know what is."

"You know well enough, *chico*," the General said sadly. "You know also that that balderdash was stolen from one of the Federal songs of the great American war. It is like trying to beat a big drum with a blue pencil. But now, instead of insulting each other's intelligence, shall we explain to our friend Taylor what is the next shot on the board? We are on our way, Taylor, to the house of a friend who lives in the outskirts of Mewstone. You know the place?"

"I don't, I'm afraid," Taylor said. "I may have known it as a boy, but I don't remember the name."

The General patted his knee consolingly. "It will come, never fear. Even if it does not come, you will not be missing anything glorious. Mewstone is on the south coast, it is said to be the third largest seaside town in England, very different from Abbot's Dean. You know the old riddle of the Sphinx: Where can you best conceal a pebble? Answer: On the beach. So, what is the safest hiding-place for a retired military officer like myself? Why, Mewstone, where you cannot spit out of the window without hitting a colonel."

"An Admiral, if you're lucky," Dr Barlow said moodily. "Even the very donkeys that draw the children's carts are RASC veterans."

"This house we are going to – I call it my friend's house," the General pursued, "because he is legally its owner. That is for me a convenient arrangement, but in fact, half of the purchase-money and cost of furnishing was paid by me, a good deal of my property is kept there, including a small but fairly good library. I and a few others can stay there quite privately when we need to do so, it is a sort of base for me. As for the other owner, he lives there in permanence, he does not consider it a nuisance when I make use of it, because we have been very close friends since my Oxford days, when we were at Magdalen together. I will tell you something about him. To begin with, he is not a retired man, nor has he ever been an officer, like everybody else who lives in Mewstone as a steady thing."

"He is not like anybody else who ever lived anywhere," Dr Barlow said. "It's his hobby. He chose to settle down in Mewstone because he is more unlike the people who live there than he would be in any other place he can think of."

The General nodded. "Well, he is his own master. What I was saying, my dear Taylor, is that my friend Arnold Fielding is a famous scholar, an Orientalist, he knows more about the Chinese especially, and their language, than they know themselves. He has been given the degree of doctor by God knows how many Universities. For myself, the Chinese are not of very great interest to me, but I have never forgotten the student days when both of us were happier, I am sure, than we have ever been since then."

"Aren't you forgetting his wife?" the doctor asked. "He was happier when he married her – or so she thinks. I don't blame her either – she could make a brass monkey happy, and I expect she knows it."

The General raised a protesting hand. "This is playing with words. There are different sorts of happiness, as there are of cheese – you know it as well as I do, Barlow *mio*. We may say that a circle is more round than a square, but where does it get us? For my part, it makes me feel sleepy, and Taylor has just strangled a yawn for the second time. That little exercise we have just had, the air of the night, the hum of our engine, the sophistry of our doctor – who could remain awake?" The General gaped cavernously, folded his arms and dropped his chin on his breastbone. "Death and damnation to the man who says a word till I have had a nap."

CHAPTER X

It was a short blast on the horn of the car that roused Taylor from sleep to the knowledge that they were moving at a much slower pace, along a broad, well-lit road with houses widely spaced on either side. "This," the General said, laying a hand on his knee, "is Mewstone. I was dreaming of mountains and forests, and I wake up in the county borough of Mewstone, which, if I must tell the truth, I do not like so well."

"And this is where we usually get out," Dr Barlow said as the car turned into a side-street and came to a halt. "There's still a short way to walk," he added as Taylor joined him on the foot-way, "because we hate to be conspicuous, and that's what we should be if we scrunched into a gravel drive in a large car at 10.30 p.m."

He moved off with Taylor at his elbow, leaving the General in conference with his chauffeur, and after some fifty paces turned in at a wooded door in a tall hedge. On the door was painted in white the dimly-visible name, "Keith House," and Taylor could make out in the darkness the bulk of a large house which they were skirting at some distance on its left-hand side. When they came out upon a broad lawn at the back, light was pouring from a French-windowed room, and by the step a man stood waiting.

"Come in, come in," he called. "Barlow, I am delighted to see you again. I heard the footsteps of two people, and as no one ever hears Justo's, I concluded that the other man must be your new friend who was coming with you, as I was told by telephone. Mr Taylor, you are welcome to our house – General de la Costa's and mine, as perhaps you know. My name is Fielding." He shook Taylor's hand with a friendly grasp and continued. "You have heard all about me, I suppose. I heard about you some time ago, while you were still lying unconscious at the Abbot's Dean place. I'm sorry to see you are still wearing bandages, but you seem to be active enough on your legs."

They were now inside the large, comfortable room, where a few long hanging manuscripts in Chinese characters on the walls gave the only clue to the special interests of Arnold Fielding. He motioned them towards a deep, broad sofa. "Sit down, sit down," he went on with the slightly nervous utterance that seemed to be his habit. "And where is Justo? He sent word that he was coming with you."

A deep laugh came from the garden. "Justo is not far away," the General said, striding over the threshold. "I had to make a few arrangements with Newlove before he went back to his own place." He took Fielding by the shoulders, over-topping him by a head, and gazed at him affection-ately. "By God, Arnold, you still go on looking younger every time I see you again. It must be the famous air of Mewstone, which keeps so many colonels alive."

Arnold Fielding's fresh complexion and slight figure certainly gave him, to Taylor's eye, an appearance of youth, which was not at all diminished by the downy yellow beard matching the short, curly hair that covered his head. He wore a suit of an unpatterned tweed so light as to be almost white, and a tie of scarlet silk completed the very unvenerable effect.

"He looks positively frolicsome," Dr Barlow pronounced. "You know, Fielding, I told Taylor here that he needed cheerful surroundings, and here you are, exactly as the doctor ordered. Which are you – a lamb or a chicken?"

"Never mind what I look like," Fielding said with a diffident giggle. "I'm quite tough, really, as you know, so don't give Mr Taylor a wrong impression."

Taylor spoke up uneasily. "I hope you won't call me Mister. It makes me feel awkward. So far I haven't been called anything but plain Taylor, and it seems to be more than doubtful whether I have a right to be called even that. I suppose you know – "

His words were cut short by the excited barking of a dog somewhere in the recesses of the house, a woman's voice ordering the animal to shut up, and approaching feminine footsteps. Taylor noted the expression with which the three others looked towards the open door of the room they sat in; it was a look of pleasant expectation, and he remembered Dr Barlow's few unstudied words about the wife of Arnold Fielding.

The woman who came into the room held up, bosom high, two bulbous, wicker-covered bottles, much as a gillie bears the bottles of whisky behind the haggis on a properly-kept birthday of Robert Burns. "Here you are, Justo!" she exclaimed. "I had to rout about in the cellar a little before I found them. I forgot all about the stuff until I heard your car hoot just now, or it would have been waiting for you with the other drinks." She placed the bottles on a sideboard where decanters and glasses were already assembled on a tray, and looked about her happily. "You'd better help yourselves," she said. "I always give people too much, you know that."

"Heaven bless you, Diana," the General said with emphasis as he went to the tray and poured for himself. "I can easily do without telque if I have your company, but the two together! As you say, you give too much. I drink your health."

"So will I, Diana," Dr Barlow said, helping himself to brandy and soda. "Speaking strictly as a medical man I can't imagine your ever having anything the matter with you, but just the same, here's your health."

"Oh, the complimentary allusions!" the lady said. "And now they're over, let your new friend have a chance at the tray. You see what there is, Mr – "

"Never let it be said!" the General broke in.

"You must be careful," Dr Barlow warned her. "He was down on Arnold like a thousand of brick just now for calling him Mister. If you call him anything but plain Taylor, you'll get yourself disliked."

Diana Fielding was by this time inspecting him with evident concern. "Well, but, Taylor, there is something wrong with you, isn't there? Those bandages, my dear man! I didn't see your head at first, with a great ox like Justo standing between us. From what Arnold was told, I thought you had quite got over your accident. Now I look at you, I'm not at all sure you ought to be drinking anything."

"There isn't any 'ought' about it," Dr Barlow said. "Taylor's as fit as you are. Those bandages are only for the sake of appearances, there's nothing under them but a few scars. But I noticed when we were having dinner that he drank very little – he hasn't got the talent for it, I should say. Still, the truth is, all three of us have been struggling with adverse circumstances tonight, and a little refreshment is what I prescribe for him. I'll do the dispensing, if I may." He poured out a little brandy, diluted it well, and handed the glass to Taylor. "There you are. And apart from this, Diana, he's had all the mothering he needs; I've been on the job ever since the railway smash. Who ran to catch him when he fell? I did."

The doctor tapped his chest proudly.

Taylor, tasting his drink with appreciation, said to their hostess, "He's quite right. He and the General saved my life between them – I don't know if you were told that – and the doctor has looked after me when I was unconscious, and made me perfectly well – bodily, that is. The only trouble with me is – "

"Your memory – yes, we heard about it from Justo," she said, gazing at him with a friendly interest that made him feel as if they were already well-acquainted. "Well, I'm bound to say Druce seems to have done his mothering very nicely – I don't mind admitting that, because it would be impossible to make him more conceited about his doctoring than he is."

Fielding, who had been watching his friends attentively while sipping from his tumbler, said, "Taylor is in rather better condition than the others, as a matter of fact. I don't know what the adverse circumstances were that Druce says they have been struggling with, but one of the circumstances has given Justo a lump on the side of his head, and Druce's chin looks a little bit swollen."

"Bah!" the General said, stretching his long legs. "Those are mice which will soon run away."

"Well, I should like to hear the story," Fielding said. "I suppose the enemy have been trying to put salt on your tail again."

The General nodded. "They have been trying, yes, but the story will not really interest you. You must know, my dear Taylor, that our friend Fielding has had much more dangerous people after him than the Ketch crowd – Chinese tokoons, Annamese music-men, Uzbeg high-hats, every sort of dubious character between the Caspian and the Yellow Sea. In Asia there is a prevailing idea that he knows too much. Well, Arnold, if you want to hear what has been happening, I will tell you, it is a simple story of a small tree-trunk on one side – or it may have been a pole

81

or a stout post – and on the other side a pair of brass knuckles, a candlestick and a revolver used as an instrument of percussion."

The General went on to describe briefly what had happened in the cottage kitchen at Abbot's Dean.

Taylor, listening and noting the effect produced, thought it was a triumph of understatement, and had the impression that the Fieldings had expected it to be nothing else. Arnold Fielding heard it with a faintly sceptical smile, his wife with that air of self-possessed benevolence that seemed to be her normal expression.

To Taylor, she was, as she stood before the hearth, a comforting person to look at. Her blue-and-yellow Mandarin coat was decidedly gaudy, she was tall and straight, her eyes were frank and friendly, her chin was decisive, her brown hair rather untidy.

She was charming, but did not appear to be at all interested in the fact.

As the General talked, she spoke a little with Dr Barlow in an undertone, and Taylor himself, as he could easily divine, was the subject of their conversation.

When General de la Costa had ended his tale, with outspread hands that told of a subject totally and finally disposed of, she nodded understandingly. "That's all we're going to be told, I suppose, and of course it was fifty times worse than you say. I wish we could hear Ketch's version. Now, Taylor, you're a newcomer here, so you had better let me show you the room I have got ready for you."

He followed her into a large hall lit by two hanging lamps of crystal carved in the likeness of fantastic fish. At the foot of the broad stairway a figure stood, a man in loose blue clothing with hands at his sides – so still that he seemed like an effigy.

"This is Lem," Diana Fielding said. "Lem, this is our guest, he is in your charge." The man came to life enough to bow slightly to each of them, then followed them up the stairs and stood silent by the door of the room to which she led the way.

It was a large, square room, so decorated that nothing in it – not even the capacious bed and the two deep armchairs – looked heavy; opposite the bed hung a long, black-and-white painting on silk, of mountain scenery in rainy weather.

"According to Justo, you've brought nothing with you," Mrs Fielding said.

She added: "That doesn't matter for him, he has quite a wardrobe here, and the doctor keeps a few necessary things here too. We can fit you out with pyjamas, though I can't promise that they will be the right size. Lem will see to that, now he's had a look at your dimensions."

She nodded to the Chinese servant, who at once disappeared from his station by the door.

"I have been wearing General de la Costa's for some time," Taylor said.

"You must have looked rather a guy," Mrs Fielding observed thoughtfully. "Now sit in that chair, Taylor, until Lem shows up again. If Druce Barlow is right about you, and I'm sure he is, it is a great thing for you to feel perfectly confident the people you are with are friendly and helpful. Well, you've come to the right shop for that – Arnold and I are made that way, and so are our Chinese servants. Lem is the butler – now I've put you in his charge, there's nothing he won't do for you – it's a matter of honour. Listen! You hear that scratching at the door. That's Lem, and it means he has got pyjamas for you and anything else I may have forgotten to supply. Now I'll say good night and go down to the others. All of you ought to be chivvied off to bed, you especially."

"I believe you're right," Taylor said, strangling a yawn. "I do feel a little tired."

"So I should think," his hostess answered. "Lem! Come along in."

CHAPTER XI

Lem, although his vocabulary was slender, had somehow equipped himself with a basic English that was equal to most of the emergencies of domestic life. Taylor went to bed in clean pyjamas in the knowledge that a bathroom was next door, and in the assurance that he would be called at seven-thirty next morning.

Mrs Fielding had forgotten nothing that a strange guest was likely to require; there was even a choice of toothpaste or tooth powder as well as of toothbrushes, over the running water-basin. There were half a dozen clean handkerchiefs among the objects on the top of the chest of drawers.

Lem had draped a black silk dressing-gown over the back of a chair. "If you wish to read," he had said, indicating with a slim hand a shelf of small books on a table beside the bed. Before them squatted a kitten-sized alabaster image of a hideousness never imagined in Europe, and carved with an amazing delicacy of workmanship; it had the body of a corpulent lion with three-toed paws, the head of a dragon with a fiendish scowl, a wide-open mouth full of needle-sharp teeth, a treble-forked tongue, a row of what looked like carven flames running down its spine, which was almost touched by its tail twisted up erect and terminating in similar flame-like tufts. "This is Tchin-teh," Lem had said with an introductory gesture. 'If you wish for light" – he had then pressed upon Tchin-teh's left fore-paw, whereupon a lamp glowed within its open mouth. "If no more light," he had then pressed upon the other fore-paw, and the lamp was extinguished.

Sitting on the bed, Taylor had looked at the titles of the row of books – *Seven Men*, by Max Beerbohm; *Geoffrey Hamlyn*, by Henry Kingsley; *The Red Pantafilando*, by Philip Trent; *In a Glass Darkly*, by Sheridan Le Fanu; *The Adventures of a Field Cricket*, by Ernest Candèze; Percy's *Reliques*; *Great Expectations*, by Charles Dickens; *Let's Be Beastly*, by Herbert Hummingbird; *That Ass Milton*, by Homer Gordon; *My Life as a Bush-ranger*, by Martin Cash; *As the Frenchman Said*, by George Holliday; *The Hunting of the Snark*, by Lewis Carroll; *The Sacred Wood*, by T S Eliot. Taylor had a vague memory of a few of these.

As he was getting into the pyjamas a knock came at the door, and Dr Barlow's close-cropped bullet-head appeared. "I just looked in to say you had better let me attend to the shaving tomorrow morning," he said. "Some of those scars will need treatment for another day or two. How are you feeling now?"

"Quite all right," Taylor answered, "and very sleepy all of a sudden. Thank you again for looking after me," he ended awkwardly, and Dr Barlow, with a nod, disappeared. Taylor, climbing into bed, was thinking of almost nothing when sleep descended upon him.

It was not until the appearance of Lem with a tea-tray that Taylor awoke the next morning.

"Good morning, sir," Lem said as he placed the tray before the bloated paws of Tchin-teh. "Sleep good, I hope."

Taylor, rubbing his eyes, said mechanically, "Thank you, very good." He was already reviewing the events of the day before. As to that day, or fraction of a day, his memory was entirely clear; as to the past, the curtain was still down. He was a man without experience, without knowledge, without property, without friends, but for the few among whom good fortune had brought him back to life.

Whoever he might have been, there was, he recognised, something in his moral being that struggled hard against the misery and fear which must oppress anyone in his situation. Things might have been a thousand times worse; that, he told himself, was certainly true, and he poured out tea for himself as Lem went silently to the window and drew the curtains to admit the sunshine of a spring morning.

As the Chinese servant returned to the bed there was a knock at the door, and he opened it to reveal the presence of Dr Barlow. "Can I come in?" he asked, and without waiting for Taylor's eager assent he was in the room, saying to Lem, "You can leave him to me now; I will look after everything. I am his doctor, you know."

"I know," Lem answered with a slight inclination of the head. "If you want, I am always ready."

With a bow in the direction of Taylor, he left the room, and Dr Barlow, who was wearing a dressing-gown of many vivid colours, came to inspect his patient at close quarters. "I can see at a glance there's nothing physically wrong with you," he said. "If you think there is, now's the time to mention it. Nothing? And as to the memory, that's the same as it was, I expect. Well, the great thing is, don't worry about it. Of course, I know that's bosh in a sense, but the inner and spiritual meaning of it is that this condition will pass away – you want to hold fast to that, and to the fact that you are in the hands of people you can trust. I've told you this before, but you can't think of it too often. By the way, you're used to having a morning cup of tea brought to you in bed, aren't you?"

Taylor reflected. "Yes," he said, "I am, no doubt. It seemed perfectly natural that I should have it when the man brought it in."

Dr Barlow grinned happily. "I slipped the idea to Diana last night that Lem should bring you tea at 7.30 a.m., and when he called you I was hanging about, waiting to see how you took it. We know you've had an English bringing-up, and it might have started something in your consciousness. But you just lapped it up as a matter of course. Now, how about a shave for you? I'd rather do it myself for another day or two. All the things are here, so we'll make a start if you're ready."

Half an hour later Taylor, his toilet completed and his bandage renewed, had been sent downstairs while Dr Barlow set about making himself, as he expressed it, pure from the night and splendid for the day. As Taylor stood on the lawn gazing at the tall trees and well-tended borders that framed the great smooth expanse of turf, he was joined by Mrs Fielding.

"Shall we sit in these chairs and have a talk, Taylor, before the others come down?" she said after the briefest exchange of civilities. "I wanted to have one last night, but it was obvious that what you needed was bed. Of course, what we were told about you before you came was enough to make anyone interested, but Druce says you are on no account to be bothered about your past life; he says you are already beginning to remember more of your early days without being cross-questioned, and are getting to be more self-confident. Well, your past life doesn't matter just now; we can talk about the present, which seems to have been fairly eventful for you."

Taylor, who found something more restful in the company of Mrs Fielding than anything he had experienced so far, lay back in his chair. "So it has," he said. "In fact it has been more or less exciting ever since I came to myself properly yesterday afternoon. Even when nothing in particular was happening, General de la Costa and the doctor made me feel as if something was. I felt it was wonderful to be with them, and I didn't want ever to lose sight of them, but I know now I wasn't quiet and relaxed with either of them, as I am with you. As for the Ketch gang, they made me feel positively murderous. Now I am getting more calm and contented every moment."

She nodded. "That's nice for both of us, isn't it? No doubt what you say about the soothing effect I have on you is true, because others have said the same. My husband used to say I was like a Chinese garden, which is his idea of a compliment. So I look after the quiet side of his life, which is the most important side, of course. You'd never think it of him, Taylor, but he is a perfect little devil for getting into difficulties and dangers – that's why he and Justo have always got on so well, I suppose."

"I shouldn't have thought that Mewstone was the place for getting into difficulties and dangers, from what I hear of it," Taylor remarked.

"No – that's why I made him come and live here when Justo first suggested it. But even here he gets into scrapes. The first summer we were here I gave a party, and the Mayor of Mewstone came to it. He has the big house next to this one, and we had got rather friendly, Arnold being quite an important person in his own line. The Mayor asked Arnold how he liked the place, and Arnold, just out of devilment, said it suited him very well, except that sometimes he was kept awake by the Mayor clanking his chain. I had quite a job calming him down after that, persuading him that all celebrated scholars were half mad, especially Oriental ones."

"Is he a colonel?" Taylor asked.

"Who? The Mayor? Lord, no – why should he be? Oh, I know," Mrs Fielding said. "You've been listening to Justo's nonsense about Mewstone being entirely populated by retired colonels. Of course, it's true that there are plenty of that kind of people in the place, but the Mayor made a lot of money in business – glue, I believe it was. Most of the colonels have much less money, and, much more sense. Now I come to think of it, Taylor, you may be a little out of date in your ideas – judging from what Druce has been telling me."

Taylor looked downcast. "Very much out of date, I'm sorry to say. I don't know how much, but a good many years."

"Yes. Well, you possibly may have the notion that retired officers are rather a benighted lot. But I assure you, Taylor, I've noticed a great change in them since my schooldays – and that's not such a very long time. Nowadays the men who have spent their lives in the services aren't benighted at all, most of them – certainly the percentage of absolute donkeys is nothing like what it used to be. That's a thing to bear in mind when you're getting used to the modern world. Most of the retired officers I know have plenty of brains; they're even well read. If you want the silly-soldier-man pose, you have to go to the theatre for it, or else to the comic artists – they're usually fifty years out of date. Colonels and Generals are as good company as any men I ever met."

"They sound to me," Taylor said, "as if they were getting back to the style of the Duke of Wellington."

"They may be, for all I know," Mrs Fielding said. "You're certainly coming on, Taylor, if you remember all about the Duke of Wellington – it's more than I do. All I know about him is that he won the battle of Waterloo, and that Blücher kissed him afterwards."

"The Duke said he very nearly didn't."

"What – get kissed by Blücher?"

"No – win the battle of Waterloo. I don't say I could tell you everything about the Duke of Wellington, but I could tell you a lot. It just happened that in my boyhood I had an immense admiration for him and read everything I could get hold of about him. I remember a great deal of it now. It's just as the doctor says – all that part of my life is getting more and more clear."

"I see." Mrs Fielding gazed at him with renewed interest. "And did your being keen about the Duke make you want to be a soldier? You have the look of a soldier, you know, Taylor – something about your shoulders."

Taylor shook his head. "All I can say is that I did want to be a soldier – you're right about that. But I wanted to be various things when I was a boy. The first thing I wanted to be, I believe, was a fireman. Later on I wanted to be an explorer, and after that a clergyman."

"You must have been a funny boy," she said consideringly. "Such a mixture of ambitions. Rather like my brother Jim – he was determined to be a bullfighter when he was about ten, then he made up his mind to be a world-famous violinist. Now he's the assistant general manager of one of the big banks, and likes it." She paused for a moment, then asked: "How do you like Justo de la Costa, if that's a fair question? You seem to have become one of his retinue somehow, but you don't know how it happened, as far as I can make out."

"I like him more than I can say," Taylor answered with feeling. "Quite apart from his having saved my life, there's something irresistible about him; I feel as if there's nothing I wouldn't do for him."

She nodded. "Yes, that's how most people who have anything to do with Justo feel about him. The ones who don't feel that way – well, they want to murder him. It's impossible to be half-hearted about Justo. You see, the key to his character is that he's a romantic adventurer. If he was a writer, he'd make a fortune out of thrillers. As it is, he lives thrillers instead of writing them. The only things he writes are papers for learned societies about ancient Indian ruins and things like that in what they call Latin America. Apart from that, he's an adventurer, as I said."

"That's the sort of impression I got about him," Taylor said, "though I never set eyes on him until yesterday. Of course, Dr Barlow has told me something about him. He seems to be quite devoted to the General, though I should say he is quite a different sort of character."

"Very different. In fact I should say the only things they have in common are courage and sense of humour. Druce Barlow is what they call a pathologist. He made a brilliant start as a GP in London, but after a few years one of his she patients, a wealthy American over here on a visit, fell for his fatal beauty and married him. She set him up in his own laboratory as a research man, which was the wish of his heart, and since then he's lived among germs and serums, inventing treatments for all sorts of ghastly complaints. His name is known all over the medical world, so I'm told. He's an FRS, and a few years ago he was Eastman Visiting Professor at Oxford, if you know what that is – I don't. But Justo came across him in New York when he was working at the Rockefeller Institute. Since then they've been as thick as thieves, and whenever Druce feels like taking a holiday from his lab, he refreshes himself by getting into mischief with Justo. I hope you like the doctor – my husband and I think a lot of him."

"I do, indeed," Taylor said. "It was fortunate for me that I came along with my lost memory when they happened to be together."

"Teamed up, as Druce would call it. He's full of that sort of talk, what with his wife and the Rockefeller – not to mention Justo, who went to an American school when he was a boy, and enjoys the society of New York toughs."

Taylor rubbed his chin reflectively. "It's a curious thing that the only people I know in this world happen to be people I feel I can rely on to any extent. There are those two men and your husband, and yourself – I feel perfectly safe and confident with all of you, and that's the best thing that could happen to anyone with my particular trouble, according to Dr Barlow."

"Yes, he's very strong on that point. I don't know about safe, though," Mrs Fielding said. "If your idea of safety is the sort of thing you've just been going through, it isn't mine. Still it's true we are all your friends, Taylor – you're a likeable sort of man, you see, even if you haven't got a past. Speaking of feeling confidence in people, by the way, you can add our Chinese butler to the list – Lem, you know. As I told you, doing everything possible for you is a matter of honour with him. His full name is Lem Hsin-shan – family name Lem, personal name Hsin-shan, which means Cultivator of Goodness, and not a bad name for a Chinese who is the right sort."

"You know the Chinese well, then?"

"Well enough to think they are the most civilised people on earth. You see, I lived among them for five years after I married Arnold, and I learnt to speak Mandarin, and took in a lot of experience that hardly any English people ever get. Now, I have four Chinese to run this house – Lem, and his friend Chiang, and their wives. Chiang's our cook, his personal name is Pao-chen, which means Treasury of Truth. As for the wives – but listen! There's Lem doing his solo on the gong; that means the others are down and breakfast's ready." She rose and led the way to the door opening on the garden. "Chiang is a perfect marvel at buttered eggs, done with bacon that's been fried and chopped up beforehand, so I've ordered that for this morning. If you don't like it – "

"But I do!" Taylor exclaimed with intense feeling. "I smelt the bacon long ago. All I ask, Mrs Fielding, is to be led to it."

CHAPTER XII

"And now that we have our hands free for an hour or two," General de la Costa said, "It is an opportunity for me to go back to what I was saying, or was just about to say, yesterday evening at Abbot's Dean, when our after-dinner talk was interrupted. You remember, my dear Taylor, that we were chatting of this and that."

The General, with Taylor and Dr Barlow, were extended in garden chairs at the further end of the enormous lawn behind Keith House, in the shade of a tall copper-beech. A little table stood near them. All about the lawn were flower-beds and trees, the taste of an invisible sea was in the air, and at a short distance a handsome Alsatian dog, preferring to lie couched in the sunshine, eyed them, its muzzle resting on its fore-paws. Taylor's first breakfast in his new life had been thoroughly enjoyed by him, although, as the doctor had remarked, only experience could teach him how unusual was the quality of anything cooked by the Treasury of Truth. Afterwards the General had asked leave to retire for a consultation with the other two, and Mrs Fielding, asking only that her husband should not be dragged into the conspiracy, had mentioned that lunch would be at half-past one.

"I remember," Taylor said, gazing up into the sun-drenched foliage above him, "that you were talking about mutton, General."

"It is true," the General said. "But mutton did not exhaust our powers of conversation. From mutton we were led on by natural stages to other matters and at last to your Elizabethans, including your Francis Drake. It was about Drake that you made a very suggestive remark, and it was just as I was going to answer you that hell began to pop, as you say."

Taylor was evidently at a loss, and Dr Barlow prompted him. "What you remarked was that you had always thought of Drake as a very rough diamond."

"So I did," Taylor agreed. "But why was that suggestive?"

Nodding at him, the General felt inside this tunic and produced from an inner pocket a small bag of wash-leather tied round the mouth with whipcord.

"Do you recall, my dear Taylor, that I spoke to you before dinner yesterday about my having invented a process, a method of production, from which I draw a very large profit, and which has made powerful enemies for me in the world of big business? Well, it happens that I can show you some examples of this work of mine."

He handed the bag to Taylor, who could feel a number of small objects inside it moving against each other, as he grasped it, with a soapy smoothness. The General pushed the little table towards him.

"Will you untie the cord, *amigo*, and put out here what you find inside." Taylor, quite mystified, undid the knot, and poured out on the table a small handful of crystals, varying in size from that of an orange-pip to that of a small grape. In shape they were eight-faced, clean and regular, and they glowed in the daylight with a slightly smoky brilliance.

Astonished at their strange beauty, Taylor stirred the little heap with a finger and gazed at the changing play of prismatic light. "And these are…" he hesitated.

"Diamonds – yes," the General told him softly.

"But not real diamonds," Taylor concluded.

"Certainly they are real," the General said, with an emphasis that caused the Alsatian to prick up its ears. "Did I not say that I made them myself? They are unpolished, that is all. Rough diamonds, as you said – a crowd of Francis Drakes! *Valgame Dios!* A sinister thought for a man of my ancestry! A single Drake was one too many for the cities and ships of the Indies in those days – and I think, my dear Taylor, that the words you found for him do him less than justice. Unpolished – yes, perhaps. But more than diamond – a living genius. But these are fancies, the stones which you see there are facts, very valuable ones. I am proud to see that you like the look of them. Try then to imagine how I liked the look of the first few specimens that I picked out of the slag when it was still warm from my furnace."

Dr Barlow, catching Taylor's startled eye, nodded. "It's true enough," he said gravely. "You are in the presence of one of the heroes of chemical research, and one of the villains of Hatton Garden. Tell him the story, General. It's a long time since I heard it, and a lot of it I never heard in detail. I shall enjoy having my memory refreshed. Don't leave out the part about the member of the Chamber of Deputies who used to travel with a nightgown and a toothbrush wrapped up in a sheet of the *Petit Parisien.*"

The General's eyebrows rose. "It is evident, Barlow *mio*, that your memory is indeed in need of refreshment, as you confess. Hercule St Gratien has never been a member of the Chamber – he is a much more important person than that, although at one time, it is true, he did not live in luxury. Now, my dear Taylor, I shall tell you the whole truth about my discovery, because I wish you to understand me and to assist me in my affairs, as you know. Also because I have taken a liking to you – all of those who work with me have been recruited on that simple principle, with the exception of a very few who work for me because I know too much about them, and they desire therefore to please me."

The small sack of tobacco was produced, and the General repeated his conjuring-trick with a cigarette paper. After a few deep inhalations, he began his story.

"You may not have heard of the ruby mines of Peligragua, or perhaps you have forgotten. In any case, you would not know that the territory where those mines were discovered was in the possession of my family, as it had been for generations. Today that land belongs to a cousin of mine. It was when his father – that is to say, my uncle Pablo – was the owner that the first successful experiments were made in the production of synthetic rubies, and we de la Costas were naturally among the first to hear of it. The process was not by any means perfect, and the stones made in this way are even today far from equal to the natural rubies in quality; but from the very beginning the thing interested me greatly, for as a boy I had spent some years at Groton, an excellent school in the State of Massachusetts, where I had been taught to know a little of science. So when the synthetic ruby came along, I was led to look into the question of making diamonds, because the diamond is by far the most valuable of precious stones.

"For that reason I prevailed on my father to consent to my coming to Europe to study in Paris, where Henri Moissan was then the Professor of inorganic chemistry at the Sorbonne. It was Moissan, as I knew, who had produced the first man-made diamonds from a solution of carbon in melted iron. That is putting it very simply, I shall not inflict a scientific lecture on you, it is enough to say that it was a matter of very high and very low temperatures and of enormous pressure. Moissan had tried, you see, to reproduce the chemical conditions in certain meteorites in which diamonds have been found – masses of incandescent matter flung out from some blazing star, and dropped here and there on the crust of our more elderly planet. So he made some tiny diamonds, too few and too small to cause any loss of sleep to the owners of diamond mines.

"I learnt a good deal in Paris. I had plenty of social life, and I succeeded in making the acquaintance of Calixte Michaud, already famous as an artist in jewellery, whom I wished very much to know. But never for a day did I neglect my work at the Sorbonne. Before Moissan died, I had mastered his technique, and I began to imagine how it could be developed. Then I went to Oxford, partly to pursue my research, partly for reasons of sentiment with which I will not weary you. For three years I was an undergraduate at Magdalen – the three happiest years of my life, as I think I told you yesterday. I am still in close touch with some of the friends I made there, Arnold Fielding among them. Also I continued to follow up my own ideas about the use of the electric-arc furnace and other technical matters."

The General pinched off the end of his cigarette, and flipped the butt at the Alsatian, which acknowledged the attention by a slight movement of its tail. Rolling another cigarette, the General continued.

"As you may suppose, I was only one of a number working here and there in the world on the lines laid down by Moissan. But no other had yet succeeded, as I did, some years later, when I had my own laboratory. Those diamonds which you see there on the table, my dear Taylor, were made by me, they are some of a large number which I produced two years ago. They are as perfect as the most faultless found in India or Brazil or South Africa, the smallest of them is of a good weight, they are a serious business proposition. In proof of this I may tell you that from time to time I have disposed of parcels of them through a firm of diamond brokers in London who are my personal friends – one of them, by name Mendoza, was at New College in my Oxford days. He and his partner Ullstein know that I have studied the making of diamonds, they prefer to know no more, what I do is not their affair so long as the diamonds I send them are true diamonds, and so long as they can trust me to deal with no other firm, and to leave the handling of the market to them. No one knows of their transactions with me except a few of my friends who can be relied upon to keep quiet about it. I have never entered their place of business. I used to see them at Mendoza's house in Grosvenor Street when I was his guest at dinner."

At this point the General produced from his hip-pocket a large flask surmounted by a silver cup, which he removed and placed on the table. "Can I persuade you, my dear Taylor," he said, " to join me in drinking a little telque? We can share the cup. It is a liquor distilled from the juice of the pelava, and it is not understood by Europeans generally. They say – our doctor here, for example, says – that it tastes like sour milk, only much more sour. This is not to be denied, but we value it for its refreshing and health-giving qualities. You would rather not – not even a *traguillo*? Well, it is not a taste that can be acquired in a day, I admit it." The General, narrowly watched by the Alsatian, poured himself a generous allowance of the liquid, drank with enjoyment, then placed the half-empty cup and the flask on the table with the diamonds and resumed his tale.

"During the time I spent in Paris and Oxford I did not take anyone into my confidence about the final object of my studies. Just the same, it was not practicable to keep altogether to myself the lines on which I was working. At the Sorbonne there was a young Frenchman named Dupont, also a student of chemistry, who tried to be friendly with me. But to me he was not an agreeable type, he was brilliant as a student, but apart from that he was nothing but a swine – in fact, I do an injustice to that order of the brutes by naming him as one of them. So I did not gratify him by discussing with him my own ideas about the development of that research of Moissan's.

"While I was at Oxford I made, as I have said, many dear friends, but I was not intimate with any of those who were working as I was at the laboratory in South Parks Road. Still, anyone who was there could see for himself the kind of thing in which I was interested. In particular, a man named Belcher, who was the Reader in chemical crystallography, knew very well that I had the idea of following in the footsteps of Henri Moissan. I was on good terms with Belcher, though we were hardly friends, and one day he made use of that expression, but I did not pursue the subject with him. Just the same, it was evident that if Belcher knew that, the information would probably be passed round.

"It was much later, near the end of my time at Oxford, that Belcher surprised me by asking if I remembered Dupont in Paris. It appeared that that individual had begun to make a place for himself in the French world of science, and that Belcher had met him at some species of international conference. It was clear that they had been putting their heads together, as you say, about Justo de la Costa. Well, I could not object to that, but in answer to Belcher's question I allowed it to be seen that Dupont had not made on me, in Paris, an altogether favourable impression."

The General refreshed himself with another sip of telque, and Dr Barlow cackled briefly. "Now that Dupont has risen in the world," he said, "there are quite a lot of people whom he has impressed in that way. What was it you actually said about him to Belcher that time? The

General," he added to Taylor, "has quite a talent for summing up the characters of men he doesn't like."

"I say about them only what is the most simple truth," the General said, wiping his moustache. "As to that I am scrupulous. What I told Belcher, as far as I can remember, was that Dupont was a repulsive blackguard, with no more character or decency than a bug, and there the matter dropped. But I continue my story. My time at Oxford was cut short by the breaking out of war between my own country and the Republic of Riesgador.

"I had already done my army service before coming to Europe. I returned home at once and received a commission in the artillery. The dispute could, perhaps have been settled peacefully, it was a boundary question which might have been submitted to arbitration, as in the end it was submitted, but first there was war – and in the Americas, my dear Taylor, wars usually are not short, they are no bush-league stuff. It is due to the temperament of the peoples. For the same reason, promotion is rapid.

"To cut short this part of my story, after two years of fighting, during which a third of the officers on both sides had lost their lives, peace was made, and I returned to civilian life with a General's rank. Also my service record had made me something of a public figure. I do not speak of that to boast about it, but only to explain how I was forced into prominence in the long and bitter political struggle which came after the war. The politics of my country are of no interest to you, my dear Taylor, it will be enough to say that at the next Presidential election I was nominated in opposition to Sebastian Verdugo, whose career I had permitted myself to describe as a justification of the worst that the critics of democracy had ever brought against it. His re-election was secured by methods of which I said at the time that history might be searched in vain for a parallel to them, and which I still think went considerably beyond the limits of what was allowable.

"At last I was free to retire from public life and to resume the scientific research which the war had interrupted. I had given much thought to this during the intervening years, I had planned in my mind how I should attack my problems when I could do so in privacy and in conditions of my own making. One of my first decisions was that this would not be practicable in Peligragua. The country was full of my personal enemies, and every action of mine would be attended by publicity.

"It was one of my war-time staff-officers, a Swiss soldier of fortune named Geiger, who suggested that his own country would be a suitable place of operations for me, and that I should make use of his services in the matter. This solved more than one difficulty. To begin with, Geiger was a close friend, he was in my confidence about my scientific project, I trusted him absolutely, as I trust all my close friends. More than that, Geiger was on the point of returning to Switzerland, where he had just inherited a very large hotel business and other property in land and houses. He insisted on treating my interests as his own, and when we travelled to Europe together a little later a complete plan had been worked out.

"I bought from Geiger a house belonging to him in the outskirts of Engelberg, a little town in the mountains above Lucerne, which he recommended as being secluded without being too much cut off. The house was just what I needed, with a large detached building, formerly used as a studio, where I could set up my laboratory. I purchased all the necessary equipment, partly in Zurich, partly in Paris, and had it installed under my own eye, although all the business transactions were carried out in Geiger's name. Finally, he supplied me with a small household staff, and an intelligent workman named Krug, who knew little of science but could turn his hand to anything, as you say, in the way of machinery and carpentry.

"So there I was established comfortably, in a delightful spot and in ideal conditions. I went under my own name, of course, and described myself correctly, because the Swiss police are of an inquiring habit of mind, as it is their duty to be, but it was given out by Geiger that he was financing the development of a new kind of refrigerating plant invented by me, which could be useful in his business. It was an excellent lie, because the producing of very low temperatures was a vital part of my problem, and the whole idea was so Swiss that nobody in the place gave it another thought.

"I had much to occupy me at Engelberg, for the experimental work to be done was very extensive, but I knew just what I was aiming at, and I did not doubt that I should get the right combination of conditions in the end. And at last the time came when my trouble was rewarded. I had my problem licked. I was alone in my laboratory, as I always was while experiments were in progress, it was late at night when the cooling was completed, and I found I had produced five diamonds of the first quality, like those you see before you on that table."

CHAPTER XIII

The General, who had thrown not a little of dramatic intensity into this account of his success, here looked directly at Taylor, who had been drinking in the story with fascinated interest. "You open your eyes, *amigo*," the General said. "Shall I tell you what happened to my own eyes at that heart-swelling moment when my first diamonds lay before me? They were filled with tears, I wept with happiness, they were the tears of relief and purification. There had been so many weeks of waiting, even at the final stage of the work. The matter of the time for the cooling of the flux had been my last problem. I had greatly simplified the conditions, but I had had a number of failures. This was a crucial experiment, and it had ended in triumph.

"When I had mastered my emotion I set to work to clean my diamonds. I sat for a long time admiring their lustre in the rays of the lamp. I got out the telque and I drank to the memory of Henri Moissan, who had shown me the way. It was an occasion for telque. Then I wrapped myself up and went for a climb up the mountain side, with the stones in my pocket. As I stood above the world I held them in my hand in the bright moonlight, and I saw it gathered up and flashed around by the diamonds I had made. The rugged peaks towering up at the end of the valley looked down on me, the clouds chased each other, there was the sound of cascades and of wind in the pine-trees and of Justo de la Costa giving himself pats on the back. *Que valentia!"*

"It was the telque," observed Dr Barlow.

"Possibly it helped," the General admitted. "For what else was it created? But the fact was enough. It was the successful end of more than six months' work, I had my formula, I felt – if I were a poet I might tell you how I felt."

"Like a dog with two tails," Dr Barlow suggested. "Your story gets better each time I hear it, General. This is the first I've heard of that rhapsody in the moonlight – up to now I've merely been told that you did the trick in Engelberg. Taylor, this is a compliment to your talent as a listener."

The General laughed lightly and rolled another cigarette. "Well, let it go. I make the tale too long. Once again I cut it short for you, my dear Taylor. After that first success, there was nothing to it. I repeated the process, on a larger scale now, allowing each time about forty-eight hours.

"What I had to consider now was the question of disposing of my stones. The first of them were made in July. A month later I wrote to one of my diamond dealing friends in London, a charming fellow of whom I have spoken already, named Mendoza, the one who had been at Oxford. He was, as I knew, fond of winter sports in Switzerland, and I made the suggestion that he might give Engelberg a trial in the coming season if it did not conflict with his other arrangements. If he should do so, I said, there was a matter which I should like to discuss with him. For Mendoza no more than that was needed, because he and his partner both knew the purpose of my retirement in Engelberg, though they knew – they insisted on knowing – absolutely nothing else. He replied to my letter, announcing that he had made his arrangements to come to Engelberg at the beginning of November and giving the name of his hotel.

"So I continued with my work. By the time when Mendoza was due in Engelberg I had enough diamonds to represent a very great fortune, assuming that the level of values was not disturbed. When Mendoza arrived I spoke to him briefly by telephone, and arranged to meet him at a spot a little above the valley where there was a cable-car terminus. From there we walked some distance along a mountain path, until we had privacy in the strict sense – nothing but a bird could overlook us.

"I did not say much to Mendoza, because it was between us a thing understood that nothing was to be said about my research, my methods, my scientific achievement. At length we seated ourselves on a flat rock, and I handed to him a small bag much like this one on the table here, containing specimens of my work."

The General took up the bag of stones and tossed it in the air, so that it fell on the table with a light jingling noise. A single smothered bark came from the Alsatian.

"My friend was much moved," the General pursued, "when he turned out the contents of the bag on the rock between us. He was pale, and he pushed back his hat to wipe the sweat from his forehead, cold as it was. He examined the stones with an optical instrument, squeezed them together, licked them, made scratches with them on a piece of glass which he had brought with him. He is a man of foresight, Mendoza.

"The first thing he said was, 'This will need very careful handling.' So we made there and then the agreement that has governed all my transactions with him and his partners from that time to this. You have already heard what it was in essence – that they were to know nothing whatever about my method of producing diamonds, and that the placing of them on the market was to be left exclusively to them. Mendoza refused to take charge of the stones, it was too great a responsibility, he said. I was to dine at his house, with his partner Ullstein, when I next came to London, and we should then talk business.

"This was very gratifying to me," the General continued. "I had never doubted that my stones were actual diamonds, because that was an established scientific fact, but I had not been certain that they would pass so easily a commercial expert's practical tests, without any chemical analysis being called for.

"Not so gratifying, but not surprising to me, was some information which my friend gave me. He told me that it had come to his ears, not long before, that a man called Cowdery, one of the big people in the diamond mining industry, was taking an interest in me and my work. That was as much as he would say, what he had heard was very vague, and besides, as he remarked, it was no business of his. But he added that he had already seen in Engelberg, on the evening of his arrival, a man who was known to him by sight as a suspicious character; he had seen him reading a paper in the Casino. Dealers in precious stones, Mendoza explained, find it advisable to have some knowledge of that class of people, and to go to some trouble to obtain it. The man in question, he said, went by the name of Ketch, he was tall and stooping, with a head completely bald.

"As I say, I was not unprepared for this. When Belcher had spoken to me in Oxford about his meeting Dupont, it had been clear to me that my research was being talked about. During the following years, when I was occupied with war and politics, it might have been forgotten, but it would have been recalled very quickly by interested persons when the fact leaked out that I had turned up in Switzerland and was engaged there in laboratory work. Geiger and I had gone about the thing quietly enough, but my identity had not been concealed, because in a well-policed modern state that would not have been practicable. It was only a question of time before it became known outside Engelberg that that mischievous devil de la Costa was planted there, surrounded with furnaces and crucibles *et tout le bazar."*

The General turned to Taylor with an eloquent gesture of his hands. "You see, *amigo,* what all this meant for me. Cowdery, about whom Mendoza had warned me, was known to me by reputation, and it was not a good reputation. If he, a very wealthy man and vitally interested in the industry, was taking an interest, as Mendoza said, in my work, that meant quite certainly that I was being watched. It meant, almost certainly, that agents of a not very scrupulous kind were being employed. And now here in Engelberg was an agent of exactly that kind, known to my friend. You see, this was not an employment for honest men. The object of anyone who was having me watched must be to get possession of my secret process, and as he could not expect to obtain it by fair means, I had to anticipate some kind of dirty work. Well, I was ready – I had been ready, down to the last detail, for a long time past."

"You mean," Taylor said, "that you were ready to defend yourself against robbery?"

The General snapped a finger and thumb. "But naturally, certainly – for most of my life I have been ready to defend myself. But this for which I was ready in Engelberg was something more serious. It was to disappear immediately and, if possible, without a trace. Not only that, but also to leave behind nothing from which could be gathered any notion about the work I had been engaged in. All this I was ready to do when I said goodbye to Mendoza on that mountain path, leaving him to return to the town by the cable-car across the valley.

"To begin with, I had always slept on a camp-bed in the laboratory. Whenever Krug was in there, I also was there. When I left it, I left it absolutely safe from intrusion."

"But how," Taylor asked, "does one make a place absolutely safe from intrusion, if the intruders really mean business? You had to reckon with the possibility of dirty work, as you said just now."

The General nodded thoughtfully. "To say the word 'absolutely' is to go too far, I admit it. But I had taken much trouble to make the place burglar-proof, as you say. Neither the door nor the window nor the skylight could be forced from outside without detonating an explosive which would blow the further end of the room, where all my apparatus was concentrated, into the air, and any walking on the floor would have the same effect. For this reason I always carried all my diamonds – much more than I had shown to Mendoza – in my pocket when I went out, and before doing so I would push over the switch, just inside the door, which brought my anti-burglar network into operation."

"You see, Taylor," Dr Barlow explained, "what the Peligraguan idea of a place being burglar-proof is. If a burglar succeeds in cracking the crib, the crib itself and large quantities of the owner's property are sent hurtling into the air. The notion has that spaciousness, sometimes mistaken for extravagance, that marks the Latin American civilisation. If you want to have a pig-sty, you build it of polished marble, with a lofty clock-tower, and a separate trough of sculptured alabaster for each pig."

General de la Costa laughed heartily. "There is a grain of intelligence in what our doctor says," he observed to Taylor. "We of that civilisation feel in our hearts that the leadership of mankind will one day be ours, when the civilisations now crumbling before our eyes are really through. So we think that a little splendour here and there is not out of place. But my arrangements for dealing with the danger of interference in Engelberg had nothing to do with that, they were simply practical. I did not wish to have anyone shoving an inquisitive snout into my highly specialised apparatus of research, that was all. If I thought it wise to disappear, I would leave no traces.

"That same night I went to my bed in the laboratory, as usual, about eleven o'clock. Krug and the domestics had already retired. After dinner I had written and posted a letter to my good friend Geiger, begging him to have the kindness to settle with my employees, and to accept the house and its contents as a proof of my gratitude and esteem. I gave a last inspection to my burglar-proofing arrangements, to make sure that not so much as the leaf of a notebook lay outside the range of destruction.

"It was the daily duty of Krug to call me at seven in the morning. That evening, as the explosion was to take place in any case, I connected the mechanism with a small clock which Krug had rigged up under my instructions, and set it so that the balloon would go up, as you say, at six o'clock. Long before that time I should have ended the down-hill walk to Stansstad on the shore of the lake, where I should wait for the first steamer to the city of Lucerne. The walk was put by my map at twenty-two kilometres, so that I expected to have a good appetite for breakfast in the restaurant of the main-line terminus. Just the same, in case of anything going wrong – you know, my dear Taylor, how in all things I am guided by prudence – I raided the larder and made myself a lot of cold bacon sandwiches."

Dr Barlow, interested as ever in any question of eating, wrinkled his nose at this. "Were cold bacon sandwiches the best your larder could do for you?" he asked. "You usually cater for yourself better than that when you're at home, General."

The General wagged a forefinger. "Bah! When it is a question of cold food, there is nothing better than a sandwich of cold bacon, cut thick, and with plenty of butter. You should investigate the matter, *chico*. Have you not read George Saintsbury on the subject of sandwiches?"

"You mean the Saintsbury who was a professor of literature – no, I haven't. But I have heard," Dr Barlow answered, "that he was a man of great judgment in the matter of eating, so I don't see what sandwiches could mean to him."

"They meant a great deal to him," the General said. "Saintsbury made it his aim to rescue the sandwich from the neglect and contempt which it had suffered at the hands of ignorant men. You see in me, my dear Taylor, a disciple of Saintsbury the sandwich-fancier. But I wander from the point – a bad habit of mine, I confess it. At two o'clock I put on an overcoat and hat, I pocketed my diamonds and a fairly large sum of money which I kept in my desk for emergencies. I put my sandwiches in a small knapsack which I carried in my hand. I turned off the lights, then I went out, set the switch and closed the door carefully. That was for me the last of Engelberg.

"Everything went as I expected – so it seemed to me. I delighted in that moonlight walk in what you call the small hours, with the torrent rushing down the steep glen on the left, and the big trees stirring and sighing on the right beyond the little railway. It was a good hard road, and as it was steep downhill, walking was almost like flying.

"When I was nearly at the end of my walk I heard the sound of a car coming down the road behind me. I was not expecting any trouble, but the place and the hour were favourable for anyone wishing to be troublesome, and as my life has always been governed by prudence, I stepped off the road and took cover behind some bushes a little way down the side of the glen. I knew that the people in the car could not have seen me, because of a bend in the road, and in fact the car passed by me without a check. As it turned out afterwards, this was just as well, because it was the only time when the gang who were after me ever had me in a quite hopeless spot. If they had seen me, shooting it out would have been no good, because they had three automatics to my one, and I should almost certainly have been wiped out and dumped into the torrent."

Taylor, who had followed this narrative with keen interest, now inquired, "How did you know, General, that they had three to your one? Could you see how many were in the car as it passed you?"

"From where I was lying, well below the level of the road, I could not see the car itself," the General answered. "I did not even try to have a look, because it seemed to me I had everything properly sewn up in Engelberg for another hour or so at least. As for the numbers against me, I was soon to know all about that, and it was fortunate indeed, as I say, that I was not seen. You see, my dear Taylor, the reptile who was behind all this wanted to have me snatched, as I explained to you yesterday, but if that could not be managed, as it could not be managed in those circumstances, he would have contented himself with having me cooled off and done with.

"When I arrived in sight of the quay at Stansstad, there was nothing to do in the early sunshine but stroll about in the wood and consider my arrangements. They were simple arrangements. All I knew about the railway service from Lucerne was that if I wished to get to London I must change trains in Paris. Also I knew that the restaurant in the Federal Railways terminus was an excellent one, and I could assume that the train for Paris would be starting at a convenient hour, so that there would be time for me to make a few necessary purchases before leaving.

"At last the steamer came chugging up to the causeway, and I came out of the wood to go on board. There, at the corner of the landing stage, a car was waiting, and it hardly needed my experience of tight places, as you say, to realise that this was the car which had passed me on the road, and that the three men in it were waiting for me. For one of them was an old acquaintance – you remember my speaking of a certain Dupont, who used to be too much interested in my research work when we were both students at the Sorbonne? Well, the man in the driving seat of that car was the same old Dupont, more fat and if possible more ugly, but unmistakably Dupont. But apart from that, it was clear they were waiting for me – when I appeared, all three heads turned round at me for one instant, after that none of them glanced in my direction, and I could not see that any of them spoke to the others. When I stepped on the deck of the steamer, two of the men from the car were among the small group who followed me on board, and Dupont remained behind. One of the two who came on the steamer was tall and stooping.

"As you see, my dear Taylor, it was clear in the first place that something had gone wrong with my plan. At the time when that car passed me on the road, it was much too early for my little automatic set-up at the laboratory to have got going. It was clear also that there was much more in Mendoza's warning than either of us had realised, for here was not only the tall, stooping man known to Mendoza as Ketch, but with him a man who knew about my diamond research work, who had discussed it with others, and who was my personal enemy.

"The appearance of Dupont lighted up the whole picture. His being here with a car, his staying behind when the others were on my trail, suggested to me very strongly that he had taken a place of his own in the Engelberg neighbourhood, that it was the headquarters of the gang who were after me, and that it would have been my place of captivity if the plan for snatching me had come off. For all I could tell, they might have been on the point of trying it on when Mendoza gave me the first news of it. But I did not give the matter much thought just then, because the situation now was entirely different – Ketch had me under his eye, and of course he would know that I had him under my eye, as I had seen him with my old college chum Dupont, and Dupont must have told him what our relations had been.

"It did not seem likely that I should get rid of Ketch and his companion anywhere short of Paris, if I did so there. They would probably assume that I was heading for London, because they would have been told that I had more friends in England than anywhere else, my own country being an unsafe place for me. Well, during the journey that was before us I did not expect an attempt on my life, because in railway trains and public places that sort of thing is not good business, especially if the man you are after knows you are around, and is capable of looking after himself. Besides, in any case they would much prefer to make me prisoner when there was an opportunity. My business was to prevent any such opportunity from arising."

Dr Barlow glanced at Taylor. "I know what you're thinking," he said. "You're thinking the General was thoroughly enjoying the situation. And you're quite right."

"Something of the sort had crossed my mind," Taylor admitted.

General de la Costa shook a finger at them. "Bah! Do not be so Anglo-Saxon. If I find myself matched up against a few crooks and thugs, must I be so God-awful serious about it? On the contrary – as our doctor says – I thoroughly enjoy it. *Como no?* If I am unable to keep to my rule of playing perfectly safe at all times, should I not at least take some pleasure in it? Well, since I was so fortunate as to know my enemies by sight, I was safer than I need have been. During the passage from Stansstad to Lucerne I ran the rule over those two birds, without being so uncivil as to stare at them. Ketch was a big, powerful man, with a typical tough-guy face – no expression whatever, a large nose – "

"Not at that time knocked sideways," Taylor suggested.

The General beamed approval. "So! You have been paying attention to my long stories, my dear Taylor. No, the accident to Ketch's nose took place some months later. May I say that you seem always so much interested, it is a temptation to me to go on reciting my experiences? I like talking about my adventures, because I have done my best to make them exciting, and the memory of them is agreeable. That is another thing that you are supposed not to do if you are English – to talk about your own doings. But if you are an American, like me, no one is surprised if you do so, or even if you boast and exaggerate and possibly tell lies to some extent. For my part, there is something in my make-up which makes me rebel against the notion of giving too much colour to my experiences. I like to make them as interesting as possible, and to let them go at that. It is the right way, believe me. The dumb Britisher, who, if he ever does tell you anything about his dangers and surprises, tries to tone them down till they sound silly – I respect him, but I prefer my own attitude towards experience. But I was telling you about my getting away from Switzerland, with those two animals tailing me."

"You mentioned one of the animals, called Ketch," Taylor said. "You did not describe the other."

The General gazed thoughtfully at the Alsatian, which, catching his eye, panted politely. "Ah, the other," he said. "Perhaps he is worth a little description, the other, because he was, and is, an unusual type to meet with in big-time criminal stuff. He was just a ferocious beast – I should say, going by his appearance, practically without intelligence, but with brutal violence and also reckless courage stamped on his face in large letters. Such brutes make one realise that being a brave man does not amount to so much as many people think – I mean, it is not enough. A vicious and dangerous ruffian may be full of courage – I have known a good many like that, including my political opponent, Verdugo, at present occupying the Presidency of my native country. Well, this thick-necked, red-faced savage was clearly nothing but a tool; it was the man Ketch that I had to think about."

CHAPTER XIV

"The man Ketch," said Taylor reflectively, as the General brought out his sack of tobacco. "Since my first and last meeting with him in Mrs McBean's kitchen I have wondered how you first came across him. I never thought of Switzerland."

"Why should you?" the General said. "No one ever does."

"But I am anxious to hear the rest of the story of the escape from Engelberg," Taylor said, "and of the baffling of the man Ketch."

The General leaned across and patted Taylor on the shoulder. "You encourage me, *amigo*. Before now you have shown interest in my long stories. Besides, our doctor has heard this one only in outline. Very well – when the steamer arrived at Lucerne I went to the railway terminus, which is near the quay. Loitering a little on the way, I could satisfy myself that Ketch and his gorilla were keeping me in view, and I thought it likely that Ketch's business was simply not to lose sight of me, and to find out where I was going to settle down when I got to my destination. That would be the sensible course for him to pursue, now that I had ducked out of the dangerous spot that I must certainly have been in at Engelberg. Well, at the station I was told that the early train for Paris had gone, and the next did not leave until the evening, so I had most of the day in which to amuse myself and Ketch.

"First I went to the restaurant, where I did not refuse myself the sort of breakfast suitable for a man who had walked about fourteen miles, and afterwards breathed large quantities of the air of the Vierwaldstaettersee. After that I went along the lake front about half a mile, looking carefully for the names of all the little streets leading away from the lake, until I came to one called Weinstockstrasse, which sounded to me attractive, so I took from my pocket a small notebook and examined carefully a page on which nothing was written. I went on up the Weinstockstrasse, which was quite steep; it was what you call a residential quarter, nothing but neat little houses and gardens, with side-streets of more neat little houses and gardens. From time to time I consulted my notebook. All this, my dear Taylor, was of course to interest Ketch and his tame cannibal, who were loitering some distance behind me. They were hardly trying to hide the fact that they were following me, because they knew I had been on to them ever since arriving at Stansstad, and it was clear that they had to follow me because they did not know what my game was, and there might be something important underlying all the banality of the neat little houses and gardens.

"When I came to a side-street called Nachtigallstrasse, it sounded nice to me, so I turned up there. At the fifth house I spoke to a man, evidently the householder, who was sweeping up leaves in the front garden. I asked him if he knew the address of a friend of mine called Biedermeyer, who had written to me a few years ago from this Nachtigallstrasse, but I had forgotten the number, and I would like to see him now that I happened to be in Lucerne for a few days.

"The householder said he did not recall the name, but he had not been long living there. He asked me if Herr Biedermeyer was in business. I said that he had been in the wine trade in Oporto when I was conducting a fencing academy there, but that when he inherited a modest fortune he had retired to end his days in his native Lucerne. Need I say that I have never known a Biedermeyer, and have never been in Oporto, nor conducted a fencing academy? It is in such a way that the mind works in moments of intense tactical activity.

"Well, the householder said that if I would come inside he would look up Biedermeyer in the directory, so my two followers had the interesting spectacle of me entering the private house of a man quite unknown to me even by name, in a place I had never heard of before."

Dr Barlow turned to Taylor. "The idea is, you see, to keep the enemy guessing all the time. They never know what you're going to do next – which is the ideal state of mind to have your enemy in."

The General nodded. "So it seemed to me. My two thugs could not possibly make sense of what I was doing, because it contained, in fact, no sense; but they would be obliged to try. Well, it turned out that there was no Biedermeyer listed in the directory as living in Nachtigallstrasse, but that two citizens of that convenient name had addresses in that neighbourhood, and those addresses I copied most carefully into my little notebook. Then I parted regretfully from my new friend, pausing on his doorstep to make sure that I had the right street-names in my little book, and that Ketch was losing nothing of the performance from his post behind a laurel-bush at the corner. The householder and I exchanged courteous gestures as I continued on my way up the street, and I devoted the next half-hour to finding the way back to the lake-front through a perfect labyrinth of charming little villas and fresh little lawns."

"You see, Taylor," Dr Barlow explained, "the General, as a military man, believes in the strategy of indirect approach."

"Bah! Who does not?" the General said. "What I believed in at that time in Lucerne was treating myself to a little harmless amusement. So we arrived at last at the lake-front, and there, in front of the Kursaal, I took a seat in the sunshine overlooking the water and meditated for about an hour. After that I began to feel hungry, so I turned into the centre of the town and looked out for a restaurant that had the appearance of being very expensive."

Dr Barlow looked incredulous. "You don't mean to tell me that the feverish passion for cold bacon sandwiches had vanished already?"

The General waved a hand. "I have not expressed anything more than a temperate love for cold bacon sandwiches, I think," he said. "But at that time, *chico*, my intention was to give a little trouble to those who were dogging my footsteps, as you say, and at the same time to continue the satisfying of an appetite which was still of the first order. You see, my dear Taylor, how these little social points can become important, even for a man like myself, to whom class distinctions are nothing. I knew well that a person with the appearance of Ketch, not to mention his attending savage, would never willingly go inside a restaurant of any luxurious pretensions, unless it was to stick up the joint. Ruffians are the shyest people on earth, when acting tough is no part of the programme – so I have found. So when I recognised what I was looking for in the Assiette d'Or, in the Alpenstrasse, I dived in there and sat at a table at the back, quite out of sight of the windows or the entrance. It was a capital lunch, and I permitted myself to linger over it to the extent of one hour and twenty minutes."

Dr Barlow nodded with suitable gravity. "It is an important principle of dietetics," he said, "to make a meal in a restaurant last as long as you possibly can, short of driving the proprietor and the head waiter to despair and suicide. And what was the next step?"

"The next step was a little tedious," the General said, "especially for Ketch. You have heard of the researches of the Dutch Senator, M de Bloch, into the moral and, in particular, the economic consequences of war, leading to the conclusion that war does not pay in any sense of the word. And you must have heard also of the Kriegs-und-Friedens-Museum, founded in honour of that statesman, in the Museggstrasse of Lucerne. I had seen this mentioned in a little guide which I found in the restaurant, so I determined to visit it. I am sorry to say that I did not find it very interesting, because it told me nothing that I, as a combatant in a very sanguinary war, did not know already. I knew that the horrors of war had impressed themselves on the mind of every intelligent soldier long before M de Bloch was born, and that the expensiveness of war was not a new discovery. Still, it had to be admitted that the display of exhibits, if that is the right word, was well arranged. It occupied me for over an hour, during which time I and Ketch and his satellite had the Museum to ourselves. It reminded me, in fact, of the place mentioned by one of your poets,

> Where no one comes
> Or hath come since the making of the world...

Then at last the time arrived when it would be reasonable to go across the bridge to the station and arrange for my transport to Paris."

"Didn't Ketch expect you would be going there?" Taylor asked. "If the gang knew you had friends in London, as I think you said they did, and the way to London was through Paris, I should have thought he would have waited for you at the terminus."

The General shook his head decisively. "That would not have been what Ketch was paid for, believe me," he said. "My being on the way to London was only a probability. And besides, more things happen in Switzerland than you might suppose. I could mention to you more than one organisation of a rather dubious kind which prefers to have its headquarters in Switzerland. In short, it was quite evident that Ketch's business was to keep me in sight and see what I did in Lucerne in the first place, and I hope that I provided him with the material for an interesting report that day.

"So I went at last to the station, about half an hour before the time the train was due to start. I did not take a first-class ticket to Paris. The fact is that in the first class the passengers are not so many – they are too few to be safe – but in the second class, with three or four times as many people, there is much less risk of any ganging-up business. In my position then, that risk was a substantial one, for Ketch might very well have had friends waiting for him at the terminus. I apologise, my dear Taylor, for boring you with these principles of railway travel, which a man in my situation cannot afford to disregard. So I found a compartment already half full, just what I wanted, and took my seat. I was careful not to pay Ketch and his assassin the compliment of looking out for them, but I knew, of course, that they would be in the same coach, and not far off at that.

"During the first part of the journey I took note of the apparent characters of my fellow travellers in that compartment. They seemed to be, and no doubt were, an elderly French priest, a French husband and wife, also elderly, and a tall Englishman with a little boy, whom he treated as a son. When it was time for dinner, the

Englishman and the little boy went to the dining-car, the others had food with them, as I had – the bacon sandwiches, as perhaps you may remember. I had already had a little conversation with the padre, talking the worst French I could."

Taylor held up a hand. "I beg your pardon for interrupting," he said, "but why did you talk bad French?"

The General smiled largely. "One of the things I like about you, my dear Taylor," he said, "is that you seem to follow my long stories with attention and that you ask, if I may say so, intelligent questions. In this case I was acting on a general principle. People are always likely to loosen up a little with a foreigner who talks their language badly, and to get a little cagey with one who talks it well. So I have found. I wanted to be friendly with these individuals, just in case of accidents. But, as I was saying, I chatted with the man of God, and offered him a couple of my bacon sandwiches, which were good enough for the Holy Father Himself."

Dr Barlow groaned faintly. "Sandwiches!" he murmured.

General de la Costa smiled tolerantly. "I must regard that subject as disposed of already – appeal has been made to an authority higher than yours or mine. At least, my padre in the train was a slave to no such superstitious prejudices. He complimented me on the quality of my sandwiches, and gave me one of several wedges of plum-cake which he had in his dinner-packet. Of course, I pretended to eat it."

"You pretended?" Taylor asked.

"Naturally, certainly," the General said. "It was only decent to do so. What else would you do, *amigo*, if someone presented you with a piece of cake? But prudence is for me a guiding star, and I make it an iron rule never to eat or drink anything offered me by people I know nothing about. All my coats have a side pocket lined with American cloth, in case I wish to get rid of food without giving rise to ill-feeling, and I assure you that in a country like my own, where hospitality is the universal rule, some such precaution is very desirable. Yes, I accepted the holy man's cake, and munched away gratefully while I was getting rid of the stuff. Then the French pair offered me a drink out of the conjugal bottle of Bordeaux, wiping the mouth of the bottle very civilly after each of them had had a go at it. It was very kind of them, as I said to them, and if they had in fact shoved in a little dope while wiping the bottle, I think I should have observed it, but just the same – " the General shrugged his shoulders.

"On general principles," Taylor suggested.

"Exactly. I just tilted up the bottle and had one or two blank swallows, and told them it was wonderful, and I could see they thought highly of my *delicatesse* in drinking so very little. After that we had a little conversation, mainly about the imperfection of the French railway system, which had just been nationalised, or de-nationalised, I do not remember which; it was always passing from one condition to the other. Later on the French couple put up their feet and had a nap, which seemed likely to be prolonged, and the padre hauled out a little book, as padres will, I do not know why, because they must have every line of the stuff by heart after many years of repetition. Anyway, he had his book, and began chewing his prayers, as they say, and the Englishman and his son came back from the dining-car, and no more words passed until it was decided by unanimous agreement to pull the shades down over the lamps.

"The next thing that I remember is our arriving at the Gare de l'Est in Paris. I had enjoyed a long sleep, and I felt ready for anything, as you say."

CHAPTER XV

Dr Barlow sighed gently. "I am glad we have got to Paris," he said. "I should like to know what happened there. All I have heard before this is that you got away from France without being followed, so that Ketch and Co. were quite some time picking up the trail again over here."

"Well," the General said, "what happened in Paris has, it may be, some interest, as it shows what use may be made of the customs and practices of Parliamentary government. When we arrived at the Gare, I got out with my little knapsack, keeping an eye open for any attempts to form a party round me in the crowd. I did not trouble myself about the two in the train with me, because I knew very well they would not be letting me out of their sight, and would try to trail me wherever I went. But I thought they might have their friends in Paris, too, waiting for me. So I did not take a taxi until I got out into the street, and stopped one as it was passing. I told the man to drive to the Palais Bourbon – the Chamber of Deputies, that is. Of course I knew I should be followed."

"Aha!" Dr Barlow exclaimed. "Now we come to the French friend who was *not* a Deputy, but something even more important. You remember, Taylor, what I said – this important French friend who had simplified the difficulties of travel by reducing his personal baggage to a nightgown and a toothbrush wrapped up in a sheet of the *Petit Parisien*.

That's all I can recollect of what I was told about him, which can't have been very much."

The General shrugged. "Bah! I had forgotten that I mentioned such a trifle. As it seems that I did mention it, that was simply to illustrate the change in the social status of Hercule St Gratien since the days when he was an obscure and badly-paid reporter on a Paris newspaper. Today he does not refuse himself the most expensive suit-cases that money can buy, with many silver-topped bottles inside, which make an impression at the *douane* whenever he has to cross a frontier, as he does very often. With ambition and study and – what is the word you have for absence of social timidity?"

"Cheek," suggested Dr Barlow.

"Ah, no, not cheek," the General said. "St Gratien is a very well-bred man, as you say, and he has the gift of tact, though this is not the word exactly. Well, I will leave it at that. As I was saying, my friend has made himself a personage. He is enormously well informed about high political and diplomatic affairs. He knows important people everywhere, from China to Peru. Although he dishes out his stuff with a right-wing slant, he never tells lies, and everyone reads his articles. They are signed with the name of Hamilcar, but everyone knows who he is, and he has Ministers eating out of his hand. We were great friends when we were students together in Paris, in his nightgown and toothbrush days – in France in those days pyjamas were uncommon – and I have seen him often since, here in England and in my own country and in New York, while he was in the process of becoming Hamilcar.

"Well, as our doctor says, it was with the idea of seeing St Gratien that I directed my taxi-driver to the Palais Bourbon. There was another reason also. I did not know how many men might be on my trail by this time, but I knew that there are always more policemen in and about the Chamber of Deputies, when it is in session, than anywhere else on earth. I had often remarked this in my time at the Sorbonne, when I knew several Deputies. At this time, standing in the entrance, I had around me enough *agents*, complete with revolver and side-arm, to storm a barricade, and I knew there were plenty more on the premises.

"Now this was a time, as I remembered, when St Gratien would be at the Chamber on the prowl for political news, listening to a debate, or buttonholing important persons about this and that. So I sent up my card to him. When leaving Engelberg I had remembered at the last moment to take my card-case, which is a most valuable aid to getting anything done in Paris, especially if the cards are two or three sizes larger than those commonly used in England. The *huissier* to whom I handed my card said, with the respect due to my military rank, that he knew where M St Gratien was and would find him immediately.

"In a very short time St Gratien came out to see me, full of *empressement*, wishing to know where I had been all these centuries, and in what way he could have the pleasure, and so forth. It is curious – we are the most intimate of friends, and would do anything for each other, but Hercule is always as polite as if he were meeting for the first time. There he stood, sleek-haired, beautifully dressed, hanging on to my hand with both his hands, his eyes half shut with pure delight at seeing me, purring over me like a cat – if I hadn't known him I should have thought he was just pretending to be tickled to death, and overdoing it at that.

"So, walking up and down the lobby, I began to give St Gratien an outline of my story. But soon it appeared that he was by no means without knowledge of it.

"I ought not to have been surprised at this, because the thing had begun in Paris, with the spying and tattling of that detestable animal Dupont, and St Gratien does hear about anything of the least importance that is going on. Anyway, he had heard of my return from Peligragua and of my settling down in Engelberg as a research worker. When I began to tell him the facts about that enterprise, he laid his hand on my arm. 'Not a word, my friend, not a word,' he said. 'You have your secret, and you are in danger, *n'est-ce pas*? That is enough; I am at your disposal.' 'You know everything, then,' I said – just to please him, because he could not really. 'I know enough at least,' said Hercule. So I told him about the gang that had been watching me in Switzerland, and what I believed their game was, and that some of them were after me at that moment.

"Hercule's eyes glistened; this was just his dish. 'Then your work at Engelberg is finished, it is in the bag?' he said. I told him that it certainly was, and that I had cleaned up after myself, too, or tried to. I told him how I had cleaned up. How he laughed! 'And now,' I said, 'I want to get from here to London without being snatched, or shoved into the Channel, or kept under observation by these birds, who are pretty certainly waiting for me outside at this moment. That is the problem. Can you help me?' And Hercule said, '*Comptez sur moi.*'

"He was enchanted with the affair. He said that the pair who had followed me, and any others who might have joined them in Paris, were certainly very dangerous men, that Dupont, who had put them on my track, was capable of anything – he was well known by reputation to St Gratien. We need not speculate, he said, about what they intended to do to me – they must just be shaken off. Already he had his plan. He took me to a room where a few of his *confrères* were at work – a room looking out on one of those charming little gardens which exist behind the scenes in the Palais Bourbon. He found me a chair and some papers to look at, and went off to do a little telephoning, as he expressed it – in fact he was gone for over half an hour.

"At last Hercule returned, full of apologies and smiling all over. He said, 'All goes well.' He had been in communication with Engelberg, but he would not tell me the news until later, when I was to be his guest at lunch at the Hotel de Bourgogne. It was the hotel where he lived, a stone's throw from the back entrance of the Palais Bourbon, and I was to meet there two friends of his to whom he had been telephoning, and who were anxious to be of use to me. I thanked Hercule warmly for taking so much interest in my affairs, and he led me out of the Palais across the little square behind it, towards the Hotel de Bourgogne, which is in a nice comfortable little Parisian street.

"Almost opposite the hotel was what you call an outfitter's shop, and Hercule steered me towards this. He said that if I was not well supplied with money I could draw upon him, but I told him I had quite a considerable sum in my possession. He said, 'What you should buy, if I may advise, is a rather conspicuous sort of *imperméable*, to be worn on your journey to England.' That garment is what you in England call a mackintosh, and what my American friends call a slicker. So we entered the shop, and I chose an *imperméable* of a light yellow colour, long and loose. I asked Hercule if it was sufficiently conspicuous, and he agreed that in it I should look like nothing human. I should put it on at once, he said, as I could not begin too soon to establish my character as a performing canary bird. Then we crossed the road to the hotel; we sat down to *apéritifs*, and Hercule got down to business.

"First he asked me at what hour I had made my getaway from my workshop. About 2.15 a.m., I told him. And at what hour was my man to have called me in the morning? I said seven o'clock. *'Eh, bien,'* Hercule said. 'Those gentlemen who were on the watch must have fine noses; they must have had their little suspicions; they decided to anticipate your domestic. I have been talking to the office of the *Lucerne Gazette*. They communicated with Engelberg for me, and their information is that an alarm of fire was given from your house about six this morning, and that the whole of your workshop was in ashes by seven. Ah, *finaud*! I congratulate you.' I said I was delighted to hear the news."

"Did it please you as much as all that, General," Taylor asked, "to have a building and a lot of valuable plant destroyed? Surely it would have been easy to make away with every trace of what you had been doing without blowing up the place."

The General shook his head decisively. "Not so easy as you think, *amigo*. It would have been hard work, and it would have taken time, and time I could not afford. It was evident, from what I had been told, that I might be attacked at any moment, and I wished to steal a march on the enemy, to be on the train to Paris before any of the gang could catch up with me. Well, I did not see how my disappearing could have become known before eight o'clock at least, because if I did not answer when I was called at seven, Krug would have called me again at eight, according to my orders.

"So it was clear that something had gone wrong with my plans. That happens so often in contests with dangerous men that I did not give it, as you say, a second thought. I knew that I must have slipped up somewhere; I never troubled to think where. When a thing's done, it's done, and one gets on to the next item on the programme. All I knew was Dupont and his friends must have smelt a rat that night. They must have acted quickly. They must have forced the door of my laboratory to see whether I had cleared out, or, if not, to take me prisoner. And when they forced that door, pop went the weasel, as you say. It would have been quite a nice little firework display, too. I know I left nothing to chance there, and I only hope some of the visitors got their fingers burnt.

"But all that is ancient history. The actual position was that I had been trailed to Paris and was being followed at that moment; they were probably keeping watch on the Hotel de Bourgogne as Hercule and I sat down to our lunch. He had his table reserved, and I was placed with my back to the wall. I asked if the two friends of whom he had spoken would be joining us, but Hercule merely looked scandalised at the suggestion. There was a fat little man at a table near to ours who seemed to be taking an interest in me, but I did not think he could be one of Ketch's lot, because he was already there when we came in, and even I myself had not known I should be lunching in that hotel until I was told so in the Palais Bourbon.

"Hercule and I talked during lunch, mainly about my research in the making of diamonds, and the disagreeable atmosphere of spying and ill-feeling by which I had felt myself surrounded when I undertook that work. Hercule remarked that this was only to be expected. He said that if I could make diamonds I should never be safe as long as I kept my secret to myself, and that if I did not keep it to myself diamonds would no longer be very valuable. All this had occurred to me already. I told Hercule that if I could get across the Channel safely I could look after myself.

"Hercule took me up to his little suite on the second floor. In the sitting room two men were awaiting us; one of them was the fat little man whom I had noticed in the dining-room. He had a small glass of cognac before him on the table, and was pouring out another for a tall, dark man whose appearance seemed vaguely familiar to me. When the introductions were made it appeared that the fat little man was M. Georges Cuvillier and the other M. Savinien de Pincorney, a Deputy from the Lot-et-Gavonne.

"De Pincorney, who was a man I took to from the first, said that if Hercule St Gratien was to be believed he and I resembled each other quite closely. I replied that I wished I could believe this. We all laughed and were on the best of terms. Cuvillier made me and de Pincorney stand side by side. He said, '*En effet!*' and Hercule clapped his hands softly. It appeared that if de Pincorney, who had no moustache, had one like mine we should be almost twins. That was the affair of Cuvillier, who was a professional wig-maker attached to the Comédie Française. The idea was, you see, that de Pincorney was to impersonate me, and he would be delighted to do so. But, I said, suppose that Ketch and Co. were to try any funny business with the gentleman who would be doing me this kindness. Nothing could please him more, Hercule assured me, because he loved getting into all sorts of trouble as much as I did, and, besides that, he knew how to make use of his position as a Deputy with any of the local authorities, wherever it might be, and, in short, I need not trouble myself about the security of my new friend. De Pincorney confirmed this in the strongest terms, and insisted on making himself useful to me – he knew something, it appeared, of my war record, and it had made a good impression on him.

"Cuvillier had with him the tools of his trade. He made for de Pincorney a moustache exactly like mine to a hair, and attached it to his lip. Hercule insisted that he must have my hat as well as my *imperméable*, because it was a rather large hat of a distinctive shade of grey, and de Pincorney said he would gladly make the exchange, although his own hat was a model from Italy, where the best felt comes from. We changed hats; they fitted admirably, and I am wearing de Pincorney's hat still.

"When the time came for my impersonator to be leaving for the Gare du Nord, en route for Calais, Hercule advised me to watch from his window, keeping well out of sight. He and my new friend, who was also carrying my little knapsack, descended, a cab from the rank behind the Palais rolled to the entrance of the hotel, then I saw my hat, my moustache, and my slicker, accompanied by Hercule, get into the cab. I could see nothing of Ketch and his follower, and I began to wonder if I had been making a monumental fool of myself, but the moment the cab began to move a large blue car, stationed in the square in full view of the hotel, also came to life. At its window I caught a glimpse of the face of Ketch, and as the car turned two men appeared from nowhere and climbed inside it. The cab and the car went off then towards the Pont de la Concorde, and I lay back reproaching myself for not having thought that one of Ketch's friends in Paris might have a large car, the perfect hiding-place in any spot where cars may be parked.

"Hercule did not return from the *Gare* after saying farewell to my hat, my moustache, my knapsack and my *imperméable*. This was by arrangement. For some hours I lay catto in – "

Dr Barlow laughed briefly. "Doggo, you mean, don't you, General?"

The General shook his head with a despondent air. "Naturally, certainly, doggo. Sometimes I slip up on these technical expressions. But this one, *chico*, I learnt from you only a day or two ago, and it had not fixed itself in my mind. I was saying that I lay doggo in Hercule's rooms, refreshing my memory of the French classics from his little library, until after six o'clock. Then he reappeared to tell me that de Pincorney had started for Calais, and that the car which was tailing them had contained five men, one of whom could be identified as Ketch from my description.

134

They also had taken the train for Calais. Hercule was unable, he said, to foresee what would happen at that destination, except that de Pincorney had no intention of crossing the Channel, and that he would probably manage to make trouble of some sort for Ketch and Co.

"So Hercule and I dined at the hotel, where I had decided to stay, as a nice room was to be had, for that night at least. It had always been a part of my plan to pay a visit to Paris as soon as possible after the successful ending of my work in Engelberg. You see, my dear Tayor, I have always been a believer in long-term plans. When I was studying at the Sorbonne, when I was only at the beginning of my research, I had already formed a clear idea of the purpose to which I should devote a large part of my very great wealth, if that research should end as I hoped it would end. So, in my student days, I had managed to make acquaintance with that famous jeweller Calixte Michaud. I had told him that one day I should be immensely rich, and that I hoped I should then be able to interest him in a programme of jeweller's work which I was considering.

"Well, that day of my return to Paris, years later, I visited Michaud once more; I sent my card to him in his *atelier*, with a note written on it recalling me to his recollection. I saw Michaud, gave him a general idea of what I should be wanting. He liked the notion very much, as I had felt sure he would, especially when I said that my first letter of definite instructions, which he would receive shortly, would contain a draft for half a million francs as a payment in advance.

"The next day Hercule saw me off on my way to St Malo. From that port I crossed to Southampton.

"I must tell you, my dear Taylor, that my plans included having a number of places to which I could retire if I was compelled to make myself scarce. You see, it was my intention to commit two or three offences and to get away with them, as you say, so that it was necessary to have a few hiding-places. Well, I had already arranged about going shares in this place where we are now. Arnold and Diana and I had had quite a correspondence on the subject while I was in Engelberg, and very fortunately Diana was all in favour of having a larger house and a much larger garden on the edge of the town; she even knew the house she wanted, which could be secured quite soon. So the first thing I did on landing in Southampton, after changing my foreign money into British, was to hire a car to take me to Mewstone and hunt up the Fielding house. It was delightful to meet again after so long a separation, and I stayed the night in the first of my English homes.

"The next day I went by train to London. I bought a few suitcases and some clothing, then went to the Savoy Hotel, where I had stayed once during my time in England before our war broke out. I registered there under my own name, of course. Next day I recalled myself to some English friends, first of all to Mendoza and his partner Ullstein. I dined with them, and we talked business – diamond business – at great length. I left with them a number of my stones, and it was arranged that they should be valued, and the price made over to me in cash when I should call for it. Also I looked up an old Magdalen College friend who used to answer to the name of Muffins, and whose actual name was Mulford – he is one of the solicitors to the Metropolitan police. I got advice from him about a few legal points. Newlove, the man who drove us here last night, used to be an assistant at the place where I kept my car when I was at Oxford. I went to Oxford; I found him still there, and I took him into my service. Now he looks after one of my two cars, as you know, and has a cottage where I can always stay in absolute privacy. The same is true of his friend Gunn, who lives in the next county. Both of them are very well paid.

"It was while I was looking up Newlove in Oxford that I heard from him of Mrs McBean, whose lamented husband had been my scout at Magdalen, and had known Newlove well. I learnt that the widow had settled down as a small shopkeeper in Abbot's Dean, where she had a married sister living. It happened that Abbot's Dean was in just the part of the country where I needed another *pied-a-terre*, and I remembered that she was an excellent cook, so I went down there. I offered to pay her rent and furnish her upper floor for myself, also giving her a decent salary for observing absolute secrecy about myself and my actions. She was enchanted at the prospect.

"All these arrangements, including the purchase of two cars, occupied me for about six weeks. For more than half that time I never saw a sign of Ketch or of anyone keeping an eye on me, but at last one day I did catch sight of him as I went out of the courtyard of the Savoy. How long it had been before he got on to me I shall never know, and it did not matter. Wherever I had gone outside London I had gone by car, and it had been easy to make sure that I had not been followed. Anyway, I was not worrying about Ketch, because I was living now in the heart of London, and I had not yet given the police any reason for troubling me – they were on my side wherever I went. But now the time had come when I must put an end to this agreeable state of things. I was established and ready for action.

"My intention was to do something suitable to Cowdery, the skunk who had been so anxious to have me snatched, or even rubbed out altogether. I am not a vindictive man, my dear Taylor, but I do not overlook conduct of that sort. So one morning I paid my bill at the Savoy and put my baggage in one of my cars, and Newlove drove me to the hotel in Brook Street where Cowdery was living at the time. I sent up my name and was at once admitted to the presence of that animal. I found him to be a large, strong man, who should have been a good-looking, agreeable type, but was spoilt by a sulky eye and a sneering mouth. We did not shake hands, although he seemed to wish to do so, and this did not please him. I said that I supposed he knew who I was, as he had received me so readily. He said he had heard of me as someone who claimed to have discovered how to make imitation diamonds of a high quality – that was the form of words which he had chosen. My answer was that I had never made such a claim, but that if the subject interested him I would tell him that I did make diamonds, adding that all of my diamonds were flawless and of the first order as to size and colour."

The General, lighting another cigarette, here began to drum soundlessly on the table with the fingers of his right hand. "When I gave Cowdery this information," he went on, "the fellow started playing this trick with his fingers on the writing-table in front of him. This annoyed me, so that I went on to say my diamonds were, in fact, more perfect and rather larger than most of the stones obtained from the diamond mines. Then Cowdery said, in an offensive tone, that I could hardly expect him to believe that, but that supposing what I told him was true, the best thing I could do was to come to a business arrangement with himself. He said that if I could furnish the necessary proofs, he might be able to make me a very advantageous offer. Then I asked him quite peacefully why I should trouble myself about him as I intended to keep the production of the stones entirely in my own hands and to dispose of them in my own way. Cowdery became very red in the face, and wanted to know why, if that was the case, I had come to him and wasted his time – a natural question, perhaps. I said that I had heard so much about him that I wanted to know what he looked like."

Dr Barlow turned to Taylor. "You see, the General was just baiting the man. Getting a bad-tempered swine to make an exhibition of himself is right in his line."

"There were possibilities of interest in the situation," the General admitted, "which could not be overlooked. As I may have said before, my dear Taylor, life must be made as interesting as possible. Cowdery did not disappoint me. He swore, he hit the table with his fists, he said that I would find he was not a man to be trifled with, that there were ways of dealing with people who would not play ball, and that I should bitterly regret having turned his offer down. Then, to keep things lively, I told him that the interview had confirmed my feeling that he was not the sort of person I should care to be mixed up with, and that I was sorry he had admitted me to his apartment, because Justo de la Costa was not accustomed to being insulted and threatened by blackguards. I said this in a tone of contempt which was quite insufferable, if I may say so without vanity. At least it had the effect which I had been playing for – Cowdery became violently abusive, he called me by more than one name of a sort which I do not permit. So I leant across the table and slapped his face."

A gentle smile softened the General's features as he recalled this incident, and he gazed into the blue sky for a few moments in silence.

"You will say, my dear Taylor, that a slap is more an expression of criticism than a blow in the serious sense. I agree, but this was a slap with weight behind it. I had been looking forward to it, I had planned it, and there was nothing wrong with it at my end. When Cowdery picked himself up, he rushed at me, but he got no farther than my right fist. This time he did not get up so quickly, because a good slam on the nose is an unsettling thing, still he did get up, and did not seem to have had enough. But it seemed to me that nothing was to be gained by prolonging the interview, so I put a knock-out punch on the point of his jaw and left him, telling his secretary in the next room that his employer was not feeling well. I went down to my car and came down immediately to this place, where I was expected. I have told you before, my dear Taylor, what happened afterwards, that a summons for assault was issued against me, which so far has never been served, and that later on I got after him where there was no company around, and gave him a real shellacking with a malacca hunting-crop, so as to imprint myself on his memory."

The General rose to his feet. "There is no more to tell you, my dear Taylor, except what you will have gathered for yourself. I have been on the run ever since that last interview with Cowdery. The police have never caught up with me. Several times Ketch's lot have done so. They are very well posted about my connections here. Once, when I went to call on a Canon of Glasminster, taking our Dr Barlow with me, and we stayed there to dinner, Ketch and his friends were waiting for us as we left the Canon's house, and there was quite a battle before we could get to the spot where Newlove was waiting with the car. That was the time when Ketch's nose was remodelled, as you may remember my telling you. The fact that Ketch and Co. were there on the spot a few hours after my arriving at Canon Gossett's house could only mean that they had been casing the joint, do you not think so, my dear Taylor?"

Taylor, so appealed to, could only look bewildered.

"I ask pardon," the General said with a self-reproachful head-shake. "That is one of the terms I picked up from Farewell Billy and his friends, and you have probably used it yourself many times during the part of your life that has been eclipsed. It merely means that they were having the house watched. They knew of my relations with the Canon – I had visited him often before, during my Oxford days – and they thought, quite rightly, that before very long I should come to the surface there. As soon as I did so, their spy was on to me, and was able to pass the word to the rest of the gang. So it was on the other occasions when they waylaid me – they knew of certain places which I should be likely to visit. But never until this last time have they got on to one of my private retreats, and it must have been a very scientific piece of trailing. I think I told you, my dear Taylor, that Ketch has a very good organisation of his own. Though he is a gorilla, and a tough specimen at that, he has brains also."

Dr Barlow turned to Taylor. "I can guess," he said, "what is in your mind. He is wondering, General, how you come to be on intimate terms with a Canon of Glasminster. I should say it would be as well to tell him about that now. You don't want to keep him in a puzzled state of mind. Besides, why shouldn't he know? Everyone who knows much about you knows it."

The General shrugged lightly. "My only purpose, my dear Taylor, in not mentioning this before was not to make myself too incomprehensible to you at the time when our relationship began. You were told of me as a citizen of Peligragua, as an officer in the army of that state, also as, I suppose I may say, a figure in its public life, and, in addition, a student at the Sorbonne and at Oxford. I thought it might sound a little too rococo, so to speak, if I told you that Canon Gossett of Glasminster is my uncle."

CHAPTER XVI

Taylor made no immediate reply to this revelation. He turned to Dr Barlow, who said, "Yes, it's true enough. But you seem even more taken aback than the General thought you might be. Come on, let's do some walking about for a change; it helps to get one's ideas in order."

Taylor got up very willingly, and the two long-legged men fell into step on either side of Dr Barlow. "A lawn like this one specially promotes the flow of thought," the doctor observed as they paced it. "It is one of the best lawns I have ever seen; it has the real springy velvety feel, which it probably gets from having been grazed on by Southdown sheep for centuries before this house and garden were laid out around it. Well, my friends, the subject before the meeting is the immediate ancestry of General Justo Hernando de la Costa, as to which he desires to volunteer a statement."

What the doctor had, on an earlier occasion, called a burst of Peligraguan laughter – loud, unrestrained and diaphragmatic – came from the General. As long as it lasted, the Alsatian barked madly, galloping back and forth, then followed with lolling tongue at the General's heels. "How I wish that I possessed your poetic imagination, Barlow *mio!*" he said. "To me this lawn is no more than a well-kept and agreeable lawn; to you it suggests an endless vista of free and unfenced mutton-raising through the ages, ending in its imprisonment within the ground-plan of a desirable residence. But our subject is, as you say, my own immediate ancestry. Well, my dear Taylor, it is not at all an unusual story, this matter which we speak of. In fact, it is very common; the best people, as you say, do it. Some of the most prominent figures in our own time have done it."

"For instance," Dr Barlow said, "Winston Churchill has never concealed the fact that he is half an American."

The General shrugged his shoulders. "Why should he try to conceal a fact that is so greatly to his advantage? His father married an American woman. My father married an Englishwoman."

Taylor smiled a little awkwardly. "So your mother was a sister of this Canon Gossett. I don't know why it should surprise me, General – unless it is that there is nothing in your appearance to suggest any trace of English blood."

General de la Costa made a highly un-English gesture of sweeping something out of existence with his two hands. "Bah! What is it, English blood? You mean that I am not fair-haired or blue-eyed, I suppose. The English are the most mixed-up lot of mongrels that was ever crowded together in one small island. The Gossett family, as I have known them, are of dark complexion and dark-haired. My mother and my uncle were born and brought up in the family house in Glasminster, which is English enough for anybody. You may perhaps remember its name."

Taylor had a troubled look. "I have heard the name," he said. "I have heard it often, I think. But I know no more about it."

"Well, don't let it worry you," Dr Barlow said quickly. "I don't think, General, I would ask him if he remembers this or that."

The General smote himself reproachfully on the breastbone. "I will not offend again. Now, my dear Taylor, when my mother was twenty years old she was taken by her parents on a visit to Oxford in Commemoration week, when balls and parties and festivities in general were taking place in the most lovely surroundings. They went there because her brother, who now is Canon Gossett, was an undergraduate at Magdalen College. He introduced them to his friends, gave parties for them, took tickets for balls, arranged expeditions on the river, and all like that.

"It happened that one of his friends, also an undergraduate at Magdalen, was my father, Don Esteban de la Costa. At that time it was a fashion among distinguished and wealthy families all over Europe to send a son to Oxford, even if it was only to make friends and to amuse himself. My own family, like one or two others in our part of the world, had decided to take part in this interesting movement, and my father, when he went to Oxford, became one of the international set which had a place of its own in the life of the University. He and my mother met at a party given by the young Gossett. She was greatly admired, and my father had always been popular, so they met at other parties as well as at two or three College balls. They had fallen in love at first sight. So now you will understand, my dear Taylor, the reason of sentiment which led me, as I think I told you, to continue my own studies at Oxford after leaving the Sorbonne."

Taylor nodded. "I can understand that, General, and it is clear to me now how you come to have an uncle who is a Canon in the Church of England. It's a very interesting story. Will you think me too inquisitive if I ask how it went on after their meeting? I mean, were the parents on both sides pleased about it?"

General de la Costa laughed lightly. "Like hell they were, my dear Taylor. On both sides there were the strongest objections. But as both the young people were as obstinate as mules, and as both of them were of good descent, and as both of them were perfectly well-bred, and as the de la Costas were a very wealthy family, the engagement was in the end agreed to after plenty of investigations and correspondence and marriage settlements. They were married up according to the rites of the Anglican Church, my mother being a most devoted Anglo-Catholic, and my father being devoted to nothing in that way, and being only anxious to please my mother. Not long afterwards he brought his young wife home to Peligragua, which she never left afterwards. Having learnt Spanish, she made a complete conquest of the de la Costas and their friends. Being beautiful, vivacious, kind-hearted, and also interested in everything and everybody, she was the most lovable woman I have ever known, and when she was killed in an accident when I was twelve years old, I did not think I should ever recover from that sorrow. Believe me, *amigo*, a man who loves his mother as I loved mine has the best of foundations in himself for a happy life, but losing her – what is the high-sounding word you have for that?" Taylor, who had been deeply touched by this unusual manifestation of feeling on the General's part, said, "Perhaps you mean bereavement."

"That is it, my dear Taylor – bereavement. Well, that is the worst thing I have ever known, and it has influenced my life, especially in a way that I may have to explain to you at a later time. As for my childhood, both my parents taught me how to behave myself, as you say, and my mother taught me the elements of religion, and I have never forgotten them – the elements, that is. I know what the feeling of reverence is, and I have it very strongly when I do have it. But that is not what is meant by being devout, of course. I have never been devout; none of my family are made that way; some of them are among the leading anti-clericals in my country, but they have always been *caballeros*, and a man of strict honour will often compare quite favourably with a man who is strict about his religious duties – so I have found. In fact, one of the most contemptible wretches I have ever known was actually a priest, and quite a success as a priest among people who were not on to him."

At that moment Dr Barlow looked at his watch and whistled gently. "We shall not be successes with the Treasury of Truth if we don't go in to lunch," he said. "The puppy pie will not be fit to eat."

CHAPTER XVII

For the next ten days Taylor led the sort of life which Dr Barlow recommended as the best for him – a very idle one, but for some daily exercise in the open air. The Doctor, on the second day after their conversation on the lawn, took off the last of Taylor's bandages finally. On the following day he disappeared – he had gone back to his laboratory, Mrs Fielding said, and she pitied the microbes there, which had probably been hoping he was dead. He had always a lot of what he called cultures going on, she explained to Taylor. "Bacteriologists' cultures are not the kind we mean when we use the word. If I speak of the Chinese culture, I do not mean something in a saucer, looking like a thin jelly, or a teaspoonful of very watery porridge. But that is all the word means to Druce. I expect he has gone back to his lab hoping that some quite invisible fungus has floated through the window and settled on one of his most deadly preparations, turning it into something which will make us all live for ever if we inject it three times daily before meals. I'm not interested in that sort of thing myself, are you, Taylor? To begin with, I don't want to live for ever, and, anyway, I hate injections."

"I can't remember," Taylor said, "that I ever had an injection. I don't like the idea of it – I don't suppose anybody does."

"Well, I suppose you were vaccinated," Mrs Fielding said, "when you were too young to know what was happening. And if you were ever in the army, our army or any other army, which you look as if you had been, as I told you, probably you had all sorts of things squirted into you whenever you went on active service. And that reminds me – I have to go to the chemist's to get some doctor's stuff for Lem's wife, and you might as well come with me if you feel you can bear it. Druce Barlow, you know, said you should do some walking every day. Mewstone isn't a bad place of its kind; it's large and has very good shops and it's much cleaner than the cleanest parts of London, it has no intellectual life worth mentioning, but you don't look for that in a resort, and Mewstone is above everything a resort. Shall I introduce you to it?"

Nothing could please Taylor better, he said. He might by chance meet with something that reminded him of his missing past, he thought, for since he had come to his senses in Abbot's Dean he had seen practically nothing of the world. His notion, which he did not mention to his hostess, was that the society of rather unusual and mentally active people probably was not a preparation for the world as it had become since he re-entered it. During his expedition with Mrs Fielding that idea was fully confirmed. The half-dozen people with whom Mrs Fielding spoke as they met in the street were totally uninteresting, though not bad. He had not expected her to be on speaking terms with anyone who was bad.

He expressed these ideas to Mrs Fielding when they refreshed themselves at a highly-civilised coffee-shop. She was contradictory: "If you think the Uffords and the Marneys and the Barhams are totally uninteresting, you have a lot to learn," she told him. "They are only English. They don't attempt to be interesting – they feel that to attempt it would be a sort of showing off – that is a form of humility, wouldn't you say? And humility is universally agreed to be one of the most important Christian virtues. As a matter of fact, they all interest me, but that's only when we're intimate, not in the middle of the Inverness Parade. Americans are not like that, they are always trying to be interesting, and usually succeeding – it's the most important of the differences between us. And as for me not being on easy social terms with anybody who's bad, why, my dear man, I know dozens of them, both sexes – people who ought to be destroyed, and would be if I could do it without being found out."

At a large and well-lighted chemist's shop Mrs Fielding presented the prescription for doctor's stuff required by Lem's wife. When it had been borne off to be compounded, Mrs Fielding said to Taylor, "I think we'll consult Mr Balmain about this difficulty of ours. He's the head man in this place, and a great friend of mine. He is a serious Scotsman, and what I always say is, what is the use of being a Scotsman if you aren't serious, the kind that has kept the British Empire going while the English were only blethering about it. I'm sure you agree with me, Taylor."

Taylor shook his head. "I'm sorry, I don't know enough of the world. But what is this difficulty of ours that you mentioned as the sort of thing on which Mr Balmain could be consulted?"

Mrs Fielding laughed. "I believe you're Scotch yourself, Taylor. You won't be beguiled into talking nonsense. Mr Balmain," she went on, as the manager appeared behind the counter, "supposing I wanted to destroy somebody, could I do it by poison without risk of being found out?"

Mr Balmain considered the question for a few moments. "It is not a method that I should recommend," he said at length, "to anyone without experience of the use of drugs. Even with that experience, it is attended by considerable risk."

149

"In fact, you are against the idea?" Mrs Fielding said.

"Aye," replied Mr Balmain.

Taylor, who had felt slightly piqued by the suggestion that he was incapable of talking nonsense in the society of a woman like Mrs Fielding, now asked of Mr Balmain, "Would you go so far as to say that you are against the idea of Mrs Fielding destroying any one, by any means?"

"There are circumstances in which Mrs Fielding could destroy a person without incurring any penalty, or even blame," Mr Balmain said slowly. "But I am afraid the matter is too large a one to be discussed in my firm's business hours. I was asked a purely hypothetical question, which I answered to the best of my ability. The medicine will be 4s. 10d.," he added as he received the wrapped-up bottle from the hands of an assistant.

"If that includes your advice," Mrs Fielding said as she fumbled in her bag, "it's cheap at the money. There you are, Mr Balmain, two half-crowns. And that," she said to Taylor as she put away her twopence and left the shop, "is as much change as I shall ever get out of that man. Nearly everybody, even the butcher's boy and the girls at the Post Office, try to be responsive when I feel like playing the fool; but not Balmain. Now we'll go to the centre of the place's life, where the Town Hall is, and then find our way back to lunch."

During the time he spent with Mrs Fielding Taylor saw nothing that struck him as being in any way linked with his forgotten years. He did not remember Mewstone at all, but he very clearly remembered the sea, and the general characteristics of a seaside place. When he asked, "Is that the Town Hall?" Mrs Fielding replied "It is indeed, and that portly man going up the steps to it is the Mayor. There is an annual conference of the Institute of Actuaries being opened there this morning, and the Mayor will be on the job, wearing his chain – you remember, the one Arnold said he was always clanking in the night, so that he couldn't sleep. But that's all forgotten, and he and I are the best of friends. I'd like you to meet him, if you don't mind, I think a Mayor would be as good as anything for your complaint – I mean important but soothing and matter-of-fact and all that. Come on."

Mrs Fielding hurried up the Town Hall steps and was greeted by the Mayor with the utmost affability. "I should like to introduce to you, if I may," she said, "an American friend of ours who is staying with us, Mr Ulysses B Taylor. He is making a study of local government in this country, and I told him this was one of the most important county boroughs."

The Mayor said that he was delighted to make the acquaintance of Mr Taylor, and would be very glad to give him any information he might need, though for the next few days the affairs of the National Institute of Actuaries would have the first claim on his attention. He expressed the hope that Mr Taylor would enjoy his stay at Mewstone, and that the weather would be all that could be desired. It was now clear that the Mayor felt that the possibilities of conversation had been exhausted, and Taylor, feeling exhausted too, took leave of him.

"Well, now you've met a Mayor," Mrs Fielding said. "Let's see if there are any other common objects of the seashore that might stir your memories. You might have a ride in a donkey-cart down on the lower parade, but from what I hear it is not the years of childhood that are missing from your recollection, and anyway for a man of your size to ride in a donkey-cart might make people think you were lacking in a sense of proportion. I'm sure the donkey would think so. We had better be on our way home, anyhow. Chiang Pao-chen is a devil for punctuality at meal times, if any dish of his cooking isn't served up on the minute, he broods over it for hours, and it isn't the least use my reminding him that Confucius was entirely opposed to fussing about anything, even food. Chiang says that he knows Confucius was the wisest of men, but he doesn't pretend to be all that wise himself."

"I seem to have heard of Confucius," Taylor said. "A Chinese philosopher, wasn't he? I don't suppose I ever studied his works, but I do remember the name."

Mrs Fielding's chin was hoisted slightly as she answered "Yes, he was a Chinese philosopher, and I am glad you remember the poor fellow's name, at least. It was really Kung Fu-tse, of course. But his philosophy, which you don't suppose you've ever heard of, was the main influence in the mental life of millions of people long before Europe had anything worth calling a civilisation. And I'll tell you another thing about Kung – his seventy-sixth lineal descendant in the male line is a friend of mine, he has given me apricot tea at his house in Chufu, in the Shantung province, the town where his eminent ancestor lived. He is the head of a family which has over half a million Kungs on its books at the present time, and every one of them is more or less a Somebody just because he is a Kung. That shows you what it means to belong to a people who respect intellect more than anything else. Who knows or cares who are the descendants of Socrates or Plato today? Not a soul. But it's no good talking sensibly to an Englishman or an American about the Chinese. They've got it firmly fixed in their minds that the Chinese are funny, and there's an end of it."

As they neared Keith House they saw, emerging from the front entrance, a short, obviously foreign man, with beard and moustache in the style of Cardinal Richelieu, and a general appearance of ferocity, who entered a taxi-cab that was waiting for him.

"That personage is called Calixte Michaud," Mrs Fielding said. "I call him a personage because he is one. You may think he looks like a caricature, but he's a type really, half the men look like that in the part of France that he comes from, and Michaud is a personage because he is the most famous of jewellers living. If you want to have a crown, or a coronet, or a necklace, or anything like that, quite unlike anybody else's, much more beautiful, and far more expensive, you go to Michaud's place in the Rue des Martyrs – that is, if you are Somebody with a big S, or if you have an introduction from the same sort of Somebody. And if he kindly consents to carry out your order, it takes about a year to design the thing. And longer than that to make it. I like Michaud myself, in spite of his colossal side – he really is a great artist, and he could make much more money than he does if he chose to make the most of his reputation."

Taylor remembered what he had heard from the General about this M. Michaud, but he thought that it might possibly have been told in confidence. His reply to Mrs Fielding therefore was, "And why is he calling at your house? Are you one of his customers?"

Mrs Fielding laughed merrily. "Do I look like it?" she said. "Besides, Michaud doesn't have customers, any more than a famous painter or sculptor has customers. No, he has been seeing Justo de la Costa. I know Justo commissioned something or other from him long ago, but he has never told us what – just like him! This man Michaud has travelled over here from Paris half a dozen times with his designs, when Justo has been staying here. Well, whatever the thing is, it ought to be something stunning. Now, here we are, in good time for lunch, and I hope you're hungry – I'm ravenous myself."

During the following week Taylor was taken out walking by Mrs Fielding or her husband daily. Arnold Fielding avoided the town: he preferred to roam over the rolling down country behind Mewstone where at the highest level few people ever came, finding a way through huge thickets of furze to open spaces in their midst where a few large rocks stood mysteriously about; or threading a path through young, sun-drenched woods, where some small animal would dart across from time to time; or visiting the deserted excavation of an ancient British camp. Fielding was not at all averse to talking, and Taylor liked listening to a man who had something worth hearing to say, especially for a man in Taylor's state, about almost everything, and who positively enjoyed explaining himself. Both the Fieldings grew to like Taylor more and more, for no more definite reason than because he was likeable, and because their friendship evidently meant so much to him.

General de la Costa, in his character of a fugitive from justice, never ventured outside the precincts of Keith House in the daytime. Once he was absent for two nights and the intervening day, having business, as he said, which claimed his attention. At no time, it seemed to Taylor, was the General's habit of vigilance ever relaxed; he was watchful always as he paced the lawn for miles each day, often with Taylor for companion. One morning, when they were together, the General paused in the shade of the great copper beech, and laid a hand on Taylor's arm.

"I should like to have your definite decision, my dear Taylor," he said, "about that offer that I made to you at Abbot's Dean, of a post in my service as bodyguard. I might have taken your conduct later that evening as implying consent – I mean your joining in the fun in Mrs McBean's kitchen without being asked, and making yourself the life and soul of the party at that. But I did not want to rush you. By this time you know me and my friends pretty well. Do you now think that such a position would suit you? – or let us say rather the position of an aide-de-camp, with duties not entirely confined to slamming people over the head with revolver-barrels?"

The colour rose in Taylor's cheek as he met the General's eye. "I am glad you made that addition," he said. "On that footing I shall be very happy to join you, and to make myself generally useful between fights – and when I say happy I mean it." They both laughed as they shook hands on this arrangement; then the General lifted a finger impressively.

"To begin with," he said, "I should like you to carry out for me tomorrow a little piece of practical and very confidential business. You know already that it is not safe for me to appear in public, and there is nothing in this small commission that cannot be undertaken by yourself, it does not call for any expert knowledge. You have heard me mention the diamond-brokers who assist me in my commercial operations, Ullstein and Mendoza. Well, I want to dispose of another parcel of my diamonds, and you, if you will be so good, will take the consignment to their place of business, also receive from them a sum of money and a cheque, and in addition a parcel of other stones which they have been collecting for me during the last few months. Some days ago I was visited by a jeweller who has been at work for me on certain plans which I have. You have heard me speak of him already, his name is Michaud. He is, as I said, an artist of the first order, and he has now brought to me here the last of the objects which I asked him to fabricate for me. It has been a long business, because he lives in Paris and I am not in a position to move about freely, as you know."

"Perhaps," Taylor said, "that was the foreign-looking man I saw leaving the house one morning a short time ago."

"No doubt it was," the General said. "That is, if the man you saw looked like a small-sized brigand of Corsica. My friend Michaud imagines, I suppose, that that appearance suits him, as he designed it for himself, and he is entitled to his opinion, as you say. Speaking as a foreign-looking man myself, I think he should be about one foot more tall, to make him look at all convincing. But there can be no disputing about tastes. Michaud has completed for me a commission of immense importance, the work has been done to admiration. I am considering entrusting him with another job of the same sort, and that is why I am asking you to bring me back the stones which my friends in Hatton Garden have got together for me, as they told me by telephone last night. Tomorrow Newlove will drive you up to London, near to the address of my diamond-dealing friends. They know that you are coming, and all will be ready, so they have assured me. You could arrive back here in time for lunch, I should think, or else Newlove will take you anywhere you would like to go, and wait for you with the car."

CHAPTER XVIII

Next morning the Fendlair, with Newlove at the wheel, took Taylor swiftly up to London through a countryside full of the freshness and colour of spring. Whatever he might have forgotten, he was no stranger to the loveliness of an English May morning; well remembered, too, was the emotion of distaste that came when the different aspects of ugliness revealed themselves, layer upon layer, as the car invaded the territory of the London County Council.

He left the car, as had been arranged, at the western corner of a massive building in Holborn which Newlove called "the Pru." Here Taylor was quite lost; all Holborn was strange to him; but with Newlove's directions, walking on eastwards, he found the opening of Hatton Garden easily enough, and soon he stood at the doorway of which the number had been given him. The building was tall and featureless. Taylor, observing the stream of passers-by, noted that those who had business in Hatton Garden were for the most part not tall and decidedly not featureless.

Entering the house, and mounting the narrow stairs to the second floor, Taylor found himself on a small and rather dim landing where two doors faced each other. Upon the door to the left was painted, in letters which had once been white, the name of the firm of Ullstein and Mendoza. There was nothing modern-looking or striking about that door. It had a small brass handle, somewhat dented, and a bell-push in the right-hand door-post.

Taylor pressed the button. He heard no sound; but after a few seconds the door unlatched itself in an unassuming manner, which seemed to leave the next move – opening it – to the visitor. Taylor, accordingly, pushed it open and stepped within, the door shutting itself after him with a ghostly click. He was in a small square room, strongly lighted by a pendant electric lamp, and panelled throughout in dark wood from the floor to the ceiling, which must, to all appearance, have forgotten long ago the sensation of being whitewashed. There was no other door visible.

In the middle of the room was a table with nothing upon it, and a wooden armchair. This was a firm, Taylor told himself, which had no belief in squandering money on expensive office furniture; for the room contained nothing else whatever.

After another brief interval, a slit opened silently in the wall to the right, slightly above the level of Taylor's head; a slit about as long as that of an ordinary letterbox, and twice as deep. Through it two eyes regarded him with as much expression as those of a fish looking out through the glass front of an aquarium.

"Your name, please," the eyes said.

Taylor gave it, adding that he had called in accordance with an appointment made by General de la Costa.

"That's right," the eyes replied. "Come right in, Mr Taylor."

As Taylor looked at the slit in some bewilderment, it closed abruptly. There was a slight sound behind him, and he turned round to find that a section of the panelling had opened door-wise in the opposite wall, disclosing a lighted passage turning to the right. Taylor's feeling that the eyes' invitation had been rather loosely phrased was increased when he entered the passage and found that after a few steps it turned again sharply to the right, ending in another doorway.

This, as he approached it, was filled with the welcoming presence of a stout elderly man with a neat grey moustache, who grasped his hand and drew him into a large apartment lighted by two plate-glass windows of unusual size. Here there was no lack of office furniture, the most prominent pieces being two glass-topped writing tables fully equipped for business, and a table before one of the windows having upon it nothing but a spacious and spotless white blotter and two small pairs of scales.

"My name is Ullstein," the stout man said. "This" – turning to one of the tables – "is my partner, Mr Mendoza."

Mr Mendoza, who rose and shook hands warmly in his turn, was a younger, thinner man with curly red hair and a freckled, clean-shaved face. "We usually have to apologise to strangers," he said, "for the little precautions we take about letting them in. Caution is necessary in our business – never so necessary as now." Mr Mendoza giggled as if this were the best joke in the world. "The jewel-thieves are a worse trouble to us than they have ever been."

"They are cleverer," Mr Ullstein said.

"I don't think it's that so much. The difference is that they're bolder than they used to be," Mr Mendoza said. "They take big risks nowadays. We have to have other precautions besides those you have seen – more serious ones. It's the same everywhere in Hatton Garden."

"Well, never mind all that," Ullstein said. "It was just a formality in your case. You were expected, and we had your description from General de la Costa. He spoke to me last night, as you probably know, and said you were to be trusted completely. The General is an old friend of ours. Sit down, Mr Taylor, and have a cigarette, if you care about cigarettes." He pushed over a long glass box as he seated himself at his own table.

Taylor, as he apologised for being a non-smoker, reflected that Messrs Ullstein and Mendoza did not measure up to such vague ideas as he had about Jewish diamond merchants. They impressed him as educated, well-bred men; they were more quietly dressed than – thanks to Dr Barlow's invincible weakness in the matter of checks – he was himself. In a corner of the room he noted a suitcase and, lying upon it, a battered violin-case lettered with the initials "JM."

He produced from his breast pocket the wash-leather bag entrusted to him by General de la Costa. "Here is the merchandise," he said.

"Perhaps you feel rather relieved at getting it out of your hands," Ullstein said as he took the bag and picked at the knotted whipcord that secured it. "Most people feel that way if they are not in the habit of carrying about a number of stones that may represent a fortune."

"A small fortune," Mendoza amended.

"It is just a phrase that is often used," Ullstein said. "It would take a larger number of stones than this, of course – even the finest – to represent a large fortune in the modern sense of the word."

"Did you ever read Dumas' novel, *The Count of Monte Cristo*, Mr Taylor?" Mendoza inquired. "To people in our way of business it's an amusing story, in a way of its own. The Count, you know, is represented as the richest man in the world – a man to whom expense meant nothing at all, who could get for himself absolutely anything that money could buy, and still be a multimillionaire – and yet the whole of his fortune consisted of a hoard of precious stones collected by a Renaissance Cardinal, which fell into the hands of Monte Cristo."

Taylor reflected a moment. "I do remember reading that story as a boy," he said. "Certainly, I got the idea that a hoard like that would be worth untold millions. Perhaps Dumas thought it would be."

"Very likely he did," Ullstein said. "In fact, most people still do. They don't realise how much the standard has changed, they believe any old heap of diamonds and what not, whatever period they belong to, would mean unlimited wealth."

"As for Renaissance Cardinals," Mendoza said with a disrespectful emphasis on the words, "they would have been perfectly satisfied with stones that no connoisseur would think much of nowadays. And the good ones they had would need a lot of expert work done on them to give them full value."

"You see, Mr Taylor," Ullstein said instructively, "the art of making a stone look its best wasn't invented then. Facetted cutting is quite a modern thing."

"I wouldn't call it modern exactly," Mendoza said. "Mid-eighteenth century, rather. But apart from all that, the most that the Cardinal's hoard could possibly have realised wouldn't have seen Monte Cristo through more than a few years, splashing it about in the way described in the story."

"To say nothing," Ullstein added, "of the probability that he was damnably swindled every time he sold a stone, as nobody knew where they came from, or where the Count came from for that matter – and anyhow he was no judge himself. And now about this little consignment – "

He took the bag to the table under the window and spread its contents out upon the sheet of blotting paper. The number of stones, Taylor noted, was noticeably less than the number of those which had been shown him in the garden of Keith House. Ullstein and Mendoza, seated on small chairs, pored over and fingered the small heap of crystals, examining them with concentrated attention through the lenses which each of them had screwed into one of his eyes. After some ten minutes of this scrutiny, which seemed to call for no conversation between the partners, each of them pulled a pair of scales towards him, and they proceeded, still in silence, to the weighing of the diamonds, marking figures upon sheets of paper as they worked. As far as Taylor could follow these operations, each stone was weighed by both Ullstein and Mendoza. Finally the two sheets of paper were compared; Ullstein added some additional figuring on his own sheet, to which Mendoza nodded his agreement; and at last the senior partner turned to Taylor with an air of satisfaction.

"I gather, Mr Taylor," he said, "that you are not an expert in this sort of thing." He waved a hand at the diamonds, which Mendoza was still fingering lovingly.

"I know nothing whatever about them," Taylor answered. "I couldn't tell the best diamonds from so many bits of glass."

Ullstein laughed indulgently. "Oh yes, you could, believe me," he said. "They are not at all like glass – a child could tell the difference. However, the point is that you aren't a judge yourself, so I had better explain what we are doing. You see, we have been doing business with General de la Costa for some time. It has become, you might say, a matter of routine. We are personal friends, we are, like yourself, in his confidence, and we know – in a general way, that is – the history of the pretty things he sends us. We do not deal with each other at arm's length. We trust him, and he trusts us. So all I need tell you, not going into details, is that we have fixed a fair price for this consignment, which he is ready to accept. That price is £58,000."

Taylor raised his eyebrows. "As you tell me there is no question of bargaining," he said, "I suppose it is not out of order for me to say, merely as a disinterested onlooker, that it seems a lot of money for those not very remarkable-looking stones."

The partners laughed gently. "You wouldn't call them that, Mr Taylor," Ullstein said, "if you were to see them when they are cut and polished. Little as you may know about diamonds, you would admire them then."

"As for the price," Mendoza added as he swept the stones together and returned them to their bag, "it is a slightly better one than we could have offered for the same lot at the time when we last did business with the General. You might tell him that. He won't be surprised. He knows as well as we do that the market has its ups and downs, though the fluctuations are not great. Our organisation sees to that, you understand. The market for cut stones is much more volatile – but I mustn't bore you with our diamond shop."

Ullstein, while his partner spoke, had risen and gone to the wall behind his office table, where, with his back to the room, he appeared to be manipulating something. Presently a door in the wall swung open, revealing the interior of a safe with cardboard boxes, small packets and files of documents in orderly array on its three shelves. Ullstein took the bag of stones from his partner and placed it among the boxes on the top shelf; then took from the second shelf a number of small packets, which he placed before Taylor on the writing table.

"As the General requested," he said, "I am handing to you £1,000 in one-pound notes. We shall give you our cheque, made out to the General's order, for the rest. There are a hundred notes in each of these packets. You will have to count them, I am sorry to say, before you give us your receipt; it may be a tiresome job if you aren't used to it, but money's money."

Taylor slipped the rubber band from one of the packets. "I don't know," he said, "that I ever counted a thousand of anything before."

"Not even sheep going through a hole in a hedge when you can't sleep?" Mendoza asked with friendly interest.

"Don't put that idea into his head, Julius," Ullstein warned him. "If he goes to sleep counting these he will only have to begin all over again. We leave you to it, Mr Taylor." And both partners turned to the papers on their tables as Taylor began his task.

Sooner than he expected he had completed the tale of notes and bestowed the packets in a breast pocket. Ullstein handed him a cheque for £57,000; Mendoza had a receipt ready for him to sign.

"Now there is one thing more," Ullstein said, as he removed a small packet from the safe. "General de la Costa asked me to collect a certain number of various stones, not diamonds, to be submitted to him for approval. We have done this several times before, and on each occasion the stones have been approved, and the price put upon them agreed to. Now in this sealed envelope, Mr Taylor, are the stones which the General asked for, together with a detailed account for their purchase. If you will sign this receipt for taking over the sealed package marked BXC, our business will be at an end for the present."

Taylor took charge of the envelope, and was about to put it in another breast pocket.

"If I may make a suggestion," Mendoza said, "it is that the safest pocket of all for small articles of value is the trousers pocket. I should carry that wad of notes there too, if I were you."

"He is quite right," Ullstein said. "There" – as Taylor made the transference – "now you are as safe from larceny as any man carrying portable property of a value running well into five figures could reasonably expect. Still, don't get into crowds on the way to your car, and don't talk to strangers. Now, when you rejoin General de la Costa, will you please give him our kindest regards. We do not forget favours received, and we remain indebted to him for the service he did us about the Peligraguan ruby mines deal, when he threw it our way."

Mendoza, who seemed to represent the humane element in the firm's transactions, shook his head slightly. "Do not think of us merely as being associated with the General in business matters, Mr Taylor," he said. "We have been in close personal relations with him. I myself have been his guest in his own country. Like all people who know General de la Costa in that way, we have a very warm feeling – affection is not too strong a word – as well as admiration for him. If he likes anyone, for whatever reason, there are no bounds to his generosity and unselfishness. He inspires attachment in other people simply by his large-heartedness, and quite unconsciously."

Ullstein nodded. "You will have felt this yourself, Mr Taylor, as you are his trusted agent. He has a genius for friendship."

"A cliché," remarked Mendoza sadly.

"Possibly it is," Ullstein conceded. "But you can't refuse to make use of an expression just because it has been said a few times before, if it happens to be what you mean."

"A few million times before," Mendoza said firmly. "John Morley used it, writing about Joe Chamberlain, before I was born."

Ullstein laughed heartily, nodding towards Mendoza as he caught Taylor's eye. "My partner is too much of an artist for this dull world," he said. "It gives him quite a pain whenever he signs himself with the commonplace words 'yours faithfully.' Doesn't it, Julius?"

"No," Mendoza said. "Because nobody is expected to take that seriously."

Taylor, joining in the merriment, took his hat. "I ought to be going," he said. "I can see you are in perfect agreement about the General, and if I can think of an original form of words for your good wishes, I will."

The partners shepherded him through the approaches to their citadel, and shook hands warmly at the outer door. "Mind you don't tell the General he has a genius for friendship," was Ullstein's parting advice.

"Tell him Ullstein and Mendoza are still in partnership, in spite of everything," grinned Mendoza.

And so Taylor, threading his way among groups of talkative Hebrews to the northern end of Hatton Garden, turned thence to the left and went on until he found the waiting Fendlair at the corner of Lamb's Conduit Street.

CHAPTER XIX

It was here that a surprise awaited Taylor. The car he soon recognised, and the thick neck and hunched shoulders of Newlove were well remembered. But as he approached the car it became evident that there was somebody inside it, bending over a large notebook, and then that the somebody was Dr Barlow. Taylor was never less than glad to see the doctor, the first man who had stood his friend in the unknown world of today; he merely wondered why he was there.

As Taylor appeared at the door of the car, the doctor tucked away his book and stepped to the pavement. He was wearing a suit of blue-and-yellow dog-tooth check which made the clothes in which Taylor had known him hitherto seem sober by comparison. "You weren't expecting me," he said, "but I was expecting you. What happened was that I rang up the Fieldings this morning to say I thought it was time I paid my patient another visit and inquired about him generally. So they told me you were in London, and I might like to come down to Mewstone in the General's car, which was to be waiting for you at this spot about this time. So here I am, hoping you don't mind."

"I am never likely to be tired of your company, doctor," Taylor said.

"Hm! Well, I've known it happen," the doctor remarked dispassionately. "But usually the people who have hated me have been people who have treated me shabbily, in the first place, or tried to. You see how it works. If a man behaves like a blackguard to me, I know that man has behaved like a blackguard, and therefore he hates me. Come now, let's have a preliminary look at you as a medical adviser. I'll go over you properly at Keith House. Yes, you seem to be thriving all right. You're standing up like a man, there's a different look in your eyes, the Fielding-de la Costa establishment agrees with you. But the memory trouble is still there, of course. Well, that may fold up any time. I should say that you are getting to be more and more like the human specimen you used to be when things were normal – before the shock came. Now, is there anywhere in London you want to go, or shall we be on our way to Mewstone? Do exactly as you like, pay a visit to the Zoo or the Tower of London."

"Thanks, I saw both of those when I was quite young," Taylor said. "If it suits you, I would rather go back to Mewstone. I expect you know where I've been, and that there are reasons for my preferring to see the General as soon as possible."

Dr Barlow nodded and slapped a pocket. "Yes, I do know. In fact, I've done the same job for the General myself more than once. It used to make me keep looking over my shoulder till I'd delivered the goods – and I'm not particularly nervous either. Well, let's get in, shall we? We shall get there easily before lunch, and they're pretty sure to be expecting you to be back by then, because the General knows how people feel who are carrying about large amounts of treasure entrusted to them. Newlove, we're ready when you are."

As the car slipped through the London streets, Taylor would ask a question now and then about some building or monument of which he had some faint memory. Then it occurred to him that Dr Barlow might be able to throw light on a few questions which had occupied Taylor's thoughts during his stay at Keith House, and which he felt shy of putting to the General.

"You remember telling me," he said, "that I came from America with a recommendation from somebody called Farewell Billy."

"It was the General who told you that," Dr Barlow replied. "But I know it was so, for I was shown the letter from Billy."

"I have often wondered," Taylor said, "who this man was who gave me such a good character."

Dr Barlow cackled slightly, then he leaned back in his corner and again looked-over Taylor thoughtfully. "I'll say this," he volunteered. "Since the first time we met, you have put on so much weight of personality, so to speak, that I don't mind telling you things that I wouldn't have cared to confuse you with at first. Very well – I know a lot about Farewell Billy, I know more than the General knows. You see, I had been on research work at the Rockefeller Institute in New York long before the General turned up with his snake-bite case, which led, you may recollect, to the General and Billy becoming so friendly. And during all the time I was there, Farewell Billy was quite a frequent subject of conversation among the people I mixed with in New York."

"Was he some sort of public character?" Taylor wanted to know.

Dr Barlow was amused. "Yes and no is the correct answer to that question. Most of the adult life of Billy O'Brien – a name by which nobody ever called him – was passed in a world where the characters do their best not to be public – I mean the world of organised crime. But Billy was such a success as a leader in that world that he became news in spite of himself. He managed to keep the peace among the racketeers, so that for years on end there were no gang wars, and there were many stories about the mixture of diplomacy and threats that Billy would use in getting his way. But I don't believe, Taylor, you understand what I'm talking about."

"Yes, I do," Taylor said. "Roughly, that is. This man who sent me over here is a criminal in a large way, carrying on operations in New York."

"That *was* Billy's position, only more so," Dr Barlow answered. "At the height of his activity he had a finger in practically every important racket, not in New York only but in many other cities. But for some years past he has been playing no direct part in the illegal world. You see, he had made a lot of money, and had invested it in different forms of legitimate business, especially in real estate, but without making the mistake of trying to cut himself loose entirely from his old associates – they would resent that, and it wouldn't be safe. No – Billy stayed on in the background as a respected adviser, an old hand whose judgment had never been at fault, and who was always ready to help the boys free of charge. And that was Billy's position when he and the General became acquainted. The General knew well enough that Billy had in his day been a greedy and unscrupulous robber and blackmailer and worse, but he liked Billy because he was afraid of nothing and nobody, and because he had always stood by any man who was a follower of his. Billy and the General were exactly alike in those two things."

Taylor nodded rather ruefully. "Yes," he said, "I see. Well, it is very much what I had guessed from things said by you and the General – only that it makes my recent past even more shady than I thought it might be."

"My advice is, forget it," Dr Barlow said. "The best thing for you is to focus yourself on now – N, O, W. For that matter, it's the best thing for everybody, so we'll change the subject. For a start, how about your visit to Hatton

Garden today? As we've both been through the same experience, I should like to compare notes."

Taylor was very ready to discuss this with someone equally admitted to the confidence of General de la Costa and the partners Ullstein and Mendoza. Dr Barlow's comments on the precautions with which that firm's affairs were carried on, and on the diamond-dealing business in general, were of a refreshing pungency; and it interested Taylor to hear that he had a personal liking for Ullstein and a rather warmer feeling for Mendoza. Ullstein was, he said, a perfectly honest man, whom you could depend on to any extent. Mendoza was, in addition, an artist, a collector of modern paintings, a figure well known in the world of music in London both as a supporter of musical enterprises and as an amateur violinist. The doctor's recollections of a few others in the same way of business who had been less agreeable characters were still being drawn upon when the car reached Mewstone.

"I'd better have a word with the Fieldings before you show up," Dr Barlow said when they arrived at Keith House. "See if you can find the General – you know where to look for him."

That personage was in fact pacing the lawn as usual, and he gave Taylor a warm greeting when he arrived and handed over the valuables entrusted to him in Hatton Garden. The General stuffed the cheque into a pocket and tossed the parcel of precious stones on to the table under the copper beech; then he said, "Now we can keep the wolf from the door, as you say. You tell me, my dear Taylor, that there are one hundred pound notes in each of these packets. Then two of these packets are for you, a payment in advance of your monthly salary under the agreement which we came to yesterday. No, no receipt if you please, no formalities of any kind between us. I shall remember the date when payment is due – I always remember dates.

You are doubtful about accepting so much? Well, it was my own proposal, and you cannot say, *amigo*, how much will be asked of you in return for it. If you find that the amount weighs upon your conscience, you can give away as much of it as you like, but do not mention the matter to me. Now sit down and cast your eyes over these stones" – he emptied the envelope on to the table – "a very fine collection of perfect gems, precious and rather less precious, but all beautiful – emerald, ruby, sapphire, amethyst, topaz, jacinth, chrysoberyl, half a dozen more. There is nothing like diamonds, either for lustre or for value, but if you want colour, what a wonderful show these things make." He took up a handful and let them slide through his fingers in a dazzling stream. "They are cut so that the very most is made of the quality of each stone. I have had some ornamental things, a few only, made by a great artist – you remember, the brigand of Corsica. They are mounted with jewels just like these, as well as with diamonds, and I do not believe there is anything to compare with them. You will be seeing them soon, *amigo*, as I hope. These stones here are intended for another piece of the same kind. Now I put them away and take you into the house; you can see Diana waving to us."

Taylor and the General were summoned into the big morning room, where Arnold Fielding and Dr Barlow were already seated, each with a glass of sherry at hand. "Lunch is twenty minutes, you two," Mrs Fielding said from her place at the sideboard. "It's early because Druce has got to get back to London. Sherry for you, Taylor, a light, wholesome wine – that's right. Here's a bottle of your private painkiller, Justo; you had better help yourself. Druce has been asking us how you have been getting on, Taylor. We both told him you had been improving every day, that nobody meeting you now could imagine there was anything wrong. In fact, Arnold said you seemed to be more strong-minded now than most of the people he comes across, though he hastened to add that that was not saying much. Anyway, you're a credit to the Fielding treatment."

Fielding, with the diffident giggle that was his habit, said, "You see, Taylor, we and Dr Barlow agreed that the thing for you was to be always learning something, always looking out in new directions, on the chance that something might click, and also because it was good mental exercise, anyhow. And we're not ashamed of the result."

Mrs Fielding, perched on the end of the settee, regarded Taylor with her head on one side. "I don't suppose," she said, "you realise how much you've changed for the better since you came here a fortnight ago. I don't mean what you feel yourself, but what other people feel about you. There are very few signs left now of the damage that happened to you in the railway smash; you've a good colour and you carry yourself well, more like a military man than ever. Instead of reminding anyone of a lost dog, you've got your tail up and your ears half-cocked, ready to pay attention, if you know what I mean."

General de la Costa, beaming benevolently in his armchair, nodded emphatic agreement, and finished his glass of telque. "It is all true, and I hope our Taylor does not object to being discussed in this way before his face."

"Quite right, General," Dr Barlow said. "Taylor is being talked over as if he were a prize pig in an agricultural show; we might as well be poking him with our sticks while we are about it. Prize pigs have never seemed embarrassed, in my wide experience of them, but possibly Taylor might be."

"You have all done your best to encourage me, and you have succeeded," Taylor said. "And I can't tell you how much good it did me to be trusted by the General today with a job that might have meant an enormous loss if I had made a mess of it. It's the first time I have been able to make myself really useful."

General de la Costa shook his head. "You forget, *amigo*, that evening in Mrs McBean's kitchen. On that occasion you were more than useful, believe me, and if nobody had his brains knocked out it was no fault of yours. I might very well have been snatched – it was quite a possibility – but for your assistance."

Dr Barlow rose to his feet. "I dare say you have had enough of the subject, Taylor, and, anyhow, you and I had better go and make ourselves presentable before the gong sounds. That drive has made me devilish hungry, Diana, and as Taylor has travelled twice the distance, and had an exciting time in Hatton Garden, I daren't think what he will do to your lunch."

CHAPTER XX

On the morning of the next day General de la Costa asked Taylor to come with him to his own sitting room on the first floor. This was a room Taylor had never entered, nor had the General himself made much use of it during the time of Taylor's stay. As they reached it, the General begged Taylor to excuse him while he fetched something from his bedroom, which was next door. Left alone in a large well-lighted apartment, Taylor found it to be furnished with that severity which seemed to be its owner's taste, and carpeted with light yellow matting whose shade was matched by the distempered walls.

There were two plain, unpainted tables, one of them with writing materials and an immense blotting-book, its red leather cover embossed in gold with an intricate design of a human figure, as forcible, Taylor thought, as it was barbarous. Round the walls of the room were three bookcases, tall and broad, glass-fronted: half a dozen volumes were ranged, spine upwards, on the other of the two tables. The largest and stoutest of the books so set out was lettered on the back, *Las Artes Populares en Peligragua*. He noted on the mantelshelf two objects which perhaps the General regarded as ornaments, one a lumpish and hideous animal figure of green stone, the other an even uglier animal of red stone, liberally spotted with discs of what looked like jade. Each beast was provided with sharp white teeth, and was snarling dangerously. In this and in no other respect they resembled Tchin-teh in Taylor's own bedroom, for nothing could be plainer than the fact that Tchin-teh was a product of the craftsmanship of a splendid and complex civilisation, whereas these two images belonged to a very early stage in the development of art.

General de la Costa, entering the room with a flat cardboard box in his hand, smiled as he noted the expression with which Taylor was looking at his sculptures. "Let us be seated, *amigo*," he said, taking a chair at the writing-table. "I am afraid that my jaguar and my tiger have not impressed you very favourably. I know that they do not make an effect of bewildering beauty on a modern mind, but for a student of the most ancient culture of which traces are left in my own country these two figures have a fascination of their own. They were carved by the Maya Indians more than two thousand years ago, perhaps not very long after they settled in my part of South America, and certainly at an early period of the great civilisation which they were building up, with their cities, palaces, temples – nothing but ruins today. These images before you were dug up by myself on one of the great mounds of decayed adobe bricks which are to be found on my estates in Peligragua, and those mounds were there, just the same as they are now, when my ancestors came over from Spain. But to see the Maya at his best you must go to Yucatan, where there are buildings with carving and ornament still surviving, beautiful enough to astonish you. My own treasures belong," the General admitted with regret, "to a primitive age of that culture. But I like them. Perhaps it is that I am primitive myself."

"You say that the Maya settled in your country. Where did they come from, then?" Taylor asked.

"Oh, Asia," the General said lightly. "Where everything comes from. The authorities believe that the Maya skipped across to Alaska by way of the Behring Strait, and then strolled south for a good many centuries until they came to a climate that suited them in my part of the world. It is supposed that there were others before them who did the same thing, and others after, but it was the Maya who began civilisation in a big way."

Taylor leaned over the over-ornamented figure embossed on the General's blotting-book cover. "Is that one of them?" he asked.

"He belongs to a branch of the family, which became too sophisticated, as I think," the General said. "They called themselves Aztecs, and this individual was a priest of Quetzalcoatl, the chief of their disgustingly bloodthirsty gods. As for the Maya remains in South America, there is a quite large literature on the subject, most of which is represented on my shelves here. I am planning to add to it myself; in fact I have added a little already. But it was not for this sort of discussion that I asked you to join me in this room. It was because I have something to say which must be between ourselves, and also to show you some baggage which we shall, I hope, manage to carry between us on our next expedition. That expedition will be made by night, and it must be made with every precaution of secrecy, including the precaution of silence. Do you remember, *amigo*, that at our first meeting I told you of my reputation in my own country for being noiseless in my operations? Well, this, too, will be an occasion for making ourselves pussycats, as our Doctor called it, and one of the things which are indispensable is a pair of rubber-soled shoes."

Liberally provided as he was with money, Taylor had in the past few days made a good many purchases of clothing, including a ready-made suit which had been passed as presentable by Mrs Fielding, and which was now being altered to fit him. Taylor, so the man at the outfitters had assured her, happened to be one of the stock tall-men's sizes, and he had felt it would be a relief to have a dark blue faint-striped change from the decidedly assertive checks which Dr Barlow had chosen for him. But rubber-soled shoes had not occurred to him. He promised that this deficiency should be made good at once.

"There is no reason for hurry," the General said. "This is Tuesday; our expedition is arranged for the night of Thursday. We shall be starting about eleven, and we may be returning here in four hours, perhaps less than that. You have no objection, I hope, to late hours from time to time?"

"My time is yours, of course, General," Taylor said. "Will anybody be with us?"

"The only person actually with us will be Gunn, one of my assistants who looks after and drives my Antelope car. Newlove, whom you know, will be somewhere around in the Fendlair, but he will be called upon only in case of emergency. And now I will declare quite candidly, my dear Taylor, that I intend to say nothing more about my arrangements for Thursday night. You will not misunderstand my silence, I am sure – after all, I have already taken you into my confidence very thoroughly; those who know as much about me and my affairs as you do are few indeed. No, *amigo*, I shall say nothing about our expedition because I wish you to be in a position to swear at any time that you were in total ignorance of my plans and had not the least idea what my purpose was. If there is anything illegal about what I have in mind, I wish to avoid your being involved in it."

Taylor frowned over this for a few moments; then he said, "I shouldn't care what you let me in for, General."

"Why not?"

"Because you would never do anything shameful."

The General rose and clapped him on the shoulder. "You put it quite simply, *amigo*," he said, "and you are quite right. But I still must insist on keeping my plans for this expedition to myself. I engaged you because I needed a protector against a gang of dangerous criminals, as I do still and shall do for who knows how long? I needed also someone to act as my aide-de-camp, which you have done already and will do on Thursday night. But if there is going to be any trouble with the law, as I say, about our expedition, I wish to take it on myself. In fact it is an essential part of my purpose that I shall do so – I will explain why afterwards."

Taylor, remembering the genius for understatement of which the General had given proofs in the past, concluded that it was useless to wonder just how much he might mean by "trouble with the law" in this case. He set the matter aside and merely asked what the baggage was which the General was going to show him.

"It is here," the General said, indicating a corner of the room to the left of the two tables. "If you will help me, we will lift these packages on to the writing-table, and so we shall have an idea of their weight and of how we can carry them conveniently."

There were six of them, all wrapped alike in brown canvas fastened with stout cord securely knotted, but of very different sizes and weights. There was one which looked as if it might contain a very large book. There was a long package which had something the shape of a pair of outsize umbrellas with exaggerated handles; but Taylor, taking charge of it, was surprised to find that it needed some little effort to raise it from the floor with one hand.

"You had better heft the lot of them, *amigo*," the General said. "I wish you to get a notion of the weight we have here on this table. What has struck you about the two or three which you have handled?"

"They are all much heavier than I should have thought from their size. And so are the others," he added after testing each of them. "The things are made of metal perhaps."

"Perhaps they are," the General replied with a brilliant smile. "In due time we shall see. Anyway, it is clear that if we two are to shift all these packages on Thursday night, and to shift them in one operation, we shall not be able to do it simply by hand. We shall need the proper equipment." Here the General produced from the box which he had brought into the room some broad bands of webbing with brass fittings for buckling and adjustment. "Will you allow me, my dear Taylor?"

Two strips of webbing were passed across Taylor's shoulders. When a large package had been suspended by its strings on one of them, and two small packages on the other, each was buckled at the hip on the opposite side. "With the goods packed that way, two strong men like you and me could hump them for miles and never know they were there. In fact the time we shall take to transport them will be very short, but it has to be done at one go, without dropping things and messing up the job. You agree with me, I can see, that it can be done easily this way." For Taylor had walked across the room with squared shoulders and a firm step.

"Well, then, that is settled," the General said. "We have everything in readiness except for the pair of sneakers which you will need for our undertaking. Now take off your equipment and let us have a talk about yourself. The difference in you since you came to stay here is very great, as we all tell you. You feel it yourself, do you not? Yet the veil is still over your past. I have spoken to our doctor about it this morning, and all he will say is that the veil ought to be wearing very thin, to judge from the records of cases like your own. He thinks you may snap out of it any time, but there is nothing we can do about it except go on treating you as one of ourselves, so that you know always that you have friends whom you can count upon. You have heard all this before, but you cannot keep it too firmly before your mind."

"But I never forget it, General," Taylor said. "I always tell myself it doesn't matter what I wake up to – if ever I do wake up – you and your friends have made a man of me."

The General produced his cigarette papers and pouch. "*Puede ser*," he said a little abstractedly. "It is possible, my dear Taylor. But, believe me, we had no man-making intentions. It was just that I and my friends all liked you, and that our doctor said we should just be easy with you. And talking about friends, I hope that you will be adding to their number on Thursday when the Fielding boys come home for their half-term holiday."

Taylor looked astonished. "I had no idea that Mrs Fielding had sons," he said.

"But why not, *amigo*?" the General asked. "Did you imagine that she would have only daughters? Perhaps you were misled by their not having talked to you about their family. They would have done, believe me, if the subject had happened to come up."

"These boys, then, go to school somewhere?" Taylor said.

"They do," the General said. "They are young – eight and ten, I believe. The name of their school I do not remember. I know it is a very good school, but the boys always refer to it as Dogpatch, and I cannot recall its true name. The elder is called Adrian and the other Jerome; they are healthy, high-spirited and well trained; the critical feelings which they have about their elders, including myself, are never made obvious. I only wish I could be sure that I was myself as satisfactory a boy when I was their age. They will take to you, because everybody does – Diana tells me that the Mayor, whom you met for a few minutes only, as she says, was asking after you yesterday with interest."

Taylor laughed gently. "That is because he wants to show off his municipal arrangements to a foreign visitor who is supposed to be interested in them. Mrs Fielding told him I was an American making a special study of British local government."

"How like her!" the General said. "Diana is never at a loss for a piece of nonsense which other people take seriously. Arnold says she picked up the habit at Girton, where she took a degree, or whatever it is that girls take at Cambridge. Now, my dear Taylor, as we have made all our arrangements, shall we go down to the open air and take a look at that large shed that is at the end of the garden, behind the rhododendrons? I have been considering the matter, and I talked it over with the Fieldings last night, and they have no objection to my making use of that shed as a laboratory. It is much smaller than the place where I completed my research at Engelberg, but on the other hand I now know precisely what space is needed, while at Engelberg half the place was taken up with the remains of past failures, and with various junk."

"I see," Taylor answered. "You mean to go on with the making of diamonds."

The General waved a hand non-committally. "I may do so," he said. "I still have a large number of rough stones, but I am always guided by prudence, and I wish to get my method of production in going order. It is possible that I shall cease to live in this country when my work here is done, as it may be pretty soon, but it might be useful to have my laboratory established here and to come back and make use of it some time or other. Getting hold of the necessary apparatus is the chief difficulty, because the essential parts of it must be specially made for me, and must be very carefully inspected and tested by someone acting for me before they leave the makers' hands. This is a task, my dear Taylor, which I could not entrust to you; it is an affair for a man with a training in science. As I cannot appear in the matter myself, I shall ask our doctor to be good enough to attend to it for me. He gets a kick out of being mixed up in my dark doings, and I expect he likes, too, the contributions which I make to the expenses of his research station. But I should not speak of it like that; the simple truth is that he and I are the closest of friends, and each of us feels pleasure in doing the other a service. Now we will go down to that shed and go into the question of leading to it supplies of gas and electricity, which are both indispensable. *Vamos!*"

CHAPTER XXI

At the breakfast table on Thursday the General mentioned that he and Taylor would be going out in his car that night, and would be absent during the small hours. Taylor expected, he hardly knew why, to hear some unfavourable comment from one or both of the Fieldings; but Arnold Fielding, who was peeling an orange, merely said, "Poaching, I suppose," and his wife reminded the General that her two sons were coming home that day, and that their sleep should not be disturbed.

"As if I, of all men, were capable of that!" the General exclaimed, stabbing himself in the chest with both forefingers. "You know very well, Diana, that I can move like a ghost when I like. Half a dozen times before, when you knew I was changing my quarters and the garden door had been left open for me, you never heard a sound from me until the next morning."

"Yes, but can Taylor move like a ghost?" Mrs Fielding wanted to know. "He hasn't practised it as you have, and I hope he won't mind my suggesting that he takes off his shoes downstairs and goes up in his socks."

"Certainly I will do that," Taylor said. "Though in fact my shoes will make no more noise than socks."

"You want more coffee, Justo," Mrs Fielding pronounced, holding out a hand for his cup. "So that was what you were after, Taylor, when you asked me for the address of a good shoe shop yesterday – you were going to get rubber-soled shoes. You are becoming secretive – catching it from Justo, I suppose."

Taylor said it was not quite that; it was just that he liked the feeling of doing things for himself, even if they were only small things. He hoped Mrs Fielding would not think he was being ungrateful.

"Of course not, Taylor," she said. "I'm not such a fool as you seem to suppose. Your feeling like that is a very good sign for you, I'm sure. Soon we shall have you taking an office in the town, with your name on a brass plate saying you are a free-will consultant."

Her husband, helping himself to kidneys and bacon at the sideboard, looked round with his diffident giggle. "You might make it a little snappier than that, Taylor," he said. "Why not a brass plate saying merely, 'Self-Help, Limited'?"

"You are a beast, Arnold," Mrs Fielding murmured.

"But that's exactly it," Taylor said laughing. "My self-help is so very limited; that is why I value so much what there is of it. Anyway, Mrs Fielding, I will make a point of coming upstairs in my socks tonight – or I suppose I should say tomorrow morning."

Mrs Fielding flapped a hand at him, as if suppressing further discussion of the subject. "Justo," she said, "What are you looking injured about?"

The General, who was eating bacon with a look of exaggerated patience, said, "I feel that I am not fit to associate with such a lot of simple characters as the present company. I am not sufficiently open-hearted, not artless, as you say – ah, no, I am secretive. I am a bad influence. It is a pity."

"I weep for you," Mrs Fielding said. "I deeply sympathise. But you know you are fond of keeping things back; you like to have a surprise up your sleeve."

The General, taking another piece of toast, repeated sadly, "It is a pity. Yes, Arnold, I believe you are right, a little more bacon would be good for me." He rose to go to the sideboard. "It will help me to forget."

"One thing you have never made any secret of," Mrs Fielding said, watching the General's proceedings, "is your appetite. It really is a pleasure, Justo, to provide meals for a man who always wants a good, large second helping."

The General, quite cured of his melancholy, said that he wished he could always give her pleasure on such easy terms; and, to Taylor's relief, the delicate subject of rubber-soled shoes was not raised again.

"One thing we had better do," Mrs Fielding said, "is to have breakfast at ten instead of eight-thirty tomorrow. Arnold and I don't care twopence when we have it, and the two boys will enjoy getting up late. Taylor, you and Justo will be called at nine. Get up if you feel like it." So it was settled.

Arnold Fielding, who had to attend a meeting of the Council of the Royal Asiatic Society in London, was driven to the station by his wife after conferring on Taylor the freedom of his library and pointing out the chair in which it was easiest to go to sleep. The General, who had, he said, a difficult letter to write, retired to his own study. Taylor, left to himself, took up a small book bearing Fielding's name, in which it was maintained that the building of the Great Wall of China was due to a wave of colossal architectural ideas which originated in Greece and the Near East in the third century BC, and which had made its impression on Chinese travellers. So much Taylor made out, but in what followed he found himself far out of his depth, and he spent most of the morning browsing at large upon Fielding's very comprehensive library, which seemed to include a little, or not a little, of everything from the epics of Homer to the *Handley Cross* of Robert Surtees.

At lunch General de la Costa was, for the first time in Taylor's brief acquaintance with him, silent and pre-occupied. Mrs Fielding, evidently recognising his mood, talked to Taylor on a number of subjects, including Cambridge University, domestic service in China, amateur photography, Quakers, the peerage, and her two sons who were to come home that evening from their school at Dodington.

At the mention of them the General roused himself from his meditations to say, "My dear Taylor, do not give any attention to what is said by Diana about her boys. Her real opinion of them is like the opinion of a tigress about her whelps, but she is so much afraid of behaving as an adoring mother behaves that she does not even do the boys simple justice. Now I tell you that they are exceptionally good specimens, they are healthy and well mannered and intelligent. You will be seeing them this evening, and will be able to form your own judgment."

Mrs Fielding looked at Taylor with an expression of helplessness. "This," she said, "is Justo in his disarming mood. I simply can't think of anything quarrelsome to say after that. I shall drop the subject until I bring the pair of them back from the station."

When Adrian and Jerome, who both resembled their mother, were brought home, they greeted General de la Costa with affectionate warmth, in which it was easy to see that admiration played a large part. But their introduction to Taylor, as a friend of the General's who had come over from America, had an effect on them which seemed to puzzle Mrs Fielding and which at least interested the General. Each of the boys as he shook hands seemed overcome with uneasiness, and whenever at dinner Taylor looked at either of them, it was to meet an unblinking gaze which was instantly withdrawn. No one, however, made any remark upon this slight awkwardness; and it was dispelled at last when the General, just before Jerome and Adrian were sent off to bed, delighted them with a thrilling eye-witness description of a fight between a bear and an alligator, which the bear had mistaken for a dead tree-trunk, possibly containing honey. The General was closely questioned about every detail of this conflict, including the noises made by the combatants, which he was fortunately able to imitate. Taylor felt that there was ground for Mrs Fielding's prophecy, after seeing the two off to bed, that there would be a re-enactment of the whole affair in their bedroom at least once before they went to sleep.

"Bah! They will sleep the better," the General said. "It is just as well that I really did see that fight; if I had not seen it I should certainly have broken down under the cross-examination they put me through. And if we do hear thumps and yells from upstairs, I beg that they may be allowed time to finish each other off. It is one of your great virtues, Diana, a virtue very unusual in an Englishwoman, that you never disapprove of anyone doing anything unless there is really some reason against it."

"Well, it's not a bad principle, I think," Mrs Fielding said. "Now, what I should like to do, unless either of you has a really good reason against it, is to have a game of Mah Jongg, showing Taylor how to play as we go along. What do you say, Taylor?" She rattled the counters in a lacquered box. "It's quite easy to learn the rudiments, and it's practically impossible for anyone to cheat, and the terms of the game are full of poetry."

Taylor was perfectly willing, and the General was eager, as he said, to wipe out the disgrace of his defeat in the last game he had played in that house, which had cost him fourteen shillings and ninepence. So Taylor heard for the first time, as far as he knew, the Twittering of the Sparrows, and by the time of Arnold Fielding's arrival from the station at nine-thirty he was an enthusiast for the game. When he asked Fielding if the game was an old game, and when the General confessed to a total ignorance of its history – if, as he artlessly said, it had a history – the sinologue in Fielding was roused, and he discoursed upon Mah Jongg.

At ten-thirty the General said that Taylor and himself ought to retire, as they had matters to discuss before going out for the evening; and five minutes later they were in the General's sitting room. He led Taylor to an armchair and took his own seat astride a small chair opposite to him.

"We have a fine night for what we have to do," he began. "I chose this night because there is no moon visible, the sky happens to be cloudy also, and it is warm and dry. A good, dark night. Tell me, my dear Taylor, have you ever been in Rome?"

Taylor, smiling at the inconsequence of the question, answered, "I shouldn't wonder."

"You should not wonder," the General said thoughtfully. "You speak lightly; you are at your ease in reminding me so gently that you ought not to be asked that sort of question. Not so long ago it would have worried you, and you would have shown it. Well, I am sorry. I should have remembered our doctor's advice. So you have no recollection of being in Rome. Now, I went to Rome for a week of vacation during my time at the Sorbonne. It was a marvellous experience, and the most important thing happened to me at the very end of my visit, in a place I had never heard of before that day. It is a church; it is called St Paul's Outside the Walls, and it has been for I do not know how long a sort of treasury of ecclesiastical splendour of every kind, to which contribution has been made by pious Catholics all over the world, and even by some not Catholics, and perhaps not particularly pious, such as one of the Czars of Russia, who had chipped in with some pillars of a most wonderful marble. And far away up under the roof was a frieze of portraits in mosaic of all the Popes from the beginning. There it was, *amigo*, that I got my big idea."

The General paused impressively. Taylor, quite at a loss, asked, "What was the big idea, General?"

"I am going to tell you," the General said. "In that row of Popes there was one – among the early ones he was – whose mother had been a British slave. So my guide assured me as I looked up, trying to distinguish faces in that far-off ribbon of mosaic. It is possible that the story about that Pope's parentage could not be proved – in fact I doubt if any of the early Popes could have produced a birth certificate – but there was no reason why the story should not be true. British slaves were common enough in Rome, and, anyway, what did I care? The point was that an English Catholic, a Duke of Norfolk, had believed the story, and had presented two fine diamonds to that church, to be the pupils of the eyes of that traditionally half-British Pope. And when I looked at them through a pair of glasses, there the eyes were, blinking at me as if to say, *'Que tal,* Justo de la Costa?' "

"What did that mean, General?"

"Forgive me, *amigo*, I should make my language clearer. Those words are just a common saying, like 'How goes it?' And the answer which my eyes gave to the Pope was, 'Fine, because your Holiness has given me an inspiration.' But I must tell you the rest when we are in the car; just now I think we should be getting ready to leave. To begin with, we will change our shoes. I have taken the liberty of bringing your sneakers here from your room."

When the shoes had been changed the General turned to the corner where lay the packages which he had shown to Taylor already. "We shall be taking with us," he said, "these articles which you saw the other day; they are to be taken to their destination tonight. We shall have to act smartly at all stages of the operation, so it will be best to get loaded up here, and not to unpack until we are at the place itself. We shall travel a little less comfortably perhaps, but it will make things much more easy."

Taylor watched the General put on his webbing equipment with his share of the canvas-clad packages hung from it, then he was helped into his own harness. The General opened the door and, stepping to the balustrade, looked down into the hall. "It is as I expected," he said in a low voice. "Our friends have left the way out to the garden free for us; they have retired into the library, I think. Now we shall go down, and not a word must be said until we are out in the open. Do not bring your hat with you – we shall have no need of hats." He led the way down the stairs and soon they stood on the turf behind the house. The General set a slow pace towards the passage at the side leading to the wooden door by which they had first entered the place. He handed to Taylor a large electric torch. "This is not for you to use now," he said quietly. "Later on you will need it. My own torch will give all the light that is necessary now."

He threw its beam before them and led the way along the asphalt path that skirted the house. "I do not believe there is any danger here at present; I have scouted all around the house very carefully at just this time last night and the night before. Just the same, we will show no light when we turn into the road. We shall go slowly to the left, and we shall be overtaken by Gunn in the car in about half a minute from now. I shall open the door and you will hop inside."

They came out on the footway in darkness, on which little impression was made by the spark of a distant street lamp to the right, at the corner of the main road. The General, his hand passed through Taylor's arm, paced slowly to the left; and almost at once a car, its engine only just audibly humming, was to be heard approaching from behind them. It slowed down, stopped as it reached them, and in a few instants the door was opened, Taylor and the General were inside, and they were travelling rapidly.

CHAPTER XXII

"There is some distance to go," the General said as he eased himself with his burdens into the off-corner of the car. "We have to go by Abbot's Dean, or to bypass it rather, because our destination lies well beyond that place. It was because Abbot's Dean lay not too far away from the spot we are going to that I chose my hide-out at Mrs McBean's. Abbot's Dean would have been much more convenient for the job, but what would you? As our Spanish saying goes, 'That which is, is best.'

"You were going to tell me, General," Taylor reminded him, "what idea it was that was given you by the half-English Pope. You said it was something very important."

"Well, yes, to me important," the General said. "It gave me an object that I have been living for ever since my time of study in Paris, when I spent part of a vacation in Rome, as I think I have told you. As I looked at those diamond eyes through my glasses, and thought that this expensive gift was intended as an act of sacrifice, the idea came to me that I would do an act of that kind, but on a larger scale and in a different way. It was to be done in memory of my mother. You have heard me speak of her, and now I will tell you something more. She was born, as she used to say, in the shadow of the Cathedral of Glasminster. All through her childhood and youth, whenever she was at home, she passed a part of each day in the Cathedral. Glasminster, as you may or may not know, my dear Taylor, is one of the most beautiful buildings in England, the perfection of Gothic. It was for my mother the embodiment in glorious architecture of her faith, which was a part of her being. More than once she said to me, when I was a boy, that it would be happiness for her to know that some small memorial of her would have a place in that building after she was dead. I promised her that when I was a man I would carry out her wish. Perhaps you think that is absurd, *amigo*, but such feelings are very real for those who have them."

Taylor looked his embarrassment at this confidence, so unusual in its tone, on the part of General de la Costa. "No, no," he said awkwardly. "How could I think it absurd? It is the very opposite of that. Whatever I may have been, I feel sure that I was never heartless and – what do you call it? – cynical."

The General's eyebrows went up slightly. "You must have been an interesting companion for Farewell Billy, my dear Taylor – that is what I often feel. But I must not wander from my story. The idea which was given to me in St Paul's Outside the Walls was that I should make a great gift in memory of my mother. It was not to be an ordinary gift. It was to mean something more than writing a cheque, or perhaps the trouble of writing my signature to a cheque made out already. It was to be a gift most carefully planned and designed, a gift which would mean a hell of a lot of trouble for everybody concerned, as well as the spending of money. You see the idea, *amigo*? And not only that – it was to mean some personal risk to be run by the giver. It is true that I like running personal risks, but that does not make it a safe occupation. So I made my resolution that day in Rome, and it has never been absent from my mind from that day to this."

Taylor, who had followed all this with close attention, wore a slightly puzzled look. "I see the idea, General, yes, but a gift so wonderful as you say – I suppose that a Cathedral like Glasminster is very well furnished already with everything that could possibly be wanted for the purposes of a Cathedral."

The General wagged a forefinger. "Glasminster used to be famous all over England for the splendour of its consecrated possessions, especially the treasures of the altar. It is very likely that you never heard about that, in those schooldays which you remember more or less. But perhaps you did hear of King Henry the Eighth – I have been told that he is the one King of England of whom every Englishman, even the most brutishly ignorant, has heard."

Taylor's expression brightened. "Yes, certainly, I have heard of him. He had six wives, and cut all their heads off."

"Ah, no, not all." General de la Costa held up a hand correctively. "Only a proportion of the total – I forget the exact number. We must be fair, even to a terrible cad like Henry the Eighth. But it is no matter, the thing I was referring to was Henry's robbery of the churches. Glasminster, a great monastery, was plundered of everything it possessed, both in lands and in goods, by Henry and the thieves who came after him. I have read much about the question, and I do not think the monasteries ought to have been let alone. What I think is that their property, when it was seized, ought to have been put to a better use than filling the pockets of a lot of greedy parasites. And I think especially that the sacred vessels and other treasures of the altar ought to have been spared. I doubt if my friend Farewell Billy's boys ever pulled anything so raw as Henry and his gang did when they treated the wealth of the Church simply as an ocean of loot for them to dip their dirty paws in. Well, all that I intend to do is to furnish the altar of Glasminster with a new outfit of treasures, even more magnificent than those which it used to have."

The General leant back, closing his eyes, and there was silence in the car as it hummed along through the darkness. At last Taylor said, "I understand very little of all this, I am sorry to say. What seems clear is that you intend to make a sort of gift that must be very unusual. And your telling me this just now, General – does that mean that our expedition tonight has something to do with that intention of yours? I feel quite at a loss."

The General pursed his lips. "I am sorry to say, *amigo*, that even now I cannot give you any information on that subject, for the reason which I mentioned two days ago – if by misfortune there should be any trouble with the law, you must be able to say that you knew nothing beforehand about my plans. That is still the case – you are as ignorant as a child not yet born. But you will not be very much longer in that condition. We are running downhill, and our destination is not far off now."

He felt in a breast pocket and produced a key – an unusual key, long and large, that had about it, even to Taylor's eye, an old-fashioned look; yet it was as clean and bright as a guardsman's bayonet.

"This would not fit on to the little bunch of keys which our doctor has insisted on your carrying, my dear Taylor," said the General. "It is the key to my problem – the problem of undoing a part of the dirty work of King Henry, undoing it very thoroughly, and in a way that cannot be concealed, but at the same time continuing to keep out of the way of all who are not my friends, and especially out of the way of the police, who have been looking out for me such a long time. This key is a facsimile of a very old key which my uncle the Canon keeps hanging on a nail in his study, and which he makes use of if he wishes to get into the

Cathedral when it is locked up – so he told me. When he was not looking I took a squeeze of it with some paraffin wax which I had brought with me for the purpose, and a locksmith in Clerkenwell made me a copy of it the next day. I have already tested it and it works perfectly. And now, are you ready to move? I have made this run at this time twice lately, everything has been reconnoitred, and Gunn knows the exact spot where he should stop."

The car, as Taylor could see, was now running slowly through the streets of a town, streets rather narrow and not very well lighted, in which no one at all was astir. "Here we are," the General said as the car came to a halt. "I get out first, you will follow me and keep as close as possible. Keep your torch ready, but do not show a light until I say. We must be silent till we reach our objective, unless something goes wrong and I have to give an order. If I do, my dear Taylor, instant obedience is the rule even if it means personal violence. Not one of the things we are carrying is to be abandoned if we have to fall back on the car, which is to stay in this place. We shall look like a couple of pedlars, but nobody, I trust, will be present to make disrespectful remarks."

He swung the door open, and closed it silently as Taylor joined him on the footway. He then led the way some thirty paces back along the route which the car had already travelled, to the corner of a wide entry, where a single lamp shone. At this point the General stopped and said, "My dear Taylor, will you place yourself entirely in my hands for a minute or two? If you will take my arm and shut your eyes, and keep them shut, I shall lead you to our destination, which I do not wish you to know beforehand."

Taylor answered, "All right, I'll keep them shut," and at once he felt himself being led to the left along a paved footway. He occupied his mind by counting the steps taken, and he had got to one hundred and fifteen when he was steered to the right and immediately halted by the General's coming to a standstill.

"Open your eyes, *amigo* – we are there," General de la Costa said, patting him on the shoulder. As Taylor opened his eyes, the darkness was complete; he found nothing visible but a very large keyhole in a small disc of light thrown by the General's torch upon a wooden door which faced him at a distance of a few inches. There was only the faintest sound as the big, bright key was fitted into the lock; then the torch went out, and with a soft thump that told of good lubrication the lock turned. The General's hand on his arm led Taylor through the doorway that now stood open, then the key rasped gently out of the lock and the closing of the door left the two visitors in total darkness.

But there was something more than darkness again. Even before the General snapped on his torch, Taylor knew very well where he was. He was in church. From earliest childhood he had known the atmosphere, and he felt that atmosphere instantly now, although he had never before been in church without a spark of light and without any consciousness of having gone to a church and entered a church. There was a sense of the magnitude and quietude of space about him and above him in what he knew to be a building, there was a coolness after the warmth of the night, there was a scent – if it was a scent – of masonry, and there was above all a feeling of awe. These things flashed through his mind before the General had pushed up the button of his torch and disclosed the surroundings of stone walls and fluted pillars vanishing upwards for which Taylor was, in that moment, quite prepared.

"You had better shine your own torch, *amigo*," the General said in a low voice. "We have not a great way to go, but it is all as dark as the inside of a cow, as you say. One may bump into things, especially into chairs, unless each man has his own light. We are in Glasminster Cathedral – did you know that? I tell you so anyway, because we have got inside without any interference, and there is no trouble to be expected now. It is a serious offence for anyone to make his way into a locked-up church, especially with a home-made key, and I have committed that offence, but I seem to have got away with it so far. That was the personal risk which I had to run. As for yourself, you are able to declare upon oath that you entered the church without knowing it. I do not think they can pin anything on you unless you insist on committing a felony while you are here – which I do not advise – that might lead them to set aside your sworn statement, and to prosecute you for sacrilege." Taylor had lit his torch as directed, and let its beams play round him. Near at hand, on the right, was an ancient tomb raised but slightly above the floor level, topped by the supine figure of a mailed knight in black marble, his head resting on a helmet, his feet crossed and his hands joined in prayer.

"We are in the south transept," the General said. "Now we have to go straight across to the other side of the nave. Soon we shall be relieved of our burdens, and I shall have done the thing that I made up my mind to do so many years ago. Now be careful about chairs, especially on your left, and of the steps up to the chancel on your right. It will be better to walk in my footsteps – as I said, I have been this way before."

He set off accordingly through the darkness. "Then all this that we are carrying," Taylor said as he followed, "is your gift to the Cathedral. It was very stupid of me not to have guessed it before, but I am afraid a man with my disability cannot help being rather stupid. And besides that, I feel as if I were in a dream."

"I do not feel absolutely normal myself," the General confessed. "I think it is because I got to know this Cathedral pretty well at one time, and I have in my mind the overpowering effect which is made by this interior. It is an architectural masterpiece. It is a strange feeling to me to be walking here with darkness in every direction, knowing that I am surrounded by all that majesty and beauty which is unseen. Is that why I speak in an undertone, I wonder, without meaning to do so? I have never noticed it until now because when coming here before at night, to reconnoitre the position, I have come alone each time."

"But so do I speak in an undertone," Taylor said decisively, "though all I know is that we are in church. The truth is simple enough. People do talk like that when they are in churches, and I am sure it is not because of any unusual quality in the architecture."

"Do not let us quarrel about our sensations, my dear Taylor," the General rejoined, "or at least let us save it up till we are on the way home. I should enjoy it thoroughly then. How refreshing it is to hear you starting a dispute with me as if you were quite determined to put me in the wrong – I have never heard you like this before. Now we turn to the right, into this corner. We shall soon be away from these immense spaces and faint ghostly echoes."

The General's torch-beam played upon a door, a plain wooden door, with an iron ring for a handle. This he turned, and saying, "Here we are, *amigo*," strode to the end of a not very large but lofty room. Here he seized a curtain of thick material and drew it, with a rattle of wooden rings, across what Taylor's torch told him was the only window.

"Now we can make ourselves at home," the General said, going to the door and switching on a bright light that hung from the beamed roof. It revealed a room severely plain, with panelled walls, pierced by the keyholes of a number of cupboards, and with the steel door of a tall safe of antiquated pattern in the wall facing the window. A few chairs stood about a long table covered with a dark-blue baize cloth; at its end was an armchair, with a blotting-pad and writing materials set before it. On the wall to the right of this chair was a large mirror, and next to it a door smaller than that by which they had entered.

"Even if there were no curtain," the General said, "the light here could not be seen from outside. The window looks out on a small lawn with high walls, they call it a garth, the door to it is locked at night and there are no overlooking houses. So, my dear Taylor, we can place our loads on the table and unfasten them at our leisure. As you said just now, these things are my gift to the Cathedral, and I should very much value your opinion of them."

Producing a knife, he quickly cut the elaborately knotted cords with which the half-dozen packages were fastened, and dragged off the canvas coverings. "I am not an expert in these matters myself, though I can appreciate beautiful craftsmanship, but I knew I could trust to my friend Michaud, who has produced any amount of this sort of thing, and knows the rules of all the religious communities – Catholic, Anglican, Orthodox. I asked him to design and make for me a specially beautiful and costly set of things which are right and proper for the service of the altar in an Anglican Cathedral, including the cover for a Gospel Book. As you can see, the plate is all of gold, with elaborate and, I think, wonderful ornamentation enriched with precious stones. You can see also that these articles are all alike in the general style of the goldsmith's work and the use of jewels. Michaud had before him, as he told me, photographs of some very marvellous church plate of the fifteenth century which he had seen and admired in Venice – he has not copied it, but he has adopted its style. Take that chalice, *amigo*" – the General raised the heavy cup and placed it in Taylor's hands – "see the grace and simplicity of the design of angels' heads on an enamelled ground around the bottom of the cup-part of the thing, and then for contrast

201

the complexity of the scheme of little niches containing enamelled and jewelled figures of the holy ones which goes round the middle of the stem – "

"The knop," interrupted Taylor.

There was a brief silence.

"I beg your pardon, my dear Taylor," the General then said in a tone of anxious courtesy. "Did you say something?"

Taylor was staring at the vessel in his hand. He said, "That part of the chalice, the place where you take hold of the stem, is called the knop. It is usually ornamented more or less, but seldom with such magnificent workmanship as this, I should think. And I would say the same of these six figures and designs on the lobes of the foot."

General de la Costa, his hands on his hips, regarded Taylor for some moments in silence. Then he said, "Do you know, *amigo*, you are always taking me by surprise just now? This sort of thing" – he waved a hand over the treasures assembled on the table – "is the last in the world which I should have imagined you would know much about. And here you are, giving me an instructive talk about knops. Now do not think, my dear Taylor, that I am trying to be funny. It is clear that you really do know about these things, much more than I do. So I ask you, what do you think about that as a Gospel Book?"

He lifted from the table a volume of quarto size, hardly recognisable as a book, so enriched its upper cover was with flat-cut precious stones of many hues. "My friend Michaud," he said, "got the general idea of this ornamentation – the cover overlaid with gold enriched with *cloisonné* enamels and jewels – from a Gospel Book which used to be in the possession of King Charles the Bald, the grandson of Charlemagne. It can be seen today in the National Library in Paris, I am told. Well, Charles the Bald reigned about eleven hundred years ago, and this book is about eleven hundred times as splendid as his book was. That blue diamond above the figure of Christ is unique, so Mendoza has assured me. The paper of the book is of a quality that is very seldom made – I left that matter to Pallingswick, the man who runs the Monboddo Press, which did the printing for me. He says that this paper will last as long as the human race, if they give it a chance – perhaps he exaggerates a little, but it is really good paper. Look at it yourself, my dear Taylor, and look at that wonderful printing – there is nothing better in that line to be had in the world."

Taylor, sitting on an arm of the chair at the end of the table, turned the pages of the book which the General had placed before him. He said again, in a low voice, "I feel as if I were in a dream."

"I shall leave the altar cross and candlesticks at this end of the table," the General said. "The cross and candlesticks in the Cathedral in Manoa, the capital of my own country, are famous, but these are much more beautiful. I place next to them the chalice and the paten – it is a simple thing, that paten, but look at the engraving! Then the cruets – what a graceful pair! Pure gold is a wonderful material, *amigo*, it has a peculiar beauty of its own, quite apart from its value as a rare metal. If it were as common as iron, those cruets would make the same effect. The middle of the table we will reserve for the best thing of all, according to my judgment" – he produced it from a nest of tissue paper in a large cardboard box.

"This," he said, "is a mitre for the use of the Bishop and his successors on occasions when the wearing of a very splendid mitre is the correct thing. As you see, it is not so tall as the mitre of that class usually is, but this more compact form is a recognised variety. Michaud tells me all this, and it was his idea to have the mitre made of ivory and gold, with the ornamentation of sapphires only. I think it will look very well indeed when it is worn. Come, my dear Taylor, you have a good head, let us try it – the satin cap inside, with the silk lining, will make it easy to fit on, I should think. Do not hesitate, after all it is still my property, it is not consecrated yet." He gently pressed the mitre down upon Taylor's brows.

"It suits you perfectly," General de la Costa said. "But no, I see you have a sentiment against wearing it." For Taylor, after a glance at himself in the mirror that hung close at hand, had risen hastily to his feet and placed the mitre with the other treasures on the table; then returned to the armchair and covered his face with his hands.

The General, not observing this sign of agitation, was still feasting his eyes on the handiwork of M. Calixte Michaud. "I shall just have to leave them where they are," he said, "along with this letter to the Treasurer of the Cathedral explaining that they are given in memory of Donna Maria Beatrice de la Costa, who never forgot the church of her girlhood. There is more in the letter than that, of course, I took trouble in writing it, but it is unsigned, and the Dean and Chapter may make what they can of it. I wish that I could lock these things away. They are not likely to be stolen, but after all there is a safe here for the altar plate, even if it is a safe that a good burglar would open by merely blowing on it. I am no good at opening safes, even the easiest – it is a pity."

Taylor, who by this time seemed to have mastered his feelings, though his face was very pale, put his hand in a trouser pocket. "Do not let that weigh on your mind, General," he said, holding out a bunch of keys. "There is a key here – this one – which opens that safe."

CHAPTER XXIII

At these words General de la Costa turned swiftly from his fond contemplation of the chalice, which he was holding in one hand while he caressed it gently with the other. He restored the vessel to its place on the table, then said, "My ears have never deceived me before. Do you really tell me, *amigo*, that the key which you are holding out to me is the key of the safe in this sacristy? I do not want to speak too strongly, because that would be against my rule, but the thing is impossible."

"It is one of three keys that I know of which fit the lock of that safe," the man who had lost his memory said with a pleasant smile. He tossed the bunch of keys on the table, and leant back in the armchair in an attitude of relaxation and contentment which made him seem a different and a larger man.

The General came to him and gently laid a hand on his shoulder. "I think perhaps you are not quite yourself, my dear Taylor."

"But I am quite myself General, that is just what I am – I am myself at last. And I am not your dear Taylor, or anyone else's dear Taylor. My name is Severn – but still I am yours, General, after all that you and your friends have done for me while I was Taylor."

"Do you mean," the General asked, pressing more urgently on the other's shoulder, "that your memory trouble is at an end, that you now know all about your past life, that you are just as you were when you entered that train which was wrecked at Molesworth? Why, it seems too good to be true."

"But it is true, General – no mistake about it. My life has been restored to me, thank God!"

General de la Costa seized Severn's hands in his and shook them vigorously. "What a moment!" he exclaimed. "I have tried to picture to myself how it would feel to me if I had most of my experience wiped out since the age of boyhood, and I must say I think it would be undiluted hell. But getting it all back again suddenly would give me quite a jar. You are sure you have the whole thing back again? And you are not feeling shaken at all? No? *Entonces*, you are of the kind that I admire, you have stood up to hell and did not let it throw you. You are a strong man, I have often thought so during these days when we did not know with any certainty what sort of man you really were. Severn, you said? It is a nice name, my dear Severn, but I shall always think of the old Taylor who made himself so very useful in the battle in Mrs McBean's kitchen. Our doctor and I, talking it over, have agreed that your conduct then was what might have been expected, as a sort of reflex action, without your ever knowing at the time that you had been a professional strong-arm guy. But now you remember the whole thing, and it all joins up, does it? As I said, *amigo*, it seems too good to be true – " Here the General paused, and his expression was clouded by something which might almost have been taken for embarrassment.

"What were you going to say, General?" Severn asked.

"Why, I was going to say," the General said, "that I have never been so very sure that your past life before you got into that train at Southampton would be an altogether pleasant one to remember, after enjoying life so much as you seemed to do in our little circle at Mewstone."

The man called Severn smiled happily. "I assure you, General, that having got my wits back does seem good to me. In fact, I have never in my life had such a feeling of relief, although I have been through some pretty anxious moments in my time."

"*Indudiablemente*, it was a part of your life to go through pretty anxious moments," the General said. "It is one of the things which we have in common. To take the most evident thing first, you are now – that is, you have become lately – a good specimen of the *genus homo*, as I have always been. You are as healthy and strong as they come, and tonight you look fitter than ever. Another thing is that you have no objection to being in a spot from time to time, you cannot be frightened."

"Well, I can be frightened and, very thoroughly frightened, I can tell you that," Severn said, smoothing his chin. "Perhaps you would be ashamed of it, General, but I'm not. For a few moments before that train was derailed at Molesworth, I was quite demoralised with fear – really, I can't describe it, or I won't anyhow. If it hadn't been over in a matter of seconds, I should have fainted from fear, I believe. But to go back to what you were saying just now, about my past life, I mean – I must tell you that you have got quite a wrong idea about it, it has not been so bad as you imagine."

The General rubbed his chin doubtfully. "It was not for me to judge you, my dear Severn. Besides, these things are relative, your standard of badness is probably a very high one now that you have got your memory back again. And anyway, Farewell Billy in writing to me about you never mentioned anything that you had actually done. Why not dismiss the matter from your mind?"

"I can't do that very well," Severn said. "You see, General, it is not a question of anything told you by your friend Farewell Billy. I haven't had time yet to make out how the mistake can have arisen, but it is certain that both you and Dr Barlow have been confusing me with someone else, right from the beginning."

General de la Costa, standing above Severn as he sat in the armchair, heard this with a stare of blank incredulity. There was silence for a moment, then he took up his familiar pose astride a chair and said, "You do not realise, perhaps, *amigo*, how difficult it is to take in what you are telling me. You are quite sure that your mind is absolutely clear? Forgive me for asking such a question, but the reasons we had for believing about you what we did believe were quite convincing reasons. It has never occurred to our doctor or to me that there was room for any doubt."

"Well, I'll tell you one thing to begin with," Severn said. "I don't know if it makes a lot of difference, but I never did get into that train at Southampton, as you said just now that I had done. I have not been in Southampton for years. I got into that train at Bridlemere, which is a long way up the line from Southampton. I have a cottage at Bridlemere, not far from the station, and I took the train to Molesworth, where I had arranged to play a round at the golf-club with a friend. Then, while the train was in the station, an elephant in a car on the other line stretched over and began interfering with our engine with his trunk, and the next thing I knew we were rushing along to death and destruction. As I told you, I have never been so terrified in my life. I have seen some fairly violent active service in the Army, I have been shot and knifed, knocked out a few times, but that was the first time I ever remember feeling frightened. So there you are – that's the whole story, as far as I am concerned, I was a simple, harmless railway passenger with a short-distance ticket. I hadn't got a passport, I never even heard of Farewell Billy. I had never carried a revolver since my Army days. In short, General, when you and Dr Barlow rescued me from that train smash, you rescued the wrong man."

The General, who had not taken his eyes from Severn's face during this speech, now sighed regretfully. "I can see that what you have told me is the simple truth," he said. "It is a pity. I do not mean, my dear Severn, that it is a pity we picked you out of the wreck and patched you up. I mean that it is a pity we had no way of knowing the truth, it is a pity that we were so completely misled. Listen, *amigo*, I had made arrangements for the man we were expecting to be in that particular compartment of that particular coach of the train. We went directly to that compartment when the smash happened, we found there one man, who had with him a forged passport and a gun with a holster. I do not think we can be blamed for leaping to the conclusion that you were our man, who as we knew would be provided with exactly those conveniences of travel. It is clear to me now that you were the wrong man, as you tell me, and that the right man was your fellow-traveller in that compartment. Do not say that you had no fellow-traveller, or I shall know that I am mad." Here the General illustratively rumpled his hair with both hands, and assumed a tragic stare.

Severn slapped the table. "Of course there was another man with me in the compartment! I had forgotten his existence till this moment. He was in the train when I got into it, he was sitting in a corner seat next to the corridor, with a large suitcase beside him. When the elephant started our train, I had my head out of the window, watching what was going on. When I drew my head in again, to get ready for the smash, I had forgotten all about my fellow-traveller, and I have only now remembered him for the first time. But he had certainly disappeared from the place where he had been sitting – I was entirely alone."

General de la Costa nodded a nod of perfect comprehension. "This makes the whole thing clear, especially to anyone like myself who has had experience of disappearing from difficult situations. May I hear more of this fellow-traveller? What was his appearance? Did you speak?"

Severn considered for a few moments. "One thing that struck me was that he was very carefully dressed, and his clothes looked new. He spoke a little like an American, but not much. As for his face, he looked like a youngish man – difficult to guess what age, because his face was completely expressionless. And yet at the same time, it was a terrifying face – I don't know why it was, but it just was. It made my blood run cold, as the saying is. I didn't mind having my blood run cold – in fact I rather liked the sensation, as it never occurred to me that the man was dangerous to me personally. I felt like a looker-on. But the moment I set eyes on him I thought to myself, I shouldn't like to have that man for an enemy, I shouldn't like to feel he was hunting me down. Perfect ruthlessness, General – that was the idea he gave me. Some people give out an impression without anything in their looks to support it, don't you think?"

"Yes, I think so, I have met with a few cases, and all of them were bad," the General said. "But I must compliment you, my dear Severn, you are a great hand at a description. Because that man in the compartment with you was certainly the man I was expecting. Your account of him convinces me. I do not know that I have actually met him, but I have known the type, and it was one of that type that Farewell Billy had sent to me. That man is known to the criminal world in New York and other places by the simplest of names. They call him the Chill – just that. I suppose Farewell Billy knows what his proper name is, though I would not bet on it, but all he told me about our vanishing friend is that he is addressed as Nick, and known as Nick the Chill, or more usually as the Chill simply. I believe that he was, or had been, Farewell Billy's trigger-man. Now can you remember any conversation that you had with the Chill, especially anything which might make him think that doing a disappearing act while you were leaning out of the window would be a good idea?"

Severn threw himself back in his chair and stared up at the light in the ceiling. "I can remember something," he said, "but it wasn't anything said by this man himself. Before the elephant began being tiresome, the guard of the train looked in to pass the time of day with me, and he mentioned that there were two police officers on the train who were on the look-out for somebody who had crossed from New York to Southampton with a forged passport. That tells you what you want to know, I should think."

"It tells me the whole thing, from beginning to end," the General said joyfully, opening his arms to their full extent. "I can see what happened, my dear Severn, as well as if I had been sitting at your side in that train. The Chill knew exactly what he had to do as soon as your railway-guard had spoken. He had to take the first chance of getting rid of his passport and his revolver, in fact he had to make a chance if necessary. He could not just step into the corridor and toss them out of the window, a dozen people might have seen him doing it. That made the situation a dangerous one for you, I should say. But it is evident from what you tell me that your elephant had the sagacity to intervene at the right moment. You know where your passport and your gun were found when our doctor climbed in to examine your remains?"

"Yes," Severn said. "He said he found them in the pockets of my raincoat, which was lying close to what you call my remains."

"Do not be offended, my dear Severn, if I make use of that convenient expression," the General said. "Your face tells me you are not that goddam nuisance, an easily offended man, and I can assure you that when we looked down through that smashed-up window into the place

211

where you were lying, you looked dead enough to satisfy the most exacting taste. You had bled over everything, including your raincoat, which had also got mixed up with a twisted metal bar from the luggage rack. Well, Nick the Chill probably acted very swiftly when you got up and craned out of the window. If it were myself, I should consider thirty seconds a generous allowance of time for unstrapping my holster, fishing out my passport, and planting both of them in the pockets of a raincoat belonging to somebody else. When that was done, all he had left to do was to grab up the suitcase which you say he had with him, and move quietly along the corridor into another compartment as if he had just boarded the train." Here the General burst into one of his formidable explosions of laughter; then went on, unaffectedly wiping his eyes, "The situation was handed to the Chill, as they used to say in his part of the world, on a platter, with parsley round it."

Severn nodded. "It must have been just as you say, of course. But there's one thing you have forgotten."

"Do not make fun of me, *amigo*," the General said, with a wry smile. "I have never liked to have anybody ribbing me, it is one of my weaknesses, though I often have to put up with it from my English and American friends. It is a social custom which makes a bad impression on any one of my race. It is true, I know, that I was not actually present when these things were done, but what I have said must be a pretty good guess. What is it that I have, as you put it, forgotten?"

"Well, let us say that you did not realise," Severn said, "that Nick the Chill changed hats with me before he vanished. The hat which Dr Barlow found in the rack, above my remains, was not my hat. I know now that I never bought such a hat in my life. It is nothing like the shape of my ordinary hats, and the hat I was wearing that day, for playing golf, was a very light, cheap unlined felt hat. Well, the hat which Dr Barlow rescued along with me was an obviously expensive kind of hat with a lining. It was not a black hat, as all my hats are, but a light brown, and it was made, according to the imprint in the lining, by somebody called Stetson, who made his hats in Philadelphia."

"I have heard of him and his hats," the General said with a smile. "Everybody in the United States has heard of them."

"Of course, I assumed that it was my hat when I was told where it had been found," Severn went on. "I looked at it quite carefully that evening at Mrs McBean's place, and I could see that, together with my passport, it made it certain that I had come from the United States. But I never put it on, because of the bandages, and when we made our escape after that free fight in the kitchen I left the hat behind. But I remember it perfectly well, and I can see now that it was no hat of mine. I got myself a hat, with Mrs Fielding's assistance, the first day I went out in Mewstone."

"It was rather rash," the General remarked, "to take her advice about it, I think. With her fondness for tomfoolery, she was quite capable of making you get a cowboy's ten-gallon hat, or an admiral's cocked hat, or a bishop's hat."

"Well, she wouldn't have made me get a bishop's hat," Severn said reflectively. "She must know that you can only wear the hat with the rest of the outfit, and she is too kind-hearted to have wanted me to make a guy of myself. Besides, bishop's hats are not to be bought at any ordinary hat-shop. I know all about getting bishop's hats."

General de la Costa rose to lay his hand once more on the other's shoulder. "Severn, my dear friend, do you know what you are saying? I am afraid this coming out of your amnesia has been too much for you. I wish to God we had our doctor here. I am so like any other man without medical training, I do not know what to do. Perhaps I should leave all these things here where they are, and get you home again. I have written this letter to the Treasurer which tells the story. Come now, *amigo*, will you take my arm, and let us make our way back to where the car is waiting for us." The General hesitated. "Do you not think, my dear Severn, that a little telque would be a good thing? Here is a bottle of water and a glass on the table, and in my pocket is the telque. It is an excellent restorative."

Severn laughed happily. "I do not need any restorative, General, I never felt better in my life. Ever since I tried on that beautiful mitre of yours, I have known all about myself. I have known that I was not Farewell Billy's trigger-man, I have known that I was the Bishop of Glasminster."

CHAPTER XXIV

General de la Costa fell back upon his chair with his arms hanging in an attitude of helplessness.

"I am not mad," he declared positively. "I do not feel mad, and" – he directed a glance at the large mirror on the wall – "I do not look mad. And yet, my dear Severn, you look as perfectly sane and collected as I do – if anything more so, because I admit to having an expression of some slight surprise, due to your tearing off a succession of the most incredible statements without batting an eyelid, in fact getting more and more calm and self-assured all the time."

Here the General sat up straight, and began telling off his points on the fingers of one hand. "Come, let us check it. To begin with, you tell me you were not the man who would be coming in that compartment of that train, although you were the only man in it when it was wrecked, and you had with you all the things which he did have, and which we were told he would have, and which nobody else in the world would have had. All right; then it seems that you never even came over from New York at all, but were on your way from your simple country cottage to a harmless game of golf in beautiful surroundings. And then – then, *amigo*, I am told that an elephant intervened in the proceedings and caused a serious railway disaster, and supplied you with the opportunity of getting the

215

incriminating evidence planted on you, besides giving the Chill the chance he wanted for a nice getaway. Just imagine it – an elephant! Believe me, my dear Severn, for my own peace of mind I would much rather he had been a tortoise. Still I swallowed him, trunk and tusks and everything, and going on from there I have lived with you day by day, gratefully accepting your help in the purpose which lies nearest to my heart, when quite suddenly, in this sacristy, you tell me that, in the first place, you are an expert in the buying of hats for bishops, and then that you are yourself the Bishop of Glasminster. That is all that we have had so far," the General said patiently, his hands again hanging at his sides. "Perhaps it is enough to be going on with, because it is the sort of statement which, as you will agree, needs a little expanding. I have always regarded you as a truthful man, because you made a good impression on me, and men who are not truthful never do that. But as regards that last assertion of yours, all that I can say is that if it is not a lie, it will do until a lie comes along. How, my dear Severn, how can you sit there and tell me that you are the Bishop of Glasminster?"

"I am sorry, General, if I made it too much of a shock," Severn said.

"But I do not object to shocks, I like shocks," General de la Costa said with outspread palms. "All I ask, *amigo*, is that the thing should not be too utterly incredible. That is not too much to ask, I hope."

Severn looked at the General with that expression of settled and humorous self-possession which had grown upon him since he had removed the new mitre of gold and ivory from his brows and placed it on the table. "Well, General," he said, "I will try to make it credible, although I admit that it is rather unusual. I sit here, as you express it, and tell you that I am the Bishop of Glasminster. Well, this is where the Bishop of Glasminster usually does sit in this sacristy. And then you have perhaps forgotten that, when we began this unravelling of the difficulties caused by my not being Farewell Billy's private assassin, I threw a bunch of keys on this table, one of them being the key of that safe. I said so at the time. There is the bunch of keys still on the table. That long, thin key is the key in question. If you will place it in the lock and turn it, I prophecy that you will find in the safe as much of the altar plate of this Cathedral as was left after the great pillage, together with other objects which have been added to it by the piety of benefactors in more recent times."

Slowly, as if hypnotised, General de la Costa rose to his feet and took the keys from the table. "Perhaps, *amigo*, I shall also find your own mitre," he said over his shoulder as he turned towards the safe. "Will you describe it to me beforehand? – then I shall know that there are no delusions at work."

Severn shook his head regretfully. "You will not find my own mitre in the safe, General, because that and my cope are kept in a specially-constructed suitcase, such as bishops usually have – we have always a lot of travelling about to do in the work of a diocese. That case is, or should be, locked up in my wardrobe at the Palace, not far from here. But I can tell you a few things which you will find in the safe, to show that you are not being deceived. There should be on the top shelf a stout leather-backed account book, with a card stuck in it for a book-marker showing a reproduction in colour of one of the stained-glass windows in Chartres Cathedral, a thirteenth-century Crucifixion, which I bought when I was there. Beside that there ought to be a tin containing dry biscuits – unless the Dean has finished them up since I was here last. Then there are some letters kept together by a rubber band, and some packets of stationery, and a half-full bottle of fountain-pen ink, the kind that you can stand up on one side when it begins to get low, and there is a ragged old handkerchief which I keep by the ink-pot to wipe the nib when I fill the pen."

"We have much in common, my dear Severn, I have always felt that," the General said. "That business of filling your own pen and cleaning the nib yourself, when you had canons and chaplains and archdeacons and churchwardens and acolytes by the dozen, to say nothing at all of the sacristan, falling over each other to make themselves useful, is just my style. It has always been my motto – the only orders which you can be quite sure of having carried out properly are the orders which you give to yourself."

As he talked, the General had taken up the bunch of keys, and placed the long, thin key in the lock. It turned easily, and the heavy door swung open. General de la Costa, having run his eye over the contents of the safe, turned to Severn with an inclination of the head.

"Everything is exactly as you have told me, *amigo*," he said. "The altar plate is all present and correct. The various objects which you said would be on the top shelf are actually on that shelf, including the biscuit-tin." He stretched a long arm into the safe and produced the tin, which he shook experimentally. "You hear, my dear Severn – there must be quite a few biscuits inside, the Dean has not taken advantage of your absence, he is a better man than you supposed. Well, then, you have proved to me the truth of your story. I ask your pardon for having doubted it."

Severn rose from his chair. "Why should you apologise?" he said. "Nobody but a born fool could have believed my story without evidence in support of it." He joined the General at the open door of the safe. "Yes, everything is here, just as it was when I was here last. Fortunately it is a large deep safe, and we shall easily be able to find room for all the articles of your most munificent gift, General. We can clear out almost everything from the top shelf and put it all on the table, there is nothing but the account-book that ought to be under lock and key. The Gospel Book could go there, lying on its side, and also that wonderful mitre, being of the convenient shape that it is, and the two cruets are not too tall to go there too, I think."

Severn leaned forward and began to clear the top shelf of the safe. As he removed the biscuit-tin he took off the lid. "Will you have a water-biscuit, General?" he said. "I'm going to. It is not much of a return for your generous hospitality, but I shall be able to do better than a biscuit for you when all this trouble is straightened out."

"A thousand thanks, not for me," the General said, as he lifted the Gospel Book to its place on the shelf. "When we have finished this job, I shall take you back to Mewstone *muy pronto*. There is nothing more to be done here, when I have placed my letter to the Treasurer among the other things, and the safe has been locked." As he spoke he fitted the altar-cross, the candlesticks and the chalice and paten into the body of the safe. "There, my dear Severn, the thing is done, if you will have the goodness to turn the key and remove it. This is a better conclusion to my plan than I ever imagined – how I would love to see the face of the person who is the next to open this safe."

"The Dean and the Treasurer have the other two keys," Severn said. "It might be either of them, or some other member of the Chapter who has been entrusted with one of the keys. Whoever it is, this will certainly be one of the major surprises of his life, I can safely promise you that, General. According to Mrs Fielding you are fond of surprising people."

As Severn pocketed his bunch of keys, General de la Costa produced his flask. "With your permission, *amigo*," he said, reaching for the glass on the table. "It is my custom to celebrate any success with a drink of telque, and this is certainly an occasion for it. Yes, I confess to you that surprising people is one of my pleasures, but it is not a pleasure that does them any harm, unless they have the misfortune to be my enemies." The General laughed loudly. "My pious gift to Glasminster Cathedral found locked up in the Cathedral safe – *Hijo de Dios*! I have never done anything better, thanks to the happy accident of your turning out to be the Bishop. And now I think we should be on our way. You must come back to our place, as I said, for a night's rest before you return to life in the eyes of the world."

"Yes, I think I should, if you ask me," Severn said. "Or if you order me to do so as your salaried aide-de-camp. For one thing, everyone at my own place is in bed and asleep, and I should get myself disliked if I came home at this hour. More important is my obligation to the Fieldings, to explain myself to them and take leave of them properly, instead of sneaking off to my Palace as soon as I realised that I had one. So if we're both ready, let's be off."

"That's the talk!" exclaimed General de la Costa. "Have you got your torch ready, *amigo*?" He opened the door of the sacristy. "This time you shall lead the way, as it is your Cathedral."

Severn did so, with a light and confident step, and they returned to the door in the south transept in much less time than it had taken to cover the distance before. The General's massive key was produced and Severn stepped out into the small porch.

"I shall never need this key again," the General said, as he locked the door behind them. "I did think of leaving it in the keyhole, just to give my uncle the Canon something to think about – his house is quite near this door of the Cathedral, and he enters it by this door as often as not, so he told me. But I think it will be better to take the key away, so that there will be no trace whatever of our coming and going, and the mystery of the getting of my donation into the locked safe in the sacristy will be well rounded off. Now, my dear Severn, I expect you know the way to the street."

"I have hardly ever made use of this way out of the Close," Severn said, fingering his chin. "The Palace is right the other end of it, but I think this pavement runs directly to the street."

"Yes, where the lamp is burning just above the entry. Though the night is so delightfully black," the General said, "you can see the spark of that lamp, and we have only to make a beeline for it. So we can do without our torches, we shall not speak, and our shoes are noiseless. We shall disappear in style. If there is anybody about in the street when we get there, it will not matter very much, because Gunn has orders to run the car up to the lamp the moment he sees us come out underneath it. Besides, we are doing no wrong. If a bishop may not walk out of his own Cathedral precincts, whose Cathedral precincts may he walk out of?"

But it happened that, at two o'clock in the morning, there was nobody about in the street.

CHAPTER XXV

As the car rushed through the darkness, both its occupants lay back in their corners, and for some time there was silence between them.

"What a marvellous night it has been for both of us," the General said at last, laying his hand on Severn's knee. "For you there has been the rolling away of the cloud that had shut you off from the knowledge of almost all your own past life, you are once more a complete personality. What a grand experience! What a blessed relief! For some time past the cloud has been wearing thin, as our doctor says, and now in your own Cathedral, something has happened to burst up the whole caboodle."

Severn laughed aloud. The General's words had hit off very happily the emotions of joy and thankfulness that possessed him. "I can tell you what burst it up," he said. "It was your coming to me with a mitre and pressing it upon my head. The last time that happened to me was when I was consecrated two years ago. Tonight, when I felt it on my head and caught a glimpse of myself in the glass, I was myself again in an instant – like switching on a light in a dark room."

"And it was a wonderful time for me also," the General said. "It was not of the same order of feeling as yours, I realise that very well, but it was glorious enough – the triumphant finish of an undertaking that had occupied my mind for years, with all its complications and difficulties, and with the new details always being added. And it was you, *amigo*, who helped me to the magnificent finishing touch of leaving all the new treasures of the altar inside the Cathedral's own locked-up safe. It was the perfect climax, and I am deeply indebted to you."

"All I did was to take a bunch of keys out of my pocket," Severn said. "You and the doctor did rather more than that for me."

"Ah well, have it your way," the General said lightly. "If you insist on being reasonable, my dear Severn, there is another way of doing me a great favour. Will you allow me to put a few personal questions about yourself as you were at the time before that smash-up at Molesworth? These things which puzzle me will not be any more easily understood by the other friends you have made in the past few weeks."

"Certainly I will answer anything you ask me. There isn't anything I want to hold back," Severn said.

General de la Costa turned half round so as to look him in the face, then tapped himself smartly on the chest. "Would you say, *amigo*, that I look like a soldier, or as if I had been a soldier?"

"Why, yes, very much so," Severn said. "The first time I set eyes on you, at Mrs McBean's place, and before I heard your rank mentioned, I thought you were a soldier, or had been one, as you say. You have what is called a military bearing, you have the air of a soldier. Is that what you wanted to know?"

"Yes, I suppose I have that sort of appearance," the General said. "Most of the men in my country have it, for they have all done, like me, their three years' national service, and it is only the youngest and the oldest who did not fight in our war with Riesgador. And an officer, of course, besides being a drilled man, has his pride."

ı't all your countrymen proud?" Severn wanted

ıe that nobody in Peligragua is short of pride," ıl admitted, "but the officers have more, and in them, in fact, it is too often excessive. More than once in my army career I have had to let some of the pride out of an officer whose manner annoyed me. But what I was going to say, my dear Severn, is that you have yourself a military bearing. I noticed that at a very early stage in our acquaintance – in fact, on that first evening at Abbot's Dean. I could see that you had been trained to carry yourself properly, and later in the evening, when we had to deal with Ketch's lot in the kitchen, I thought that you must have had experience of fighting at close quarters. A man of peace, you see, may get into a fight and may do his best, but if he is just a beginner half his blows never get home, he does not know where to land them or how to put his weight behind his punches. But in that scrap, *amigo*, though I was quite closely occupied at the time, it seemed to me that you never wasted an ounce, and our doctor afterwards said to me just the same. He warned me, though, not to speak of this to you, because of his idea that you should not be worried about your past life, and I think he was quite right, at that. Then afterwards, at Keith House, Diana said to me that she felt sure you had been a soldier."

"She said something of the sort to me," Severn said, "but she didn't press me about it – perhaps she remembered that I was not to be questioned. But now, General, I will tell you the simple facts. Before I left school I had got to be quite good at boxing – I think I told you that once before – and I kept it up afterwards, at Cambridge and in the Army."

General de la Costa snapped his fingers triumphantly. "I knew it!" he exclaimed. "You were an officer like myself."

"Yes, for three years I served in the Coldstream," Severn answered. "When the war came along I left the University and qualified for a commission. I found that I liked soldiering, and as for what we were fighting for, I was only too glad to have a hand in it in spite of all the muddle and misery. But I had always meant to go into the Church, I knew it was what I was intended for, and as soon as I could get out of the Army I went back to preparing myself for the ministry. I was ordained when I was twenty-five, I became a curate in North London, after that I was vicar in three places where there was plenty of hard work to be done, and I was a bishop at forty-nine. There you have the bare bones of my record."

The General nodded. "They are very bare. You must have been very active in the affairs of the Church, you must have earned a great reputation. And here you are, after all those years, still looking like a soldier."

"Well, I am feeling like one, if it comes to that," Severn said, rubbing his chin. "In clerical life there is always something to be conquered – difficulties of one sort or another. If you ignore them or dodge them, you get nowhere."

"And if you do not ignore or dodge, you get to a bishopric and a seat in the House of Lords. Yes, I understand that," the General said. "May I put to you another question? When we picked you out of the train wreck at Molesworth you were wearing a blue jacket and grey flannels and an open-necked shirt – at least, you were wearing the remains of that costume. I thought it was a strange one for a New York gunman, because gangsters are very snappy dressers as a rule, but you had the passport and the gun and the hat, and they settled it. But was it not an even stranger costume for the Bishop of Glasminster?"

"You remind me," Severn said, "of the time, long ago, when I was rather surprised to see Dr Winnington Ingram, the Bishop of London, playing a round in exactly that get-up. I had finished my own game, which I had played in black clothes and a dog-collar, and as it was a very warm day I determined on the spot that I would follow his example for the future. As he was my own Bishop at the time, I considered it was my duty to do so, and I have done so ever since. Does that set your mind at rest?"

"Completely at rest, my dear Severn. Anything is easy to believe, when one has accepted the fact that you, once a Guards officer, are today Bishop of Glasminster."

"But really, there is nothing so very incredible in that," Severn said. "If it had been your business to keep an eye on our Church affairs, you would know that there have been in recent years a number of cases of officers leaving the Army to do as I did, and I am not the only one who has been advanced to a bishopric."

"I am delighted to hear it. The more the merrier, as you say," General de la Costa yawned cavernously. "I hope you will pardon my being drowsy, my dear Severn, the excitement of this day, or rather this night, has made me a little tired. Ah! You are yawning also. The best thing for both of us will be to fall asleep."

Severn was awakened by a hand on his shoulder. The car was slowing down, and the General was lighting a cigarette. "We are stopping," he said, "just at the point where we entered the car. For you the world is changed since then, and I – I have fulfilled a vow. It was a memorable journey." He opened the door and stepped out, followed by Severn. "Thank you, Gunn. It was all very well done."

The driver turned a satisfied face towards them. "It's always a pleasure," he said. "Guv'ner," he added, "there's something Newlove asked me to pass on to you. He 'phoned me about it just before I started on this journey. You remember the bloke you gave a thrashing to, soon after you took on me and Newlove. Cowdery, the name was."

"You are right, Gunn, that was the name," the General said. "What has he been doing? Or has somebody been doing something to him? I should be glad to hear of that, I do not claim a monopoly in the business of doing things to Cowdery."

"Nobody won't do anything more to him," Gunn replied. "Newlove said he had just heard as Cowdery had been killed instantly, running his car smack into a tree near his place in Surrey. Newlove's petrol station is close by the spot."

General de la Costa stood in silence for a few moments, then shrugged his shoulders lightly. "Very well, Gunn. Will you let Newlove know I am obliged to him for putting me wise so quickly? And now, on your way."

The car rolled off, and the General, with a hand on Severn's arm, began slowly to traverse the short distance that led to the side entrance of Keith House.

"If this news is confirmed, it alters the arrangement of my life," he said thoughtfully. "You see that, do you not, *amigo*?"

"You mean that Ketch and his gang were being paid by that man Cowdery," Severn answered. "Yes, if that was the case, it ought to mean that they will give you no more trouble. They have had enough proof that you are a dangerous man to tackle, and I don't suppose they will go on trying just for the fun of the thing."

General de la Costa waved a hand lightly. "No doubt you are right in thinking they will lay off snatching me, as soon as they hear this news. But there is another thing which to me is more important. You remember that the disagreement between the police and myself arose out of my taking no notice of a summons to appear and answer to a charge of assault brought by this man Cowdery. Well, my dear Severn, no man can bring that charge except Cowdery himself, because there was no other person present when he was assaulted – on both occasions he was the only witness. So now there is no charge for me to answer, and the police have no longer any interest in me as a fugitive from justice."

"Good!" Severn exclaimed. "Then you are a free man again, unless you are threatened by some other enemies I haven't heard about. You can go about openly, live where you like and go where you like without any precautions. I congratulate you, General."

Once more the General shrugged his shoulders. "I thank you, *amigo*. I suppose this new state of things is, as you say, good, it must mean for me a change of interest at least. But I will confess to you that I shall miss the way of life in which you have seen me until now. For nearly three years it has kept me on my toes, as you say, always sharp and watchful. It has suited me. Ah, well, never mind, one can always make new opportunities. And here we are at the corner of Keith House. Only think, my dear Severn, of the amazement of our friends when they hear at breakfast-time that they have been entertaining an angel unawares – or a bishop, which is practically the same thing. For the present, remember that we must not make a sound."

CHAPTER XXVI

When Severn awoke next morning from a sound sleep it was with a lightness of heart such as he had not known, he told himself, since boyhood. He had gone to bed happy and tired, this morning he was happy and fresh. It was going to be no easy task taking up the threads of his life where they had been broken; the threads were so many, and some of them were so hard to handle. But he felt equal to all that, equal to anything, this morning, with the rays of the sun making a broken pattern on the floor just beneath the drawn curtains.

He took the watch from beneath his pillow and pressed, as Lem had taught him, the left paw of Tchin-teh. The light pouring from the image's hideous jaws showed that the hour was twenty minutes to nine. He pressed the other paw and lay on his back, giving himself up to thanksgiving and meditation.

At last there was a gentle knock, and Lem appeared with the tea-tray. As he placed it by the bed with his usual greeting he added, as he went to draw the curtains, "I think master coming."

As Lem withdrew, Arnold Fielding announced himself with his usual appearance of shyness. "I thought," he said, "I would like to see if all was well with you after your adventures in the small hours. But I needn't have worried – I have never seen you look so well and happy."

"And I never have been, under your roof," Severn rejoined. "I should think I must look like a different man. Can you guess what happened to me during those small hours?"

A delighted smile lightened up Fielding's pink face. "Why, yes, perhaps I *can* guess. When Barlow was here last he told us of something that was likely to happen at any moment. Was that it? Have you recovered your memory?"

"That's it," Severn answered. "The cloud is entirely gone, not a trace of the trouble is left." He finished a cup of tea.

"What a deliverance!" Fielding exclaimed. He stretched out a hand, and exchanged with Severn a cordial grasp. "Justo, you know, had the idea that when this happened you would get a disagreeable shock. Well, one look at your face is enough to dispose of that. He seemed to think you had been some sort of bad character. Of course, that made us think so too."

Severn laughed. "It isn't for me," he said, "to give myself a certificate of character. But I can tell you what I have been and what I still am. I must warn you that you will find it hard to believe, or even impossible, but I assure you it is perfectly true. I am a bishop."

"Just so," Fielding answered unemotionally. "Do you mind if I sit on the side of the bed? Let me pour out another cup of tea for you. A bishop, yes."

Two faint perpendicular lines appeared between Severn's eyebrows. "I can see you think I have gone out of my mind, you sound as if you were trying to humour me. Well, I'm not surprised at that, but I can only go on telling you it's perfectly true. I actually am a bishop."

"Of course you are," Fielding agreed. "Bishop of Glasminster. This is a great honour for us."

Severn stared at him. "What a let-down!" he gasped. "How on earth did you know? But yes – of course. You have been talking to General de la Costa."

"Not a bit of it," Fielding protested. "When I passed his door just now he was snoring loudly. Lem has just gone in to wake him. No, I didn't hear of it from him. I heard of it last night. In fact, I heard of it before you and Justo left the house. And who do you think told me?"

Severn rubbed his chin in bewilderment. "This is beyond me," he said.

"It's simple enough," Fielding told him. "It was the boys who gave you away. Did you notice how they stared at you all through dinner? Well, they had recognised you the moment they saw you. When they were told you were a friend of Justo's from America, and when they heard us calling you Taylor, they didn't know what to think. I'll tell you what happened as soon as you and Justo had gone up to your rooms to get ready for your outing. Diana went up to the boys' room to see if they had settled down to sleep, and found them waiting for her – they wanted an explanation, because they were perfectly certain you were Dr Severn, the Bishop of Glasminster."

Severn, sitting up in bed, massaged his scalp vigorously with both hands. "And how did they come to know me by sight as well as all that?"

"That was what Diana wanted to know, because we haven't any bishops in our circle of acquaintance. Well, they told her that not long ago you had spent a couple of days with the headmaster of Dodington – "

"Where your two sons are at school," Severn broke in. "I see, I see. I didn't realise they were at Dodington, the General told me they called their school Dogpatch – he couldn't remember its proper name. So they saw me there. But, you know, I still don't understand how they could recognise me as I am now. My face is all over scars that weren't there when I was staying with Dr Brackenbury at Dodington. I thought they had changed me for life."

Fielding brushed the suggestion away. "Scars of flesh wounds on the face don't make a very serious difference if the features haven't been knocked out of shape, which yours are not. Besides, resemblance depends on a score of details that have nothing to do with the face. The boys noticed the scars, and wondered how you got them, but they were never in the least doubt about your being the Bishop of Glasminster. They knew you by your eyes and your voice, which are both very distinctive, and by your whole bearing. To them you were quite certainly the Bishop, with a badly scarred face."

"Yes, I see," Severn agreed. "It's true, I know, that the face isn't everything. I remember I have often recognised someone at a distance simply by his walk, and even a man's back view can be quite unmistakable."

"Just so," Fielding said. "And mind you, the papers all had photographs of you when your disappearance was in the news, and both Diana and I saw them. We talked about it, and we saw nothing for it but the conclusion that most people seem to have come to – that after the accident you had got out of the wreck and wandered away unnoticed, with your memory gone. Where you went to was anybody's guess, and is still – and some of the guesses have been decidedly tragic. When you came to us a fortnight later, and when Barlow had taken off the last of your bandages, it never occurred to either of us to connect you with the pleasant-looking prelate of the pictures. We'd never seen you in the flesh. The boys had seen you, alive and, so to speak, kicking. By the way, they recognised a mannerism of yours, too – the trick you have of rubbing your chin with your thumb and fingers, as if feeling whether you needed a shave."

Severn, who was in the act of doing that very thing, smiled a little bashfully. "Like this, eh? Well, now that I am performing the trick, I find that I do need a shave, not to mention a shower. But tell me, what did your wife do when she was told this, with the General and me still on the premises?"

"Why, she told the boys she would try to clear up the mystery, and that now that they had got it off their chests they must go to sleep. Then she came down and told me. She was quite convinced, and on thinking it over I agreed with her. But we couldn't see what we could do about it, after all Druce Barlow's insistence on not questioning you about your forgotten past. So when we heard you both going out we waited till you were safely away, then we put a call through to Barlow's house in London, and were lucky enough to get him, just home from a dinner party. I told him all about it."

Severn, now busy with a shaving brush, remarked quietly, "Not all exactly. The one thing you could tell him was that your two sons believed they had recognised me as the Bishop of Glasminster. From what I know of Barlow, I shouldn't think he would swallow that easily, as he had excellent reasons for thinking I was somebody quite different – the same reasons that General de la Costa had until one o'clock this morning or thereabouts."

"You're quite right, of course. As soon as I had told him what I had to say, I heard over the wire that sound which in the case of Barlow does duty for laughter – you know, a noise as if he had just laid an egg. But when I assured him it was serious, and told him why I thought so, he began to be interested. What impressed him most, as it had impressed me, was the evidence about the way you have of fingering your chin from time to time. And the end of it was that he said it was his duty as your doctor to come down here and look into the matter, so I told him we should be expecting him this morning and that lunch would be at two o'clock. He is coming in his car, and must be on his way now – in fact, he may be here at any time.

Now I'll leave you and go down to break the news that you have found yourself, and that you are the Right Reverend – "

"Not in this house," Severn broke in hastily. "This will be my last day here, and I should like my memory of it to be as pleasant as all the rest has been. It will be ruined if there is any formality. I've always hated that – in fact, I'm famous for hating it, I believe. Can't I go on being just as I was, when I was supposed to be a professional criminal with a defective memory, and we were all on the best of terms?"

"If you feel that way about it," Fielding said, "it would certainly suit all of us. I have come across a good many ruthless desperadoes in my time, but you are the only one I really liked, and Diana says she simply can't bring herself to talk to you as if you were respectable. I'll go and tell her what you say."

When Severn and General de la Costa appeared at the breakfast table, the atmosphere was almost as if the experiences of the past night had never been. Mrs Fielding, who was in hilarious spirits, hoped that Severn would not mind her slipping into calling him Taylor from time to time, as Taylor had come to be his name in that house, and none of them would ever think of him as anything else. Severn said that it was a better name than the one which his oldest friends called him by, and he would be delighted to answer to it.

"I can't help wondering, all the same, what your oldest friends call you," Mrs Fielding confessed. "Is it too bad to be told?"

"Your oldest friends are the ones who were at school with you, I suppose," Fielding ventured. "Schoolboys are capable of anything."

The two schoolboys, his sons, sitting side by side at the table, giggled without reserve. "Please, sir, was Dr Brackenbury at school with you?" Adrian Fielding asked.

"We were at Wellington together, yes," Severn said. "Do you want to know what I was called at Wellington?"

"No sir, thank you, we know," Adrian answered.

"You see, sir," Jerome explained, "the day you came to Dog – I mean Dodington, Wakefield minor happened to be standing by the door when you got out of the car, and old Prawn Dr Brackenbury, that is – came down the steps and said, 'Hullo, Piggy.' That's how we know."

"Yes," their father said, "and after that you were known to the whole school as Piggy before most of them had seen your face or heard your voice. I know, I know. A bishop called Piggy made an irresistible appeal to their hearts. Now, you two, you've had enough to eat, be off and try to forget Dr Severn's improper name."

When Adrian and Jerome had left them, General de la Costa sighed audibly. "I cannot help saying, *amigo*, that you ought to have stopped all that at the beginning. If when you are at school you find that some insulting name is being applied to you, the remedy is in your own hands. I remember that I met with that unpleasantness at my American school, Groton, and it did not last long. It was only a matter of a few fights, not more than thirty perhaps, before they gave up calling me Gila."

"And why did they call you that?" Fielding inquired.

"It was short for Gila Monster, a very hideous reptile which was believed to be found only in the Latin-American countries. After that I came to be called Conk, which I did not mind."

"It sounds a disgusting name to me," Mrs Fielding opined. "Why did you put up with Conk, if you took such a serious view of Gila?"

"It was started by one of the masters, who taught mathematics," the General said. "When he had some question to put, he would often ask in a tone of badinage, 'What does our Conquistador say to this?' – or 'How would you do it, Conquistador?', or something like that. That I did not object to, because my family was founded by a famous Conquistador, besides the man liked me, and I liked him. Of course, among American boys Conquistador naturally became Conk."

"But I can't agree with you, General," Severn protested, "about my school name being an insulting one. There was no malice about it. It was simply the inevitable result of my having been christened Charles Piggott. As soon as that fact had leaked out, I became Piggy to the whole school, and the name has stuck to me ever since. All the same, I didn't realise that Dodington had got hold of it. I suppose that was why the address I gave in the chapel was heard with such breathless attention – because I was Piggy."

Mrs Fielding directed his attention to the sideboard. "That reminds me – try some of that sugar-cured ham. It goes very well on top of the hot dishes, and you ought to have an appetite after what happened last night."

"But he had a late supper, Diana," the General said. "He had a water-biscuit in the sacristy of his own Cathedral just before we left."

"Well, I don't care, I'm still hungry," Severn said, "I've got a nickname to live up to now. Thank you, Mrs Fielding, I'll cut myself a slice. Getting back my memory has made me ravenous."

Just then the door of the hall was opened by Lem, who stood aside bowing as Dr Barlow came briskly into the room. "Good morning, everybody," he said. "You see, Diana, I didn't lose time. Your story over the wire was far too good for me to delay about seeing my patient. I slept on it a few hours, I breakfasted lightly, and then fled down here like a maddened stag. Do you think I could have a cup of coffee? No, nothing else, thank you – just a cup of coffee."

He turned to Severn, who was preparing to attack the ham on the sideboard, and looked him steadily in the eyes. "Something has happened since I was rung-up last night, I can see that," he remarked slowly. "At that time, so I was told, you still had no idea who you really were, though the Fielding family had just made the discovery. But this morning – " he turned to the others. "This man is no more a mental case than I am – not so much, perhaps, taking it all round. Let me carve that ham for you – that's right. Every man to his trade. Even for a minor operation like this an FRCS has an advantage over an amateur." He shaved off half a dozen miraculously thin slices of ham and handed the plate to Severn.

"It was Justo who was at the bottom of it all," Mrs Fielding explained. "He took Taylor out with him last night, to help him in doing a deed without a name somewhere, and brought him back a bishop – the missing Bishop of Glasminster. Here's your coffee, Druce."

"And we haven't yet been told how it happened, or why, or where," Arnold Fielding told him. "You've come just in time to hear the whole story, and the person to give it us is Justo, obviously. I suppose you were the only witness, Justo."

"Yes, and don't make it ordinary and unexciting, as you tried to make the story of the fight in the kitchen at Abbot's Dean," Mrs Fielding cautioned him.

General de la Costa, leaning back in his chair, twisted his moustache thoughtfully. "You overrate my ability, Diana. If I wished to make this story ordinary, I really could not do it. To begin with, the bare idea of Taylor being what he is was totally unexpected by every one of us, excepting those two boys. Besides that, I myself did the best I could to prevent the story from being ordinary. As for my being the right one to tell the story, I am ready to start it, as I was the originator of the whole thing, but I should like the Bishop to take his part in it whenever his recollection does not agree with mine, or whenever there is something which he knows that I do not. And I should say something before I begin – there are a few matters of fact which had better not be circulated outside this present company. I shall leave those matters to your discretion; you will realise that everything that was done was not completely in accordance with law and custom."

Dr Barlow, having drunk his coffee, had now dumbly asked and been granted leave to light a cigar. "It wouldn't be your story, General," he declared, "if everything in it was perfectly correct, but of course you can trust all of us to sift out the unmentionable parts if we ever have to talk."

"That is all I ask," the General said, and at once launched forth on an account of all that had happened from the moment of leaving Keith House the night before. The Fieldings, it appeared, had heard long since of the General's vow to establish a memorial of his mother in Glasminster Cathedral, but about the nature of it, and the commission given to M. Calixte Michaud, they knew nothing. "It is a habit of mine, Diana," the General said apologetically, "to disclose nothing about any plans I may have until they are actually carried out. I hope that you will see the new treasures of the altar very soon, when they have become officially a part of the Cathedral's consecrated possessions. The bishop may allow you to examine them privately – they are worth looking at, and so is the mitre which I have presented with them, the only one of its kind in this country."

The General's narrative moved quickly over the course of events up to the entering of the Cathedral, the passing over to the sacristy and the unpacking of the treasures there. It was at this point that Severn held up a hand. "I had better say something here," he said, "because the General does not know exactly what happened. He placed the mitre on my head, as he has just said, because he wished to see how it would look when it was worn, but when he saw that I did not like this, he turned again to the chalice and the other things on the table. He did not see that being crowned with the mitre had made me a different person – made me the man I had been before the cloud of amnesia had settled down on my mind. It was very sudden – like switching on an electric light. I felt confused for a few moments, then I came to myself and thought about the safe, which the General was saying he wished he was able to open. And I knew immediately that I had a key to that safe on the keyring in my pocket. I produced it, and gave the General a surprise by offering him the very thing he wanted."

The General, sitting with folded arms, nodded gravely. Dr Barlow, with a beaming face, exclaimed, "And who was it who insisted that you should always carry in your pockets the things you had there when you were knocked out? That's the advantage of carrying out your doctor's orders strictly – you find yourself in a sacristy with a million pounds' worth of valuables that ought to be locked up, and there you are with the key."

"And that," the General said, still nodding gravely, "was only the start of the business of making a monkey of me. First there was the producing of the key, which made me think you were out of your senses. Then there was the revelation that the whole of the story I had built up about you being Nick the Chill, formerly Six-gun Pete the Wyoming Wonder, was merely bunk. After that you led me on, so gently, by telling me that you knew all about buying bishops' hats, and then, when I tried to induce you to come home quietly and be put to bed with a hot-water bottle and a powerful sedative, you gave me the information – and proved it, too – that you were the Bishop of Glasminster. Just like that!" With a light introductory gesture the General fell back in his chair.

Mrs Fielding laughed delightedly. "How well you tell it, Justo! You understand that sort of thing so thoroughly – keeping people guessing and staging surprises."

"Yes," Dr Barlow said. "Now you know how it feels to have somebody holding out on you that way. But what you have just told us was no more than a sketch. We have had the full story only up to the time of Taylor realising the truth about himself. We should like to hear the rest unexpurgated and unabridged, if you don't mind."

The General wagged a mildly negative forefinger. "Not from me, at least. We have come now to the development which I foresaw, the part of the story about which the Bishop knows as much as I do, and more. It will be better for him to carry on with it and bring it to an end, while I go to the telephone in your study, Arnold, if I may, and put through a call which ought not to be delayed."

When the General had left them, Dr Barlow turned to Severn. "It seems, then, that you cleared up that little misunderstanding which had led the General and me astray. You explained that you were not really the Chill, in spite of all the evidence that made it a lead-pipe cinch that you were the Chill, and couldn't possibly be anybody else."

"Just as you say," Severn answered. "I did persuade him that I was not the professional assassin he thought I was. But I had better tell you the rest of the story in detail, as you suggested. I shall enjoy doing it, because it all made up one of the most wonderful experiences of my life."

"We shall all enjoy it," Mrs Fielding said. "I shall enjoy it especially, because I cry when I am much wrought up, and you can't think how enjoyable that is. Now Taylor, don't keep us waiting. Go on from where you took out your bunch of keys and told Justo that one of them would open the Cathedral safe."

Severn did his best to reconstruct the scene of the undeceiving of General de la Costa, and was rewarded by the spellbound attention of his hearers. "So that," Dr Barlow exclaimed, "is the explanation of how the apple got into the dumpling! Ever since the truth about your identity was sprung on me last night, and ever since I woke up this morning it has had me puzzled. I was mulling it over all the time I was driving down here, and I couldn't see a loop-hole anywhere. Well, could anybody? Could you, Arnold?"

"Most of this is new to Diana and me," Arnold Fielding said, "but it does make sense of the General's mysterious hints that Dr Severn's forgotten past might turn out to have been rather a murky one when he did recover it. And I agree that, on the evidence you and Justo had, it was impossible not to assume that the man you rescued was the man you were expecting."

"Well now, let's hear the rest of it," Mrs Fielding said. "I want to hear how Justo was led up the garden, as he says he was. I don't believe you did it on purpose, Taylor, that isn't in your line. But after your memory came back, you told him about the elephant, and about its wrecking the engine of your train, and about the man who was with you sneaking out when your back was turned. When you explained how it was that you weren't the man who was expected, why couldn't you have told him at once who you really were?"

Severn, rubbing his chin between his thumb and fingers, looked uncomfortable. "Yes, that sounds so simple, but somehow I found I couldn't do it that way. For one thing, the plain truth would sound such a totally incredible lie that I couldn't blurt it out without any preparation. For another thing, the General's perfectly natural belief about who I was had been suddenly knocked to pieces, and I had a strong feeling that I ought to break the whole truth to him gently."

"That's a kind of feeling," Mrs Fielding declared, "that is quite wasted on Justo. He can be gentle enough, if he wants to, in handling other people's feelings, but he prefers to be told the truth the hard way, as he calls it."

Severn went on with his story of how the hard way had been avoided in informing General de la Costa that his accomplice in illegally entering Glasminster Cathedral had been no other than the Bishop of Glasminster. His account of the steps by which he had overcome the General's disbelief, and especially the detail of the tin of water-biscuits, delighted the Fieldings and produced from Dr Barlow a yelp of joy. "How I wish I'd been there!" he exclaimed.

"And I wish you had been there," said the General, who had silently entered the room at that moment, "because I am always glad to have your company, Barlow *mio*, but as far as the unveiling of the mystery of our friend Taylor goes, you would not have been happy to be there, you would have been in just the same miserable situation as I was. You had fallen, just as I did, for the set-up that made a wrong gee, in spades redoubled, of the Bishop of Glasminster. So, when all that folded, you would have felt like kicking yourself, just as I did."

"Never mind, it all came to a happy ending," Mrs Fielding consoled him. "At least, it will be a happy ending, I suppose, when Druce has driven Taylor back to his Palace, and handed him over as a mental patient completely cured. Of course, it won't be so happy if the people at the Palace say they never saw him before in their lives – but you can cross that bridge when you come to it. By the way, does anybody mind if the boys come in here now? I know they are interested in the only bishop they have ever seen at close quarters, and he won't be here much longer."

Severn, when the boys were recalled to the room, greeted them with a genuine pleasure that improved their good opinion of him. General de la Costa, however, had another matter of business, as he described it, to broach. "Just now," he said, "I was talking on the 'phone to an old friend of my student days – you know him, too, Barlow *mio*, Sandy Mullins. He is one of the solicitors to the Metropolitan Police, and I have not communicated with him, of course, since I became a fugitive from justice. He said he was delighted to hear of me again. I asked him, did that mean that he knew about the death of Cowdery, of which I had been given private information just before the Bishop and I returned to this house very early this morning. His answer was that the news had just reached him, though it had not yet been made public, and that he had been glad to hear it, not only on general grounds, but because the police would not now have to waste any more time trying to arrest me."

"That was a relief for you," Arnold Fielding observed.

"Not so much of a relief," the General rejoined. "I have always been a few jumps ahead of the police, and so long as that was so, it has been nice to feel that I was in request. No, what I really wanted to ask about was if Scotland Yard would be interested in having something really serious to tie on to the leading members of the Ketch mob, including Ketch himself. He replied that there was nothing that Scotland Yard would like so much. He was very emphatic about it; in fact, I gathered that when Scotland Yard woke up after dreaming that it had caught Ketch with the goods, it cried to dream again, like the character in Shakespeare."

"That was Cannibal," remarked Jerome Fielding.

"He means Caliban," his brother amended. "We did *The Tempest* at school last term. Jerry has a foul memory for names."

"I must be careful," the General said, "to lay off literary allusions in my conversation. They only lead to unpleasantness. What I was trying to say was that Ketch's crowd have done a number of important jobs lately, using their methods which the police recognise easily, but as usual leaving no proofs against them. So Scotland Yard is suffering terribly from frustration, and would welcome any escape. Mullins has just been telling me all this, and you should have heard his cry of joy when I asked if several cases of aggravated assault and attempted kidnapping, and one of burglary, would be any good. When he asked about evidence, I told him that I could swear to Ketch himself in all these cases, and to five of his gang in several of the cases. I added that you, Barlow *mio*, would give evidence in support of mine. Besides that, I gave the name of Mrs McBean, who can swear to the man who called at her shop on the evening of the burglary. So the Yard is making a date for all three of us, when they will pull in the Ketch lot and ask us to do our identifying."

"Then you don't think I shall be wanted," Severn said.

The General shook his head. "I should not think it would be necessary, and there are reasons, as you can see, for keeping you in the background. From your own point of view, I mean. To begin with, you are likely to have your hands full for some time to come, when you go back to your ecclesiastical duties. Am I not right? Being mixed up in a prosecution, even when it means only a few appearances as a witness, takes time, and you will have no time to spare."

"That," Severn agreed, "is terribly true."

"And, of course," the General resumed, "your activity on that evening, which was so invaluable to our side, might not fit nicely into the picture of a suffering victim of mental disorder."

"You broke one man's arm," Dr Barlow pointed out. "I heard it snap. And you knocked another one out cold. I won't say you danced on his face, because the light was too bad for me to see, but he was certainly under your feet at the end of the mix-up. So, if the prosecution can manage without you, I shouldn't insist on figuring if I were you. And now, if you agree, I will go and ring up the Palace, Glasminster, and say that you have been found. I shall say I am your medical adviser, and that you have been suffering from amnesia, and that you have only just come out of it and told me who you are. I shall say I am bringing you home in my car after lunch. That all right?"

"I should think so," Severn said. "It's all true, as far as it goes, and I had rather you did the explaining about my mental trouble. And now you'll want to discuss the Ketch business with General de la Costa, I expect. May I go in the garden and arrange my ideas, Mrs Fielding? If I am wanted, I shall be there, under the tree."

CHAPTER XXVII

Severn had hardly taken his chair under the great copper-beech when he found himself cornered there by two small, familiar figures in neat blue jackets and grey flannel trousers. They had a look of eagerness which meant, he could guess, some appeal to himself.

It was the elder of the pair, Adrian, who opened with, "Please, sir, may we ask you something?"

"We thought you wouldn't mind," Jerome added. "General de la Costa said we could ask you."

"Oh, did he?" Severn said. "When did he say that?"

"It was just now, sir," Adrian explained. "While he was waiting for the London number he wanted, we asked if he could tell us another animal story, because he told us such a lovely animal story last night, about a bear and an alligator fighting."

"And he said," Jerome proceeded, "he couldn't tell us one just now, but we should ask you for an animal story, sir, because you knew the best animal story he had ever heard."

"And when we asked if your animal story was a true story," Adrian said, "the General said you never told stories which weren't true."

"And he said," Jerome added, "that you were in the story yourself, sir, so it must be true."

Severn, not denying the force of this argument, was asking himself how much of the story could be told. He thought he recognised the General's curious sense of humour in the suggestion that he might tell these juveniles a story which had its inevitable end in a chaos of destruction, death and horror. As for the comparatively harmless opening chapter, he realised that it was about the steepest story he had ever heard of, but he was not afraid, quite apart from the General's sweeping testimonial, of being written down a liar. He felt sure that in the past he had never been even suspected of this weakness. He knew, too, that truth is sometimes quite as strange as fiction. Besides that, it was obvious that a part at least of his "animal story" must have been reported in the newspapers at the time. So he said to the expectant pair, "Well, I will tell you the story that General de la Costa means. It's about an elephant – an elephant that went mad in a railway train."

The rapture of both boys was expressed in the syllable "Ooooh!"

"And it's true that I was in it," Severn pursued. "That is, I saw what the elephant did. Hasn't either of you ever heard about it before?"

"No, sir, never," Adrian declared with emphasis; and Jerome added, "We didn't know elephants went in trains. Do tell us about it, sir. Was he a great big 'normous elephant? What made him go mad? Were you in the train with him, sir? Did you sit near him? Did you...?"

Severn lifted a hand. "You must let me tell the story my own way, and you can ask questions afterwards if you like." He recalled the events of those few close-packed minutes in the station at Bridlemere, beginning with the first intimation he had had of the presence of Chuny in the neighbouring train – the sudden crash of splintering wood and the heavy thumps. Severn could tell a story well when he liked, and he possessed that far from common gift – a good visual memory; when he came to the moment of Chuny's bursting through the wall of her boxcar, the sight of her furious head, with lifted trunk and glaring eyes, was vividly present to his mind, and he described it in awe-inspiring detail.

He kept it in mind that he must not tell even this part of the story too well. He made no mention of David Hopkirk's being plucked from the engine cab and dashed, a dead man to all appearance, on the permanent way; and while he described as much of Chuny's wrecking activities as he had been able to see, and did full justice to her performance on the whistle, he did not say what to himself at the time had been evident – that the starting of the train had been Chuny's work, with its natural climax in a fatal railway smash. Severn's tale ended with his own train leaving the station, and his own last vision of the hideous head thrust out of the shattered boxcar.

"I never saw the elephant again," he concluded, "so that's the end of my animal story." He was thanked with the warmest sincerity; and then followed the inquiry which he had felt to be inevitable. "Please, sir, can you tell us what noise the elephant made?"

"I couldn't make a noise in the least like it," Severn protested. "You have to have a trunk, to begin with, to make even an ordinary elephant noise, and this elephant was making a noise not at all like any other I ever heard."

"Have you heard lots of elephants, sir?" Jerome naturally wanted to know.

"Yes, a good many," Severn said. "When I was in India. But all those I saw were tame elephants, though they made a deafening row when a lot of them were all trumpeting together. Some of the Indian princes keep a good many elephants."

"Just to show off, I suppose?" Adrian observed.

"Yes, exactly that," Severn agreed. "To have a number of elephants shows how important you are. When I visited the Rajah of Wusserthanbad he had over thirty elephants – so I was told."

"But this elephant in the train had gone mad, hadn't he, sir?" Jerome inquired. "Do mad elephants make a special noise?"

"Well, I've always heard that they do," Severn answered. "And this one in the train certainly did. It was a sort of a fearful roar and blood-curdling screech mixed up together. He was making that noise when I went past him in the train."

"And what did he look like then, sir, when you were quite close to him?" Adrian asked, while Jerome, capering slightly, shrilled, "Did he see you, sir? Did he try to get hold of you?"

"I don't think," Severn said, "he saw me in particular – there were other people looking out of the windows besides me. But I could see him very well as we went past; the train had only just begun to move, you see. I could see right into his huge red mouth, and see his trunk stretching straight up in the air, and his staring eyes all white round the edges, and his great ears sticking out flat on each side of his head, the way an elephant's ears never do in the ordinary way. And he was screeching all the time."

Severn paused. It seemed to him a good ending for the story. The boys gazed at him fascinated; then Jerome came a pace nearer and half whispered, "Please, sir, would you care to see my white mice?"

E C Bentley

Complete Clerihews

In 1905, Edmund Clerihew Bentley published a volume of nonsense verse consisting of a series of four-liners designed to poke fun at distinguished personalities. Illustrated by Bentley's lifelong friend, eminent critic and author G K Chesterton, they were known as 'clerihews' and became as popular as the limerick form. In *Complete Clerihews* the entire collection is presented, with original illustrations. The assortment of over 100 participants includes Karl Marx, Jane Austen, Mussolini, Henry VIII, Noel Coward, Tennyson, Dante, Leonardo Da Vinci, Dorothy Sayers, Aeschylus, Keats, President Roosevelt, Cleopatra and Lewis Carroll.

Trent Intervenes and Other Stories

Artist, connoisseur and private detective, Philip Trent, features in this classic and unputdownable collection, comprising eleven short stories. Including 'The Genuine Tabard', in which a clergyman and unique *objets d'art* are involved in a neat confidence trick; 'The Foolproof Lift', in which a blackmailing valet is found murdered; and 'The Ordinary Hairpins', in which a golden-haired opera singer commits suicide – but Trent is wisely suspicious.

E C Bentley

Trent's Last Case

When a scheming American capitalist is found dead in the garden of his English country house, two immediate matters confound amateur detective Philip Trent: why is the dead man not wearing his false teeth and why is his young widow seemingly relieved at his death? The newly widowed Mabel Manderson – 'the lady in black' – has a disarming effect on the refreshingly fallible and imaginative Trent, in this classic detective story that twists and turns as a result of the irresistible combination of ingenious deductions and misplaced assumptions.

'One of the three best detective stories ever written' – Agatha Christie

'It is the one detective story of the present century which I am certain will go down to posterity as a classic. It is a masterpiece' – Dorothy L Sayers

Trent's Own Case

The murder of a sadistic philanthropist sparks off an elaborate investigation led by artist and amateur criminologist Philip Trent, who had been painting the portrait of the man who was murdered. Two subsequent murders and the disappearance of an actress provide subsidiary mysteries in this inventive tale, which sees Trent in an elaborate maze created by ingenious criminal schemes.

E C BENTLEY

THOSE DAYS

The title of Edmund Clerihew Bentley's memoirs refers to those days that began in the 1880s and ended with the outbreak of war in 1914 – a date he feels draws an abrupt line across history. Bentley is particularly interested in the contrast between those days and the time at which he was writing this volume, first published in 1940.

Schooldays at the renowned St Paul's, London are described with particular note to the uniquely gifted author G K Chesterton, who became his lifelong friend. And at Oxford University in the 1890s, Bentley describes his acquaintance with Hilaire Belloc and John Buchan, among other notable individuals.

The launching of his career in journalism, the inspiration for the famous 'clerihew' and how he came to write what has been described by Agatha Christie as 'one of the three best detective stories ever written' (*Trent's Last Case*), are discussed with honesty and eloquence. But Bentley also looks outside his own life and shares his thoughts on the politics and culture of Britain during this interesting period.